THE DISTANT HILLS

A MARRIAGE NOT FOR LOVE . . .

Angela Burns on her mother's death travelled with her younger sister Nellie to Australia to live with their adopted Aunt Kara, only to find her aunt had died while they were on the high seas. Angela is frightened, for they have no money and nowhere to go, but Gilbert Lawrence, Aunt Kara's great-nephew and owner of her rich cattle station, comes to the rescue and offers Angela marriage. For Nellie's sake she accepts. A marriage not for love between two proud people who misunderstand each other's motives is the theme of this stirring romance by our favourite Lucy Walker.

by the same author

THE MOONSHINER
WIFE TO ORDER
THE LOVING HEART
LOVE IN A CLOUD
THE STRANGER FROM THE NORTH
KINGDOM OF THE HEART
MASTER OF RANSOME
HEAVEN IS HERE
COME HOME, DEAR
SWEET AND FARAWAY
THE ONE WHO KISSES

CHAPTER ONE

Angela, holding a travelling-case in one hand and a tweed coat in the other, walked down the gang plank of the small coastal ship on to the long jetty that stretched out into the Ocean Bay like a mile-long, crooked finger. Half-way down that gangway she turned her head to see if Nellie was following her. Nellie was there, one hand holding the rail and one hand holding her case.

Angela was forever turning her head to see if Nellie was following, or even there at all.

They were sisters; Angela, the elder, was eighteen years old and Nellie, the younger, was thirteen. They had come thirteen thousand miles, first by ocean liner and then by coastal trading ship to this remote and little-known cattle port on the western coast of Australia. They had left England in search of someone who, in the interim between their arranged departure and their arrival in Australia, had died. Now they were simply in search of a place to go and the only place Angela could think of was their original destination, Red Gorge. This was the nearest town to the cattle station Naroo Downs where Aunt Kara Anstey was to have given them a home.

They had a little money . . . what was left after the sale of their mother's cottage in a village in Yorkshire, but it wasn't very much. It had to be guarded with thrift.

Angela hadn't any idea what would happen to them now, but she had courage, she had a good reference from her former employers where she had operated a calculating machine in a bank in the town near her home village. She had a sister to maintain and rear, and this very responsibility gave her courage, and oddly enough, a sense of confidence. She was not alone and Nellie had to be looked after. Something would not only *have* to be done about it, but something *would* be done about it.

Angela stood now on the long wooden plank jetty and waited for Nellie to descend the last two steps of the gangway.

" Angela, it's hot," Nellie said and her voice hinted of tears. Nellie was afraid of the vast emptiness of the ocean behind them and the great desert-like country sprawling under a dust haze before them. She was cross with Angela for being so certain that everything would be all right when they got to

Red Gorge: for thinking that everything anyway would always be all right. Nellie longed for the soft grey skies and gentle greens of her homeland just as formerly she had longed to leave them and become interesting to her school friends as the "girl who is going to Australia."

"I don't like it, Angela. I want to go home," Nellie said.

"We can't go home, Nellie. There isn't a ship to take us just now. We'll go home by and by when I've saved a little money, and you've had some more schooling."

Angela, whose slim body had not yet lost the gentle lines of youth, and whose face still proclaimed her to have been until recently, little more than a child herself, now stiffened her back-bone imperceptibly and pressed her lips together in a firm line.

"I think we get on this funny little train to go down the jetty to the town, Nellie. Come on. It will be fun to write to Nora and Kate and tell them about it. Just imagine their surprise on hearing about a jetty so long there has to be a train to take everyone down its length."

"But it's dusty . . ."

"Very well," Angela said gently but firmly. "We'll walk, shall we? I believe it's only a mile and it's not so terribly hot after all, is it?"

"I don't want to walk. It *is* hot."

"Then let's get on the train and not make such a fuss about it," said Angela and she proceeded to do just this. As usual she had to turn her head to make sure that Nellie was following. As she did this she did not let her eyes rest for one pathetic moment on anyone else's eyes. She had to pretend she knew just what she was doing, where she was going, and that everything was going along for Angela and Nellie Burns as prearranged.

Angela was probably the only girl in the world who was at that moment terrified of advice and friendliness; above all of sympathy or helpfulness. She had told so many stories out of pride and anxiety on that seven-day trip up the coast that she couldn't now tell the truth. It was too late.

Angela's mother, a widow who had lived until her death a year before in a small Yorkshire village, had had a lifelong friend who, way back in what Nellie called the "olden times," had married an Australian and gone back to that country with him. This friend and Mrs. Burns had corresponded with one another all their lives. "Aunt Kara," as Angela and Nellie grew up to call her, had twice been on visits to England and she had stayed with the Burnses in their cottage. Angela remembered her as being tall and slim and browned with a life in the open air. She had told them all about her life on a cattle station; how her husband had been first head stockman and then manager of this station for his uncle who owned it.

Years later one of her letters told how the uncle had died and he had left the station between "Aunt Kara's" husband and a great-nephew called Gilbert Lawrence. Aunt Kara wrote that this was a wonderful thing for both herself and her husband as Gilbert Lawrence was a lot younger than they were and there would be someone to leave the whole station to as she herself, sadly, had no children.

It was about this time, since Mrs. Burns herself was now widowed, that Aunt Kara had begun to write and say they should all come out to Australia and live with her. There was a huge homestead on this great property.

> "Room for a dozen families," she wrote, "and a wonderful life for your two girlies. As I love them as my own it would be like having children of my own about me. And if your darling Angela could only hurry and grow up we could marry her off to Gilbert. But she will have to hurry. I've just added up, he's ten years older than Angela and really could marry anyone he wanted to right now. He says he's not interested in women, only in Naroo Downs. All the same I tell him I've got a lovely English daisy already planned for him. Also I don't have to add that though I long to see him married I'm frightened to death he might marry the wrong person, or some person who won't get on with *me*. You've no idea how frightful that would be when you're hundreds of miles from your nearest neighbours."

This sort of letter came at fairly regular intervals, though they didn't all refer to Angela—who was no more at that time than a long-legged schoolgirl carrying a satchel to school every day—as the prospective wife of Aunt Kara's beloved Gilbert Lawrence.

"It's because she has no children of her own," Mrs. Burns had said sadly. "If I took you and Nellie out there, Angela, she'd appropriate you too. She feels you belong to her because she and I have been lifelong friends."

"It sounds like a wonderful life. All those horses . . . and the cattle musters . . . and camp-fires . . ." Angela had said with a feeling of divided loyalties nagging a little at her heart.

Mrs. Burns had wavered about going to Australia. She didn't think she would ever go. Her cottage was so comfortable, and though they had had very little money there was every prospect of things being easier when Angela left school. Already a friend of her late husband had said Angela should be trained to go into the bank. As he was in the bank himself he would help get a post for her there.

On the other hand what was to become of Angela and Nellie if her own health didn't improve?

As Mrs. Burns's health gradually deteriorated she began to turn more and more to her friend's letters from Australia. She wrote that she felt now that she herself would never make the trip but if anything happened to her would Kara look after Angela and Nellie?

Aunt Kara wrote back urgently. The girls must come to Australia. They would be looked after as her very own.

Then she added what she had not referred to for two years:

> "And my sweet Angela shall marry my stubborn, self-willed but adorable Gilbert and live not only happy ever after . . . but rich, too. You must know, Hetty dear, that we've made a great deal of money in cattle . . . and sheep, too . . . in recent years. You must let me know what you need."

But Hetty Burns, knowing in her heart that her girls would be safe, and barely waiting until Kara Anstey had sent the passage fares for them all to go out to Naroo Downs, closed her eyes and gave up her interest in life.

It was not until Angela, now employed in the bank, went sadly through her mother's letters that she learned of the contents of the recent correspondence. Her mother had spared the girls the knowledge of her own approaching death and therefore of the last desperate measures she had taken to ensure their future.

Angela sat at the round table in the window of the cottage and read through the bundles of letters that had accumulated over twenty years of faithful friendship. On top of her mother's papers she had already found the bank passport with the sum for their passage money to Australia.

Though she had been aware of Aunt Kara's references to

Gilbert Lawrence and her own girlish charms, she had not given them a thought. She was too deeply concerned with her personal loss, and anxiety about what to do with Nellie.

Nellie . . . pretty, dainty, delicate, spoiled Nellie . . . was only twelve years old then.

How was Angela to educate her and look after her at the same time? A junior clerk was not so well paid as all that. Their mother's pension died with her. There was the little cottage, a few savings and the passage money to Australia, that was all.

Whichever decision she made . . . to stay or to go . . . would have far more lasting repercussions on Nellie's welfare than her own, Angela thought. She was at that time seventeen, but she felt that she was grown-up, independent, and could manage life for herself. She could not afford to be afraid, so she was not afraid.

But Nellie?

Nellie wanted at that time to stay at school and go on being bosom friends with Nora and Kate Thomason for ever. Nellie didn't even want to go to the neighbouring town to interview the solicitor who was disposing of Mrs. Burns's affairs because it would mean a day away from Nora and Kate. Nellie's life was an hour to hour affair and it consisted entirely of what Nora, or Kate, or she herself said in each of those hours.

So Angela decided to try and manage as they were for a trial period. She wrote and told Aunt Kara all about it. Aunt Kara cabled back a plea for them to come to her.

It was the following winter and Nellie's recurring almost chronic colds, that settled the issue. Angela could not go to work and earn their income and at the same time stay home and nurse Nellie. Things were going wrong with the cottage too. There was a leak in the attic, and the water pipes into the kitchen were corroded. A wind storm had blown down the garden shed and the snow was so deep and thick and lasted so long into what should have been spring that there wasn't really quite enough money to buy coal.

Suddenly Angela knew it was all too much. She could never keep up the repairs on the cottage, let alone look after Nellie properly. She wrote and told Aunt Kara so, sadly admitting her failure as if she herself had been to blame. She was a little ashamed of accepting Aunt Kara's home and Aunt Kara's help but she had to do so for Nellie's sake.

Aunt Kara wrote she would come down from the north and meet them at Fremantle port. She was delighted, and oh so happy, that the girls were coming to her. They must sell the cottage at once and did they have enough money? She also told them to bring plenty of cotton wear for the climate was extremely hot.

Angela was now eighteen and Nellie had had her thirteenth birthday. The responsibilities that had sat on Angela's shoulders had given her a rather old-world air of seriousness but not even the weight of care could take from her the clear candour of her grey eyes, the sweetness of her rare smile or the rich colour of her light-brown hair. There was a firmness about her mouth that seemed to have grown there since her mother's death but it added to the real if somewhat girlish dignity of her whole bearing.

Nellie had fair hair and pretty blue eyes, that occasionally lit up with mischief, but she was slim with fine bones, and small ankles and wrists that made Angela think she was frailer than in fact she was.

Thus, in their neat, simple and inexpensive clothes, they set out across the world to Aunt Kara's station at Naroo Downs, down under.

There was nobody to meet the girls when the ship berthed at Fremantle.

Bewildered but determinedly unafraid Angela went to the office of the Travellers' Aid Society which stood beyond the customs sheds on the South Wharf. There she told them she had expected to be met, and by whom.

An office girl was dispatched to take Angela and Nellie to have some morning tea and arrange their passage through the customs while inquiries were made.

Angela remained unafraid. It was funny, she thought, how unafraid one was when one couldn't afford to be anything else. She had . . . she just *had* to keep up a front for Nellie.

"Aunt Kara's probably an unpunctual kind of person. They have all that time . . . up there on that cattle station in the north. They don't get used to worrying about it. I believe they don't even have clocks. They get up with the sun and come home from mustering at sundown. Aunt Kara told me . . . that time she came to England . . . the stockmen always look up at the sun or at the shadows on the ground to see what time to sit down and have their lunch."

Nellie was unco-operative in this belief and besides, she was tired from the long wait going through the medical and immigration inspections, so she sat on a step and watched while Angela explained to the customs officer what they had in their cases. He was a nice officer for he did not open more than one case and he marked all the rest with a white cross.

When they returned to the Travellers' Aid office there was tragic news for them. There had been an accident with a car coming down overland from the north a few days before. Aunt Kara had been in that car. In going to meet Hetty Burns's children she had lost her own life.

Angela went a little pale when she heard the news. She did not feel so much the personal loss or that the ground had suddenly sunk from under their feet as that Aunt Kara had given up her life for them . . . Angela and Nellie.

Somehow she couldn't let Aunt Kara down now. She had to keep up a front for Aunt Kara's sake, as well as Nellie's sake.

It was this feeling that she had to do everything with dignity and fortitude more than anything else that made her tell her first " story."

" We will be quite all right," she explained to the Travellers' Aid people. " We will go on to Red Gorge, the nearest town to Naroo Downs. Mr. Gilbert Lawrence is expecting us. Would you please tell us where to find the shipping office so we can book a passage up the coast."

" Well, you could go by air, you know."

Aunt Kara in more than one of the early letters had told about minor happy adventures on the ship journey up the coast so Angela thought that this was the proper prescribed way to go to Red Gorge. She couldn't show her ignorance to the Aid people for fear of their pity. That would undermine her own confidence and she could not tell them she and Nellie did not have enough money to go back home. Under no circumstances could she let even these kind people think she had very little money and absolutely nowhere to go.

She had to say she was going to Red Gorge by ship and that she was expected.

" We don't like travelling by air," she said. " Yes, we will be met at the port." She hoped she didn't blush.

She was directed to the shipping office and as it was the off-season for travellers she found she could get a berth for herself and Nellie on a trading ship that was leaving in three days' time. The Travellers' Aid people booked them in a hostel for the three-day wait.

"We don't like travelling by air," she said, and hoped again she didn't blush. She knew air fares always cost much more than ship fares.

On the ship kindly people asked Angela and Nellie where they were bound and with whom they were going to stay. It was then that Angela told the next of her stories. She had no idea that vast though the north was everyone knew who everyone else was who lived there. The sheep and cattle stations were so huge, that the owners were sufficiently few in number and their stations, their names and their fortunes were known to everyone.

"We are going to stay with Mr. Gilbert Lawrence at Red Gorge . . . two hundred and fifty miles out . . ." Here Angela blushed and stammered. She hadn't known that. But she couldn't tell these kindly curious people her terrible plight. She couldn't have borne their pity nor would her pride have let her accept their help. Besides, she had to pretend in front of Nellie that she knew everything, and that everything was going to be all right. She could never, even in her weakest moments, let Nellie see that she was assailed by doubts and that the immediate future was as much a mystery to her as it was to anybody else.

Angela was so afraid she would make some serious mistake in what she said of her expectations of Red Gorge and was so ashamed not to be telling the truth that, hard though it was on a small ship, she deliberately avoided her fellow passengers from then on, and even when approached she pretended to be so shy she didn't have a word to say for herself. As a matter of fact she was suddenly and remorselessly assailed by a shyness, partly born of embarrassment, partly of anxiety, that she hardly understood herself.

She did not caution Nellie about what to say and what not to say to fellow passengers for Nellie had taken to sea-sickness as an antidote against her dislike of the small cramped cabins after the spacious ones on the great liner that had brought them out from England. Laid low in her bunk Nellie was certain of constant care and coddling from the stewardess. And she liked being interesting.

She liked telling the stewardess, in Angela's absence, that she was a poor little orphan girl; that she was very delicate; and (which was true) she was top of her form at school. She always won the prize for needlework too.

"You'd better not be too delicate up in the north," the

stewardess cautioned Nellie with a frank eye to the fact that Nellie was only sick when someone came into the cabin. "It's a tough climate for the likes of you. And where are you to stay once you get off at Carnlow?"

"Red Gorge," said Nellie loftily. "We're going to live with Mr. Gilbert Lawrence at Naroo Downs."

"Well, let's hope he meets you at Carnlow for the only way to get to Red Gorge from Carnlow is by car or truck and it's about six hundred miles. And Mr. Lawrence's station is another two hundred and fifty miles out. You'd better get good and well mighty quick, young miss, or they'll go without you. You've got to be fit to take that kind of travelling in this country. Day temperatures about a hundred and eight . . . if you're lucky."

Nellie's eyes widened. This was the first she knew that Red Gorge wasn't near the ship's port of call. Why hadn't Angela told her? And she didn't like the way the stewardess was implying doubt as to the authenticity of her present state of *mal de mer.*

"Of course he'll be there to meet us. He's going to marry my sister. He's a very rich man, isn't he?"

"Oh, so that's what's in the wind, is it?" The stewardess looked at Nellie with renewed interest. This was more to Nellie's liking. "Yes, my Aunt Kara arranged it. Before she died, you know. That way both my sister and Mr. Lawrence can inherit the station."

"You mean Mrs. Anstey from Naroo Downs? You mean she was your aunt?"

The stewardess was impressed. She eyed Nellie with doubting eyes, however.

"She died, unfortunately," said Nellie with the right amount of tragic sorrow in her voice. "So, of course, my sister will have to take her share of the station now. Oh, well, it will be easy enough when she's married to Mr. Lawrence. I mean Gilbert Lawrence."

"What do you make of that?" the stewardess later said to the steward over the teapot in the steward's pantry. "The older girl, the pretty one who never says a word to anyone, is going to marry Lawrence of Naroo Downs . . . *so the young one says.*"

The stewardess winked knowingly.

"I expect the Naroo Downs boss will be in when we berth," the steward said later to his Number One passenger in the best berth on the ship. " I hear the young English lady has come out to marry him."

The Number One passenger told his fellow passengers over the bar that evening. The next morning the ladies discussed it at breakfast. By eleven o'clock each and all of the dozen lady passengers on the boat had made an attempt to speak to Angela. But Angela, terrified of more mistakes or more stories, barely breathed a courteous " good morning " in response to their advances and fled to her cabin. There, Nellie obliged by having another attack of sea-sickness and insisted that the only thing that would take her mind off it was a Cologne-soaked handkerchief on her forehead and Angela reading her a story.

When Angela emerged at nightfall the ladies were as much afraid of her " proud reserve " as she was of their finding out she was nobody with nowhere to go and very little money to do it with. She had pride, as the ladies properly guessed, but it was a totally different kind of pride from what they feared.

" What a dark horse Gilly Lawrence is!" was the most repeated remark over the bridge tables that night. " Wonder if she knows how lucky she is."

" Oh, I don't know," one person ventured to say. " I think she's rather sweet myself. And Gilly Lawrence will be a pretty hard nut to crack. I wonder if she really knows what she's in for? Wonder where she met him?"

" Somewhere where he was dressed up and looking the handsome devil he is," another said.

" And a devil he is," added a third. " I believe he drives the men out there at Naroo Downs with a stock-whip."

" If he does they still stick to him," said the first woman dryly.

" He probably salves their wounds with pound notes," put in a new voice. " He's got it."

There was a general laugh.

" All the same he would be a hard man for a nice little girl like that to marry," said the first speaker again. " And I think she is nice. I think she's really more shy than reserved. She has a charming little face. There is something rather affecting about that young dignity. I like her."

Angela was unaware of the gossip and speculation that was going on about her and, as none of the passengers was disembarking at Carnlow, there was none of them to discover anything more about her except that Gilly Lawrence was not at the boat to meet her.

It was mystifying to the passengers and food for further speculation as the ship travelled north, sailing out on the next tide.

Meantime Angela and Nellie had been taken by the jetty train down into the small township of Carnlow.

CHAPTER TWO

The wife of the proprietor of the Carnlow Hotel was very quick to sense something of the predicament of the two young girls sitting by their cases in the lounge. She knew everyone who came in and out of the tiny port, or if she didn't know them she knew they were strangers and soon knew something of their business.

She was a kind motherly woman and she hid her surprise when the older of the two girls inquired about means of travelling to Red Gorge.

The only way to Red Gorge was by a red earth track for six hundred miles through spinifex and semi-desert. It involved spending one night camping by the road unless one was lucky enough to get a lift from some adventurous person who left town between three and four in the morning and travelled the whole day and early evening to make the distance without recourse to an overnight camp. There were no regular cars or trucks to Red Gorge and getting there depended entirely on the chance of someone going and being prepared to take passengers along. The proper route for travellers to Red Gorge from down south was by air. Inland people only went to Carnlow if they had their own cars and because they wanted the sea trip.

None of these things did Mrs. Appleby of Carnlow Hotel tell Angela as Angela stood by the reception desk and politely and innocently asked her astounding questions about getting to Red Gorge.

Mrs. Appleby put her finger thoughtfully to her lip and looked at Angela with a veiled but sympathetic curiosity. Then her gaze went beyond Angela to Nellie, whose face, at this moment, was very white.

"That child needs to sit down," she said, rising and coming round from behind her desk. "Come, I will take you into a little private lounge we have here and you can settle your things while I make inquiries for you."

"Thank you so very much," Angela said gratefully. She managed to sound matter of fact but she did not deceive the experienced eye of Mrs. Appleby. Mrs. Appleby had seen all kinds pass, sooner or later, through this tiny outback cattle port. Only last week the governor had been here and right now, out under the trees on the gravel square at the back of the hotel was a trio of the toughest gambling stockmen who had ever hit the town. In the best room on the south wing were two security officers making a routine check of the people who came and went on a route that led to the new Tolnado terminus of the rocket range territory. They were masquerading as commercial travellers but they did not deceive Mrs. Appleby, any more than this slim girl with the English complexion and the grave eyes deceived her.

"Now here we are," she said, installing the two girls in comfortable chairs. "Take off your hats. Nobody wears hats up here in the north except when they're out in the sun. Then, of course, you *must*."

She took Nellie's hat from her and put it on a small table. "Here, child," she said. "Here is a fan. I always keep fans handy for visitors. There's one on the table now by you, too, Miss . . . What did you say your name was, dear?"

"Burns," said Angela quietly. "Angela Burns."

"Well, Miss Burns, I'm going to send you in some tea. And this young lady too. And I'll make some inquiries for you."

She smiled benignly on the girls and went out of the room looking thoughtful. She went in search of her husband who was polishing down the bar top after serving some beer to two men who had taken the tally of the stores unloaded from the ship.

"Harry," she said, catching his eye and managing to convey a forewarning of the oddity of her next remarks. "There's two young girls in the lounge wanting to go to Red Gorge. They think there's a train or tram service there probably. They're new chums, I fear."

"Two of 'em?" said Harry. "Girls? You mean young girls?"

"That's just exactly what I do mean . . . and they want to go to Red Gorge. To-day by the sound of things. They didn't ask to book in here."

"For crying out loud, there mightn't be anyone going to

Red Gorge for a week." He looked across the bar at his customers. "Any of you blokes know anyone going to Red Gorge?"

"Sure," said one man. "Bill Smiley. But he's leavin' in about an hour. He can't take any two girls. He's camping overnight."

"In that case," said Mrs. Appleby, "he's leaving early tomorrow morning. And he'd better see his spare tyres are okay because nobody'll be wanting a blow-out on this trip. Where is he right now?"

"Down at the garage filling up."

"Then you go down and fetch him up here right away. Tell him I want to see him and don't tell him what for. There'll be beer on the counter for you when you get back. Meantime I've got some tea to make, a room to get ready and a coupla baths to run."

As Mrs. Appleby went through the door her husband caught the eye of the remaining customer.

"Must be a coupla duchesses in there," he said.

"Yeah?" his customer drawled. "They're the two girls got off the ship when she came in on the tide. One of 'em's going to marry Gilly Lawrence . . . so they say."

Harry Appleby's hand ceased rubbing a cloth along the counter.

"*Gilly Lawrence?* Him getting married? You sure? Why isn't he in here to meet 'em if that's the case? And what they doing not going to Red Gorge by air?"

The other man shrugged his shoulders.

"He took off for down south last week in his own plane. After Mrs. Anstey got killed in the car crash, it was. Maybe they got their dates wrong. Maybe there's nothing in the story at all. How'd Gilly Lawrence meet two girls from England, let alone marry one of 'em? He hasn't been out of the State in three years."

"I don't know," said Harry Appleby, resuming his polishing.

Both men ruminated in silence, the one rolling a cigarette as he leaned his back against the bar, the other rhythmically weaving figures of eight with his polishing cloth on the counter. Gilbert Lawrence was a big name in the cattle industry. Bigger than ever now, probably, since Mrs. Anstey had gone. Marrying someone outside the cattle circle gave food for thought. Marrying anyone at all, for that matter, gave food for thought. Somehow one just couldn't see Gilly Lawrence tied down and playing the domestic routine.

"You know what," said Harry Appleby, rolling up his cloth and putting it in a hideout under the counter. "I reckon that calls for a beer on the house."

"Agreed," said the other, turning round and facing his host. "Say, listen, Harry . . . can you see it? I mean can you see Gilly Lawrence playing the husband? Playing anything but his mighty self?"

Neither man admitted even to himself he had no right to call Gilbert Lawrence by any name, much less the familiar "Gilly" of legend.

Angela Burns was never to forget that drive to Red Gorge as long as she lived.

Mrs. Appleby had given the girls their evening meal and a comfortable room. She had had them called in the small hours and dispatched on their way with Bill Smiley the truck driver. She had provided a hamper for all three and it included two bottles of beer "on the house" for the driver. She had charged Angela and Nellie the minimum amount for their accommodation for so far she was the only person north of latitude twenty-six who discounted the story that the elder of these two girls was to marry the great Gilbert Lawrence.

"A snake yarn," she told her husband scornfully. "Something someone dreamed up on a night out. You know what those ships are for talk . . . and gossip. I'll bet a hundred pounds those two girls haven't got that much to rub together . . . and they've no idea where they're heading for. Fact is, I've given Bill Smiley a note for Hannah Smith at the Red Gorge Hotel to give them the watchful eye. Only I didn't tell *them* . . . the girls, I mean. The elder one would rather die than show anyone she's lost. Just plain lost. The younger one will make out. She knows just how to catch the sympathetic eye and get everything done for her. Not that she's not an innocent one too. Just spoiled, I'd say. And a bit on the delicate side."

Angela and Nellie had ridden up in the cab of the big truck all the six hundred miles of that wild desolate country. Bill Smiley had been silent and taciturn at first, occasionally mentioning he'd lost twelve hours in getting to Red Gorge "all on account of that interfering grandmother Mrs. Appleby at the pub."

As Angela had no knowledge of what he was referring to, this particular grumble did not disturb her.

After daybreak and a stop for a quick snack Bill Smiley had become more talkative and presently Angela found him interesting. He knew all sorts of odd things and odd stories about the track over which the great truck was speeding with a four-wheel drive and immensely heavy double tyres. Each time he turned and caught Angela's inquiring eyes his voice softened a shade.

She was a nice girl, he decided. Ah, well, 'suppose a bloke could give someone a lift now and again. And they didn't talk a babble full of girlish rot in his ear all the time. The young one looked delicate too, poor kid.

So through blazing blinding heat, across grass hummock, red claypan and stony outcrop and treeless spinifex plain, Bill Smiley drove them six hundred miles to Red Gorge.

He only swore once, too. That was a remarkable feat of abstinence for Bill Smiley. It was when a pack of kangaroos raced alongside the track out into the desert.

"Eat all the grass," he snarled by way of explanation and apology for his one loud, vehement and unprintable, word. "Them too," he said, watching with a baleful eye a flight of yellow-combed cockatoos. "Eat the shoots of the trees—where there's a tree. Kill out the whole country if they had their way."

Kangaroos, cockatoos, emus and wild donkeys, Angela learned, were the curse of Australia. The heat and waterlessness he not only took for granted but seemed to enjoy. "Where there's water you got no excuse for drinking beer," he said. And he liked the open frankness of Angela's sudden smile when he said this.

"She's a real lovely girl," he thought to himself. "And has she got courage! Outside the Birdsville Track this is about the worst stretch of country in the continent, and not a grumble out of her." The heat was a hundred and fifteen in the shade.

It was seven o'clock in the evening when Angela and Nellie were discharged at the Red Gorge Hotel and Bill Smiley handed over his letter from Mrs. Appleby to Mrs. Smith.

Angela had learned from the truck driver in advance that Red Gorge was a mining town on the edge of the cattle country. Until the war there had been nothing but great gorges slashed like canyons in the middle of the cattle runs. All around there were cattle runs but right in Red Gorge itself there was only the mining company, its employees and the tradespeople who served them.

"Hotel, mine office, school, hospital," Bill Smiley had said. "Them's the four corner-stones of Red Gorge. You can't get lost because there's always one of 'em in sight."

The hotel was a pleasant surprise and a great relief. It was big and modern and air-conditioned. It had lovely shrub-decorated patios and lounges, and when Angela and Nellie were shown to their room they found it decorated in modern colours and with hot and cold water serving the wash basin in the corner. The bathroom at the end of the passage was fit for a palace.

This, in the middle of that terrible spinifex plain and desert! Angela found it hard to understand!

Because she thought her drowsy sister was in need of a good sustaining meal, Angela insisted they put on fresh frocks and go to the dining-room for the late meal Mrs. Smith had told them would be waiting for them.

It was a very large dining-room with tables covered with snowy-white cloths, bowls of bush grass for decoration and patterns of shining silver set about the tables. There was one small group of men at a table at the end of the room when Angela and Nellie entered. They turned their heads and looked at the girls and went back to their cigarettes, coffee and conversation with which they were ending their meal.

Mrs. Smith herself brought a hot covered dish to each girl. "Waitress has gone off duty now," she said with a smile. "But I kept this hot in the pantry for you."

"Thank you so very much," Angela said. She felt nonplussed at the degree of kindness she was finding from these people in the north. She wondered why. Nellie, on the other hand, took it all for granted but when she lifted her silver covered dish and found a beautifully served plate of roast lamb and green peas she looked mollified.

"Expected to find fried kangaroo or stewed spinifex, I suppose," Mrs. Smith said with a knowing smile. "Young lady, we might be in the never-never here in Red Gorge but this is the best hotel south of the equator. I know, because I run it. Now, while you two eat, do you mind if I just sit down here and rest my tired feet? It's nice to have someone new to talk to. All we get here is mining people, station people, an occasional American dropped in to buy a yard or two of manganese or asbestos."

"Yes, please do sit down," Angela said hastily. "I'm so sorry our late arrival has put you to so much trouble."

"No trouble at all," said Mrs. Smith, sitting down and pouring herself a tumbler of water. "You are new up north, aren't you? Come up the coast on the ship . . . so I hear."

She said nothing of the letter Bill Smiley had given her from Mrs. Appleby at Carnlow.

Nellie had tentatively taken a small bite of roast lamb and there was a look of sudden surprise on her face. It not only looked good, it tasted good.

"Yes, we are new to the north," Angela conceded with a touch of embarrassment. This was the end of the road. Where did she go from here? She looked up at Mrs. Smith's face and instead of idle gossiping curiosity in the other woman's face she read real interest and a touch of motherly concern.

The pride Angela had used to hide her predicament while on the ship was no use now she was here in Red Gorge. She knew it, and she knew she had to ask advice from someone. For a long minute she looked at Mrs. Smith and then she dropped her eyes to her plate as delicately she sliced a small piece of lamb and put her fork into it.

"We were coming up here to see someone," she said, still keeping her eyes down. "She has since died, but I thought I would like to come on." She looked up now and then said with complete frankness, "I would like to get some kind of job in Red Gorge. Do you know if that is possible, Mrs. Smith? I mean, are there jobs available?"

"What kind of job can you do? Are you a nurse? A school-teacher?"

"No. I worked in a bank. I was a computer."

"A computer? For crying out loud! What's that?"

"Operating a calculating machine. It works out money, percentages, averages. Adds up and multiplies . . . and . . . well, things like that."

"We got three bank branches here in Red Gorge but they're small little shows. The only place that's got an office full of machines and things is the mine office. And I do know they never can get people to work those machines. Not in Red Gorge, anyway. They get girls up from the south but they don't stay. They like to go back to the city lights. Here, now, I'll ask Mr. Morton over there. He's the mine manager."

"Oh, please *no*," begged Angela. "You see . . . we've come a long way . . . and Nellie's nearly asleep. And I mightn't be dressed right."

Mrs. Smith was already on her feet.

"Please," begged Angela. She swallowed hard. "It's so very important for me to get a job that I would like to look my best."

"You look pretty good to me," said Mrs. Smith firmly. "And there's nothing like striking while the iron's hot. Besides, I do a lot for Mr. Morton. Has his swanky-doodle friends from down south and even America in here all kinds of odd hours. No extra charge either since the mine brings us all our business. Now you sit still there a minute."

Mrs. Smith walked in a matter-of-fact way in the direction of the only other occupied table in the dining-room, and Angela tried to swallow the piece of lamb which a minute before had promised to be delicious and which was now an indigestible lump in her throat. From behind her she could hear the scraping of chairs as someone rose at Mrs. Smith's approach.

"*Work*," said Nellie, looking at her sister aghast. "I thought we were going to live on a cattle station. And ride horses and keep dogs . . ."

"Ssh!" Angela begged. "I'll explain it all to you later, Nellie. You see, I would like to work *first* . . . and then be invited afterwards to a station . . ."

"But Aunt Kara said in those letters you were reading that she wanted you to come here to marry Gilbert Lawrence . . ."

"That was fairy-tale stuff she wrote for small children years ago," said Angela, suddenly at the end of her patience. "Nellie, will you please wait until we are in our room before you say anything. Anything at all. Please, promise me."

Fortunately Nellie was too tired after that long overland journey in the heat to protest at the tone of Angela's voice, or even at the prospect of Angela working in Red Gorge. It was all too bewildering to her and suddenly all she wanted to do was go to sleep. She put her head down on her arms which were now resting on the table.

"Please, Nellie . . ." Angela pleaded, for she thought her younger sister was about to burst into tears. At that moment she heard Mrs. Smith returning to the table, and there were other heavy footsteps accompanying her. Angela closed her eyes to say a little despairing prayer when a new thought struck her.

She was in luck. There was nothing to be unhappy about. She hadn't been in Red Gorge two hours and here was someone bothering to come to her on the subject of a *job*. Why, that was wonderful! It might have been weeks. Even if she didn't get a job, something was being done about it already.

Mrs. Smith brought two men to the table, an older man in his middle forties and a younger man who might be in his late twenties. The younger man smiled at Angela with such a fresh friendly smile that tired though she was her spirits rose even higher. Both men were dressed in summer tropical clothes and they looked like businessmen.

"This is Miss Burns," Mrs. Smith said to the older man. "Miss Burns, this is Mr. Morton from the mine. And this is Mr. Richards who is an accountant at the mine."

The younger man, Mr. Richards, smiled even more engagingly but Mr. Morton merely nodded his head.

"Will you please sit down?" said Angela, her back a little stiff and her head a little high, but she smiled politely as she returned their greeting and half-rose in her chair in deference to the older man's position in the town.

Mr. Morton leaned over her table and stubbed out a cigarette in her ash-tray but he didn't accept her offer to sit down.

"Mrs. Smith tells me you have office experience and are looking for a job," he said, giving her a sudden sharp look from between his half-closed eyes. "You understand machines, I gather."

"Yes. Comptometers," Angela replied quietly. "I can also type."

"Well, have a chat here with Mr. Richards. You might come down to the mine office and see me in the morning." He turned away to join the third man in his party who was on the point of leaving the dining-room. "We start at eight in the morning," he added, giving Angela another quick appraising look. "Good night to you."

"Good night, Mr. Morton," Angela said, almost breathless with shock in this sudden turn of events.

In a dazed way she watched Mr. Morton leave the dining-room and did not, for a minute, notice that Mr. Richards did sit down at the table, that Mrs. Smith was now herself tidying up the other table just vacated by the three men, and that Nellie, who had some minutes earlier put her head down on her arms, had not moved.

Slowly Angela brought her eyes away from the door and looked across the table at Mr. Richards. He was watching her face and his smile now broadened into a friendly grin.

"He's okay," he said, meaning the now absent Mr. Morton. "Don't let him worry you. If you can work a machine you'll get a job handed to you on a golden plate. We've got two of the things lying idle up in the mine office right now." He paused. "You have got qualifications, I suppose. And you don't look the kind that has a criminal record." He laughed.

"You mean a certificate of training and a reference?" said Angela. "Yes, I have both from the bank where I worked." She added a little shyly and quite modestly, "I *think* they're quite good."

"You bet they are," said Mr. Richards encouragingly. He turned from looking at Angela's bewildered face to Nellie's head bowed in her arms on the table. "That kid's asleep," he said. "Mrs. Smith said you've come from Carnlow to-day."

"In a truck," said Angela and then added firmly, "It was *fun*."

Mr. Richards threw back his head and laughed.

"I've only made that trip once," he said. "And if you call that fun, young lady, I'd hate to see you really enjoying yourself flat out. But come on, let me help you get this youngster to her room. She's too heavy for you."

The young man stood up and walked round the table to Nellie's side. He was above medium height and quite striking-looking with a good forehead and nose, bright blue eyes that smiled a lot and a mouth that smiled a little unevenly but showed a very good set of polished teeth.

"Oh, please," said Angela, pushing her chair back. "Nellie can walk . . ." She bent over her sleeping sister to wake her but Mr. Richards held up a protesting hand.

"Don't be so big sisterish," he said with a tease in his voice. "Leave the poor child to her dreams. I'll carry her."

"But she's thirteen . . ." began Angela.

Gently, almost tenderly, this strange and pleasant young man put his arms under Nellie's legs and shoulders and lifted her.

"She's thistledown," he said. He turned and in an effortless way began to walk down the dining-room with his burden. "What do they feed you on in England?" he asked. "This poor child is all skin and bone. I could play battlecock with her."

"How did you know we were English?" asked Angela as she held open the door for him. "And we have lots of good food at home, only Nellie's been sick."

"That's why you came to Australia?" he asked over Nellie's

head. "And I knew you were English for three very good reasons. One . . . that pink and white complexion which we'll brown for you up here in three months. Two . . . you don't speak the way I speak, now do you?"

His eyes over Nellie's head were laughing at her.

"And three?" asked Angela.

"Something about mad dogs and Englishmen. Know it? Now which is your room?"

"The end one, I'm afraid," said Angela. "I'm sorry it's such a long way . . ."

"I'm not. I can talk to you longer. I love hearing the way you speak, that's for sure. Well, here we are, you open the door and I'll deposit the sleeping beauty in her bower."

He walked into the room and put Nellie, still sound asleep, on one of the beds.

"Don't you wake her up to get undressed," he cautioned. "She won't care a fig what she's sleeping in so long as she can sleep."

"I think perhaps you're right," said Angela, looking down at her sister's sleeping face with the compunction one always feels when looking at the young and defenceless.

When she looked up Mr. Richards was looking at her and not at Nellie.

"You're tired, too," he said. "I won't keep you up, but come and see me before you beard the manager in his den in the morning. I'll give you the drill about what to say to him. After that you'll get a job, certain sure."

"But it won't be any good if I haven't the qualifications to do what he wants to be done."

"Dear child," said Mr. Richards. "If you can use a Comptometer you'll be working for *me*." He grinned and walked to the door.

There was the droning sound of a plane taking off somewhere near at hand. Mr. Richards cocked his head and listened.

"That's the Cessna," he said. "I thought for a moment it might be the DC coming in with the mail."

"What is the Cessna?" Angela asked because she thought she was expected to say something.

Across the distance of the room she liked the look of the friendly Mr. Richards even better. She still couldn't absorb the total load of kindness and good luck she had had poured on her in so short a time. He would be nice to work for, she knew this instinctively.

"The Cessna is Gilly Lawrence's plane. He's a big station owner and flies his own way into town. He owns a nice slice of the company interests in the mine, too. You'll meet him."

"You mean he's a mining man too?" asked Angela, and then bit her lip. Mr. Richards folded his arms and leaned on the door jamb.

"So you've heard about Gilly Lawrence already, have you?" he said. "Well, you'd have to, sooner or later. He's the biggest gun in and out of the town."

"I knew Mrs. Anstey, who lived at Naroo Downs . . . when I was a child in England."

Mr. Richards brought himself upright with a jerk.

"For heaven's sake," he said. "You're the niece that was coming out from England?"

"Not a real niece. Aunt Kara was my mother's oldest friend. We just called her Aunt."

"Then what . . ." He stopped short. In the tiny silence that followed, the plane could be heard droning a circle round the town.

"He's just been down south," he said, nodding his head in the direction of the window through which the sound of the aeroplane could be heard. "He's testing out before he takes off for Naroo Downs. Didn't you know he was in town today?"

"I've only just got here myself," said Angela. "But, Mr. Richards . . .?"

"Yes?"

"I would like that job in the mine office, please. I've come here to work, not to visit Mr. Lawrence."

Mr. Richards gave Angela a long appraising look. She was standing very straight and still on the other side of Nellie's bed. Her grave eyes were clear and firm.

"Okay," he said. "You'll get it." Then added mischievously, "That's if the qualifications and references are up to standard. Have to have them for the files. Mr. Gilly Lawrence might look 'em over."

Angela smiled and her shoulders relaxed perceptibly.

"As for him up there . . ." Mr. Richards nodded his head again to the window and the sound of the plane engine. "He comes in over roof-tops whenever he wants. There's plenty of time for you to meet *him*."

He waved a hand and went through the door, shutting it after him.

Angela walked slowly to the window and looked out. She caught her breath for she had not known before how much a night could have of beauty.

Beyond the dark shadows of a few houses on the slope of the town a silver plain stretched away to the rim of dark mountains. There were the sounds of laughing voices somewhere, and the clatter of crockery in the hotel kitchen department. Yet it seemed as if the world was silent all around, and from pole to pole. The sounds . . . voices, crockery, the droning of a plane . . . were local. Beyond was endless silence, limitless plains, a vast hood of blue-black sky studded with brilliant lamps; and in the near distance, the dark mountains.

As Angela stood at the window and looked at the night, the plane completed its last trial circle. She could follow its flight by the winking port and starboard lights. Like two coloured fire-flies in the night the red and green lights passed along a sky trail through the moveless stars towards the mountain ridge. The sound of the two engines grew fainter and the lights passed over the range into the unknown distance beyond.

"He's gone," thought Angela. "He's gone."

For a long time she stood and looked at the sky and the place between two stars where the plane had disappeared, Gilbert Lawrence, Aunt Kara's beloved nephew, with it. For the first time she felt the real impact of Aunt Kara's loss.

She felt suddenly overcome with tiredness, almost as if life, or the spirit at least, had gone out of her. She turned away from the window, switched off the light and lay down on her bed, fully clothed, as Nellie was.

"In a minute I'll get up and get undressed," she thought.

But she didn't open her eyes again until a maid brought in the tea at six o'clock next morning.

CHAPTER THREE

"In this part of the world the distant hills are always blue," Mrs. Smith said as she stood with Angela at the office window of the Red Gorge Hotel. "Pity of it is, when you get to 'em they're just grey and stony and hot like the rest of the north. 'Cept where the gorges are. They make up for everything."

"It's in the gorges they find the blue asbestos?" asked Angela.

"The world's best. But there's a lot more to 'em than

that. Every metal under the sun. Red Gorge, the big one, is red with iron, copper and bluestone. There's manganese out on the plains. They say Gilbert Lawrence has got hundreds of miles of it . . . right on the surface, you can see it from the air . . . out at Naroo Downs."

"Have you ever been to Naroo Downs, Mrs. Smith?" Angela asked.

The older woman shook her head.

"Too busy," she said. "This place keeps me running morning and night. Some day, I'll go. Mrs. Anstey used to ask me. They say it's lovely out there." She sighed and turned away from the window. "Well, that's why the hills that are distant are always blue up here," she said. "Somewhere lovely and cool we always want to go but never do go. Now come along, young miss, you look at this little map of the town and I'll show you how to get to the mine office."

"You are quite sure I'm not imposing on you by leaving Nellie asleep upstairs?" Angela asked, looking at Mrs. Smith with a small cloud of anxiety in her eyes.

"Of course not. That child's exhausted. If she wakes up before you're back I'll get the housemaid to give her some breakfast, and I'll bring her along here to keep me company."

"I couldn't wake her properly for morning tea."

"Should think not. She's tired. What's more . . ." Mrs. Smith broke off and looked at Angela thoughtfully. "As a woman with a grown-up family I don't mind telling you that child doesn't look too strong to me. She mightn't take too well to this heat."

The shadow deepened in Angela's eyes. She looked down at the road map with unseeing eyes. When she looked up her her own face was a little pale.

"I'm afraid we have to stay for a little while. You see . . ." She hesitated as she saw the thoughtful inquiring look in Mrs. Smith's eyes. Once again pride came to her aid. "We've made a long journey and we need to get over *that*," she said with an attempt to show confidence and firmness. "After we recover, we may move on."

After Angela had made sure of her directions to the mine office, picked up her hat from the chair by the door and once again thanked Mrs. Smith for looking after Nellie, she went out into the wide palm-decorated patio of the hotel. Outside, the heat, although it was only half past seven in the morning, struck her like a blast from a furnace. Its glare wounded her eyes so she was thankful for the sun glasses she had bought from the barber's shop on the liner coming out from England. They were of the very latest design and by putting them on Angela unconsciously added a touch of the mysterious and reticent to her otherwise simple appearance. The white straw hat was not only simple, it was becoming, and the few people that were in the wide dusty roadway looked at her curiously more than once.

Any stranger in town was interesting and one whose slim figure and unusual appearance would have been attractive anywhere was doubly interesting in Red Gorge.

As Angela walked down the road to the mine office she was quite unaware she was as cool and fresh as a flower to sun-faded eyes that never saw a flower except in certain seasons round the pools at the bottom of the gorges farther to the east.

In the hotel office Mrs. Smith wrote a note to Mrs. Appleby at Carnlow. One never knew, a truck or car might be going through that track and the letter could wait on the shelf for a mailman.

> "You are right," Mrs. Smith wrote. "They're strangers without any ties in Red Gorge. And they've not too much money. The older one was looking for a job right away. There's something worrying them and maybe they came out here for the younger one's health and someone told them Red Gorge would be a good place to come because there were always jobs hanging out like figs on the trees. I've my doubts as to whether the young one will stand up to this climate. She's a nice little kid but spoiled. As for the older girl—well, you're quite right—she really takes my heart. Straight as a die, too. You can always tell it when you're in our business, as you know. We meet all sorts. Well, she's gone down to the mine office to get a job and judging by the look in young Mr. Kevin Richards's eyes, she'll get it. Then we'll see how they make out. I'll keep an eye on them, never fear. But I wouldn't let them know. Lots of pride and that sort of stuff about the older one. I'll let you know how things go."

As she folded the letter and put it in an envelope she made a further comment to herself:

"*May move on!* Landsakes, and in a continent that could take the whole of Europe with room over! Like Kevin

Richards said, there's mad dogs and Englishmen but no one ever said anything as smart as that about *Englishwomen*."

At the mine office Angela immediately left the heat behind as she crossed the threshold. This building, like the hotel, was air-conditioned. Moreover, it was the most modern-looking office Angela had ever seen. It shone with polish, carefully chosen restful colours. Behind a glass panel the receptionist's desk and office furniture was of tubular steel and discreetly coloured chair slings. Beyond the glass wall of the outside office Angela could see the same modern streamlined office comfort of the interior rooms.

She was early so the only two people inside that building were the receptionist, now taking off her hat and hanging it on a wall peg beside her table, and the bent head of Kevin Richards in an office area beyond.

This was *business* so Angela carefully avoided looking in Kevin Richards's direction. He had only to lift his head to see her through the glass wall. She took off her sun glasses, blinked her eyes in the new light, and smiled shyly at the receptionist, who was looking at her with the kind of curiosity that showed surprise and an acute interest in the other's sartorial effects.

"I hope I am not too early," Angela said politely. "But I do have an appointment with Mr. Richards at ten minutes to eight. Perhaps I could wait . . ."

"No, you don't have to wait," the other girl said, still looking at Angela with such curiosity that she almost forgot her manners. "He told me to expect you. You're the new girl for the Comptometer, aren't you?"

Angela blinked again, this time from sheer surprise.

"But I . . ." she began to say. She stopped. It mightn't be wise to add she hadn't yet been taken on by the mine. Goodness only knows what Mr. Richards had in his mind, or what he had really said to the receptionist.

"That's all right," the girl said, suddenly pulling herself together. "I'm sorry I'm staring but you do look different from anyone else who comes in for a job."

"Do I?" said Angela uneasily. Didn't she look efficient enough, she wondered?

"My name's Janette Wells," the receptionist said. "Come round through that door and I'll tell Mr. Richards you're here."

As the office was a glass house Angela could see that Janette's way of telling Mr. Richards was to rap on the glass wall. She could also see the pleased amused smile with which Mr. Richards received this message.

"Perhaps they're very friendly," Angela thought.

Kevin Richards opened the door for her.

"Well, here you are," he said. "Looking as fresh as any English daisy. By the way, what does an English daisy look like? I've never seen one."

"Like me. You just said so," said Angela with a smile and then suddenly bit her lip. Was she allowed to talk to him the way he talked to her?

"Well, well!" he said. "Now I really do know."

He placed a chair for her and then walked round his table to the chair on the other side. He sat down, moved his blotting-pad and then looked up. When he had done this Angela saw that his personality had gone through a transformation in that short minute between sitting down and touching the blotting-pad. His eyes were still friendly and he still smiled but this time it was the business executive interviewing a possible employee.

He took the parchment envelope Angela handed him across the table, opened it and read the contents of certificates and reperences. When he finished he put them back in the envelope, handed them across the table to Angela and sighed.

Angela flushed.

"Won't they do?" she asked.

He shook his head.

"They're too good to be true," he said. Then corrected himself with a hint of his former friendlier grin. "I mean you're too good to be true. You'll give us a few weeks' service and then flit to higher salaries and more rarefied places elsewhere. Or . . ."

"You mean . . . you don't think . . ."

"Of course I think. How do you think I run my job if I don't think? Of course, you'll be taken on. We'll get what work we can out of you in your short stay, Miss Burns, and then give you a farewell tea-party, a snakeskin belt as a parting souvenir, and wave you off on the aeroplane to promotions elsewhere. Or . . ."

"Please, Mr. Richards," said Angela puzzled, "I think you're joking."

"I'm not, Miss Burns. The work you've been doing is on IBM, Hollerith, or Powers machines. We've got IBM machines here but so has every really modern office in the country. What we haven't got is half enough girls to work them. A girl, or man for that matter, who has had this training is worth her weight in soft gold that's been rolled in diamonds."

He leaned across the table and pointed a finger directly at Angela.

"Do you know what, Miss Burns?" he demanded. "In this country for every one hundred girls there are a hundred and six males. What do you think that means?"

"They, I mean the girls, get married."

"Exactly. And that's what will happen to you if you don't put on a uniform of sackcloth, get some freckles on your nose and wear flat-bottomed fishboats for shoes. I'm warning you. Also in this town there are only fifty girls to every hundred males. Above average for bachelors, you see?"

"I do," said Angela gravely.

Kevin Richards leaned back in his chair and folded his arms.

"You're eyes don't light up? You don't leap out of your chair? Perhaps you knew these interesting vital statistics before you came to Red Gorge?"

Angela blushed, this time with annoyance she could barely conceal.

"I did not, Mr. Richards," she said with considerable dignity. "I came for my sister's health. Though Australian bachelors in general and Red Gorge bachelors in particular may wish for a wife, they can hardly wish for *two*. And anyone who takes me takes Nellie too."

She thought this was the most extraordinary business interview she had ever had in her life.

"In that case," said Kevin Richards with equal gravity, "all you've got to do is name your own salary."

"Name my own salary?"

"Precisely."

He got up from his chair, walked round the table and stood beside Angela's chair. He rested both hands on the table and leaning forward on them looked down into her bewildered face. Suddenly his own face broke into a smile.

"Miss Angela Burns . . ." he said. "Last night I told you if you saw me first I'd give you the low-down on how to deal with the G.O.M. in there." He nodded his head in the direction of one of the glass walls through which Angela could now see Mr. Morton hanging his white tropical hat on a peg. "Don't take any notice of steely eyes or flinty hearts," he added, still smiling and looking straight down into Angela's eyes. "They're straight façade. I've put all the trumps in your daisy-like hand. Go right in there and play them. Don't forget to name your own salary."

Angela took up her envelope of credentials and stood up.

"Mr. Richards, I don't know how to thank you—and everybody . . ."

"Don't forget I'm one of the excess bachelors of Red Gorge, and may I sit at your table for dinner to-night? You'll be able to afford to pay for your own dinner," he finished with a further grin as he went to the door and held it open for her.

As Angela, after a polite knock, passed into Mr. Morton's office Kevin Richards went across the outside office to the receptionist's desk.

"Janette," he said with an affectedly sad air. "When you relay that telephone message through to Naroo Downs about the journalists coming up here to photograph the gorges you'd better tell Gilly Lawrence the lost Burns children are *found*. They're right here in Red Gorge. He was in a heck of a fluff yesterday about having to go south again to look for them. I wasn't going to tell him of our golden find but on second thoughts I'd better lead a frank and open life with him. He swings a nasty stock-whip when he's out of sorts."

Janette Wells was a pretty round-faced girl with dark hair, dark eyes and an expressive mouth. Her eyes were a little sharp and bright now as she tapped her teeth with a pencil.

"I can understand how sad you are," she said. "She's really pretty, isn't she?"

"But there's *hope*," said Kevin Richards. "After all, Gilly Lawrence only thought he had to find out where they'd got to because of Mrs. Anstey. When he knows they're here, and safe in our keeping . . ."

"*Your* keeping, you mean," said Janette sarcastically.

"Why should you worry?" demanded Kevin. "You've got at least six admirers to my knowledge."

"So I have," said Janette, turning to her typewriter. "That's just why I'm not worrying."

"But you haven't caught the big fish? You haven't got Gilly Lawrence on the list. Is that it?" asked Kevin teasing.

Janette gave him an oblique look under her lids.

"*Him!*" she said. "Huh! I'd as soon be tied up to a rock python as Gilly Lawrence. Besides, there's talk of Stella Winton being out there at Naroo Downs, now Mrs. Anstey has gone."

Kevin Richards whistled.

"The beautiful Stella Winton!" he said. Janette typed furiously. "Ah, well!" he added. "Give me the English daisy!"

"You would!" Janette said without looking up, and swinging the machine carriage across with a bang.

Kevin Richards lifted his shoulders from the window frame against which he had been leaning.

"I suppose I'd better do some work," he said. "I'm only sorry I don't rate a private secretary in this house."

"And that there aren't brick walls," added Janette, still not pausing nor looking round.

When Kevin Richards walked through to his own office her fingers stopped and for a moment she sat looking down at the typed sheet on the roller. Then quietly she turned her head and stole a look through the glass walls to where Angela Burns was just rising from her short interview with the manager. Janette sighed, and went back to her typing. When Angela came through she managed a smile. This girl was a nice girl, you only needed half a glance to see that. It was not her fault there were always manpower problems in Red Gorge.

"I'm to come back after lunch to start," Angela said. "Perhaps you would be kind enough to show me where I'm to work."

"Congratulations," Janette said, standing up. "I hope you stay a while with us. We're terribly short-handed in the office."

"Oh, I will," Angela promised fervently. She felt as if standing on the office floor she was standing on a gold mine. *Twenty pounds a week!* And she hadn't named it. Mr. Morton had. She had yet to learn that it cost nearly twenty pounds a week to live in Red Gorge, with the only compensation that one lived well because one had to live on what was sent up from the south. And it was all expensive, but all good.

Back at the hotel she was so excited she could hardly tell Mrs. Smith of her good fortune.

"I'm to work the big calculator, not just the the Comptometer," she said. And then suddenly broke off. Nellie! For the first time since her mother's death a whole hour had passed in which she had forgotten Nellie.

"Is Nellie all right?" she said. "And, oh, Mrs. Smith, what shall I do with Nellie while I go to work?"

"She's still in bed asleep, and you'll send Nellie to school like everyone else."

"Is it a good school? And can she get good companions? And qualifications . . ."

"It's a new school and the pride of the desert. She can get the same certificates as any child down south, and in Red Gorge the mine manager's child and the station owner's child sit alongside the miner's child. Now, young miss, you've lived near enough to Scotland to know what that means."

"Oh, yes, I do indeed," said Angela breathlessly. "If only Nellie can make a friend. At home her whole life was taken up with her friends."

"You walk up to that school as soon as you've had a good cup of tea. One look inside it and you'll wish you were back at school yourself. On your way back call at Mrs. Sharman's, the fourth house from the town on Emu Flat. She takes in boarders."

"Boarders?" said Angela, suddenly coming back to earth again.

"Yes, boarders," said Mrs. Smith, folding her hands and nodding her head. "This place costs twenty pounds a week for *one*. Only the manager can afford to live here. And Mr. Richards and one or two others have their evening meal here."

"Where does Mr. Richards live otherwise?"

"He has a State house. Out along Emu Flat. They're all State houses here, big and little."

"Could I get a State house, do you think?"

"And do for yourself? If there's one empty you can get one, they have skeleton furniture but you have to put the frills in yourself."

"Then that's what I'd like."

"You take my tip and move into Mrs. Sharman's while you're looking around and waiting."

"Yes, perhaps I'd better do that. Mrs. Smith, you have been so awfully kind. I wish I knew how to thank you."

Mrs. Smith looked at Angela's radiant face. All the shadows were gone. Anxiety was banished.

"She doesn't think of herself at all, that one," Mrs. Smith thought. "All she asks is a secure job and a house in which to bring up her young sister. Most girls would drop dead at the thought of having to spend the rest of their lives amongst strangers, and in this climate."

"Come on, now," she said aloud. "I'm going to give you a

cup of tea in my own sitting-room. By the time you get back I'll have young Nellie up, bathed and fed. Then we'll see how *she* looks at this new world."

It took Nellie a big scene, a flood of tears and a near fainting fit to begin to look at the new world as a place in which she might live for a few years.

For once Angela, who had returned from entering Nellie at the school, was adamant. Necessity made her firm. The girls had no alternative and Nellie had to be made to see it.

"Darling, wait till you see the school. It's lovely. The paint on the walls is new and of heavenly colours. The headmaster is a Scot. The children all wear the nicest clothes and they're as happy as can be. There's a radio in every room. And Nellie, a swimming-pool. Just imagine, the children go swimming every afternoon."

"Is there television?"

Angela had to shake her head.

"Not here," she said regretfully. "Only down south."

"Then let's go down south. Why can't you get a job down south?"

"First I have to earn some money here." Laboriously Angela explained to Nellie how they had spent a certain amount of their limited capital and it had to be replaced before they could make further inroads in it.

"But why can't we go and live on Aunt Kara's station?"

"Because it's not Aunt Kara's station any more. She only had part of the income from it for her lifetime. It now all reverts to Mr. Gilbert Lawrence."

"Why can't he take us to live with him? Why can't you marry him?"

"Nellie," said Angela with sudden severity, "if you even mention that subject again I'll have to do something desperate like putting you in a boarding-school. That would mean sending you hundreds and hundreds of miles away. Besides, I couldn't afford it. You've just got to face the facts of life, even though you are only thirteen. Mr. Lawrence does not want to marry me. I do not want to marry him. We're bound to meet him sooner or later and if you say anything near him about staying on his station or about marrying I'll be forced to send you to boarding-school."

For once Nellie was silenced by Angela's anger. She had never seen Angela angry like this before. She supposed Mr. Gilbert Lawrence was really an ogre. When she had asked the housemaid about him this morning the housemaid had said:

"My, he's good-looking. Big tall man, he is. But he's got a terrible reputation. Drives his men with stock-whips, so they say. All the same, when he comes in here, to the hotel, I mean, he's always nice to the staff. Very polite and all that." She had nodded her head thoughtfully. "But I wouldn't cross him, on horseback, all the same. He might use a stock-whip on me."

Nellie had listened to this talk about stock-whips with wide eyes. She had liked the picture of Gilbert Lawrence being tall and handsome and polite to the people in the hotel. But *driving people with stock-whips?* She wasn't sure she wanted Angela to marry him after all, in spite of a million-acre station, and horses to ride every day.

Nellie had no idea that *Driving men with stock-whips* was only a local saying and meant that he worked his men very hard. She had a mental image of a tall man flaying men's backs with a great long lashed whip.

"Why don't they ride away to some other station?" she had asked the housemaid, meaning the men whom she thought were the victims of the stock-whip.

"That's the funny thing about it," said the maid. "His stockmen always stick to him. But they're a hard-riding tough lot themselves. Maybe they can stand a boss like Gilly Lawrence, the same as they can stand this awful climate up here. They don't ever go south, not even for their holidays. There's stockmen out there at Naroo Downs were born on the place and the farthest west or south they've ever been is Red Gorge and this hotel."

The maid rather liked Nellie's awed interest and she went on to dilate on the tyrannies of Gilly Lawrence and the toughness of his men, forgetting that she too, a minute before, had shaken her head in some doubt.

"Why do you call him 'Gilly Lawrence?'" asked Nellie. "Why does everyone call him 'Gilly Lawrence?'"

The maid shrugged.

"He's just the big shot round the place," she said. And then she winked and added, "They don't do it to his face. They wouldn't dare. Everybody just likes to talk about him, whether they've met him or not."

"What do you call him when you meet him?" asked Nellie.

"I call him 'Mr. Lawrence' and mightily politely at that."

"Well, I shall call him Gilly Lawrence to his face," said Nellie, tilting her chin. "And if he lifts a stock-whip to me I'll have him put in prison."

"That'll be the day!" said the maid, giving a final rub to the dressing-table mirror.

"People aren't allowed to be cruel to children in this country, are they?" asked Nellie, suddenly doubtful.

"No," said the maid, determinedly swatting a fly which had dared to escape into the sanctum of a Red Gorge hotel bedroom. "You put him in gaol and I promise I'll be there to see it. Now there you are, this room's nice and tidy and when you go along to the office Mrs. Smith's got a pleasant surprise for you."

"Nothing," said Nellie, "would surprise me any more."

The maid went out, closing the door behind her.

"Put Gilly Lawrence in gaol!" she said with a chuckle. "That would be a wonder day, for sure. Like those two cattle owners up there in the Kimberleys accusing one another of cattle stealing. And taking one another to court over it too. Ought to have known better . . . at their age."

An hour later Nellie could see Angela's point about not wanting to marry Gilbert Lawrence. All the same, she was dying to see him. He had grown to the proportions of a legend by the time the housemaid had finished with him and in an odd incomprehensible way Nellie thought it wouldn't be such a bad idea to stay in Red Gorge for a little while. It would be like seeing the villain out of a Wild West film.

Odd, but this was the Wild West. She was right here, in the middle of it. It might be fun, after all.

Nellie had not then been outside the air-conditioned luxury of the hotel. She had yet to savour the heat of Red Gorge.

She remained very quiet after Angela's unusual outburst. She said nothing because she was not used to giving in to Angela and she wasn't sure it was wise to do so now. There were lots of other things in her life about which Nellie wanted her own way and only Angela could give them to her.

Besides, she had never lived in a luxury hotel like this before. She had never even been inside one. If the rest of the world beyond those palm-decked patios, those fern-bowered verandas, those sealing glass doors, was like it, it mightn't be so bad, after all.

"Angela," she said, lying back luxuriously in the long-backed lounge chair in which she sat. "I do feel tired. Could I please have a lemon drink?"

Angela noticed the film star pose but she was so relieved to put a period to this little scene that she smiled.

"Of course, dear. I'll get it."

"No. Just ring this bell," said Nellie, and she put out a thin tired arm, and with an air of infinite boredom, pressed the button on the side of the table.

The thinness of that arm made something catch at Angela's heart.

"Nellie, darling," she said. "I'm so sorry I was cross."

She decided this time not to chide Nellie for calling a steward for attention. Mrs. Smith had been so good and Nellie couldn't possibly understand.

Three days later Angela had already smoothed out most of the immediate problems of her life in Red Gorge. She and Nellie were to move the next day to Mrs. Sharman's until a State house, one of the smaller, less expensive ones, was vacant for them. Nellie was already installed in the school and though she had been very difficult about making the walk in the heat she had liked the school once she got over the first half day and the strangeness. The bright colours everywhere and the modern equipment fascinated her and when Angela bought her a swim suit and she learned she could be taught swimming as well as be free to swim in the pool her whole horizon lightened. But she did not tell Angela any of this for fear Angela would not understand that the walk was too hot and too long and that Nellie had to lie down and rest when she got in, in the afternoon.

In the mine office, Angela found that Kevin Richards was not only kind but very efficient in spite of his somewhat breezy manner. For two nights he had sat at her table for dinner and each time his friendliness could almost be mistaken for courting. Angela was careful not to misconstrue this, however, for she noticed he often had, in unguarded moments, the same manner to the typists and particularly the receptionist Janette Wells. Angela also noticed that Janette Wells was always cross with Kevin Richards and often spoke sharply to him. After one of these sharp utterances, which Kevin always received with an amused grin, Janette would follow his lean figure as he walked away, with her dark eyes a little inscrutable.

In the machine room Angela quickly grasped the work she had to do and she did this with a kind of tireless efficiency that made Kevin Richards whistle.

"Don't be too good," Kevin said once with a smile. "Or the G.O.M. will marry you himself in order to hang on to you."

" But he's married already. Nellie sits next to his little girl at school. And there's a boy in a higher class."

" You were the one who first brought up the subject of two wives," said Kevin. " You never can tell about a place like Red Gorge. Anything can happen here, *once.*"

CHAPTER FOUR

This was the day Angela heard the Cessna coming in over the roof-tops. She knew nothing of Kevin Richards's message to Naroo Downs that the " Burns children had been found," or that Gilbert Lawrence had any interest or responsibility in finding them at all. Nevertheless when she heard the droning of the small plane and saw it quite literally coming in over the roof-tops she felt her heart suddenly beating faster.

What was he really like, she wondered? She supposed that one day she must inevitably meet him. Already she had seen that though Red Gorge was a widely scattered town it was in reality very small. Everything in it was related in some way or other to the big mines out of town. In the morning she had seen some men going out to the mines in trucks and in the afternoon she had seen the first shift coming back in those same trucks.

Her eyes, each time she had looked from her window in the hotel, or from her glass wall in the office, had wandered to the blue hills in the distance. Beyond them was Aunt Kara's station. She wondered what it would have been like had Aunt Kara lived. She wondered what Gilbert Lawrence was really like and whether Aunt Kara had loved him only because she had no children of her own or because he was in any way worthy of that love.

She felt proud of the fact that when she did meet him she would be independent and he would not feel she had come to Red Gorge to get aid from him.

Seeing the shadow of the plane pass over the roof-tops she had no idea it was her own presence now in Red Gorge that had brought Gilbert Lawrence in from Naroo Downs, and that in a few minutes she would indeed meet him.

Her back was turned and her head was bowed over her work when she knew by the sudden draught of hot air that someone had entered the office.

A quarter of an hour later the bell on her table buzzed and Angela lifted the receiver. It was Mr. Morton.

"Would you come into my office please, Miss Burns?"

"Yes, Mr. Morton. I will come at once."

She wondered if he had some new work for her, for she was already assured by Kevin Richards's manner that her work was good. All the same, she could not help feeling her heart-beats quicken. In any country and any office a summons to a junior officer from the manager must mean something of a sense of expectancy.

As she went through the main office she could see the back of a tall man dressed in khaki drill clothes. She could see a wide-brimmed hat such as the sheep and cattle men, some of whom she had already seen round the town, wore.

As she knocked and went into the office Mr. Morton stood up and the tall man turned round. Angela, because Mr. Morton was the manager and she his employee, looked at him and not at the stranger.

"Yes, Mr. Morton?" she said. She waited for him to speak and while she waited she felt the tall man looking at her. Mr. Morton was a trifle ill at ease.

"I understand you've not yet met Mr. Gilbert Lawrence," he said. Then coughed and added, "Mr. Lawrence of Naroo Downs."

"No, Mr. Morton," Angela said and once again, as if fore-warned, her heart beat a little faster and a faint flush began to tinge her cheeks.

"Well, this, eh, this is Mr. Lawrence of Naroo Downs." Mr. Morton made a small gesture with his hand towards the tall man beside her.

Angela slowly turned and raised her eyes to meet a pair of unsmiling grey eyes in the face of the most relentless, tough good looks she had ever seen.

On second thoughts he wasn't handsome. His face was powerful and browned by a life in the open air. His mouth was a straight line. His square brow and nose were straight, like his mouth. His dark hair, parted at one side, was thick. There were threads of silver in the black over his temples and when Angela thought about him afterwards it was this she remembered most. This, and his height and the unsmiling grey eyes. It was the whole aspect of strength that gave the impression of handsomeness.

Quietly and uncontrollably the flush in her cheeks deepened

to a blush. Her heart beat very fast so that she would not trust herself to words.

There was a moment's silence and then Mr. Morton coughed again. Gilbert Lawrence slowly put down the papers he held in one hand, turning away a little as he did so. He then turned again to Angela and held out his hand. All his movements were slow and considered. Yet they gave an impression of being able to spring into a lightning speed if necessary.

"How do you do, Miss Burns," he said. His voice drawled and seemed to come through half-closed lips. It sounded as if it was used rarely and then sparingly, but to effect.

Angela lifted her own hand and when he took it he gripped it a little too hard as if he was used to shaking hands only with men of powerful frame such as himself. His eyes showed no expression, yet they summed her up.

"How do you do?" Angela said in a voice so low she hardly heard it herself. She knew she would never forgive herself for that blush.

Of what had she been guilty that this man should look at her like this and that she herself should blush for her crimes?

It was the unexpectedness of the meeting. There could be no other reason.

"I missed you at the ship at Fremantle," Gilbert Lawrence said . . . still in the same drawling voice that was deceptively soft. His eyes were looking at her with the same grey blankness that was a mask for interrogation. "I am very sorry."

"I am sorry if I put you to any trouble, Mr. Lawrence," Angela said. "I did not expect you. Only . . ."

She was going to say "Aunt Kara" but the words died unuttered on her lips.

Gilbert Lawrence's eyes glinted a moment as if they forbade her to go on.

Of course! If Aunt Kara had not gone to meet her and Nellie she would have been here to-day. If he had had a regard for Aunt Kara he would be thinking that now, as Angela too was thinking it.

Suddenly there was a lump in her throat. She could say no more because of it, but she did not allow her eyes to waver away from his. To do that would admit guilt, and perhaps defeat. She would never do that to this man. It had been Aunt Kara who had bade her come and not she who had asked to come.

He turned and picked up the papers again but did not glance at them. Slowly he turned back to her.

" And your sister? You brought her with you? She is well?"

" Yes. We are here together. She is quite well, thank you. That is, it will take her a little time to get over the journey, and used to the new environment."

" You intend to stay, Miss Burns?"

Miss Burns, indeed! In Aunt Kara's letters it had been Gilbert and Angela. That " Miss Burns " was meant to show her just what their relationship was.

Mr. Morton was standing, both hands on the back of his chair, watching them. Vaguely, at the back of her mind, Angela was feeling very sorry for Mr. Morton. He must find this a very odd meeting. It was the only friendless meeting Angela had experienced since the morning the big ocean liner had docked at Fremantle.

" Yes, I intend to stay," said Angela. " I didn't quite know where to go, Mr. Lawrence. So I came on here. I hope you did not think it was with any intention of bothering you." She saw something like a fleeting grim smile change the expression of his eyes. It was so quickly come and gone that she could not tell what it meant. All she knew was that for a single moment the expression of his face had changed. Her back stiffened a little. She would have liked to add . . . " I'd rather be shot than be a charge on *your* hands," but she had to keep up the role of politeness for politeness's sake.

" I had no idea, of course, how far north, and inland, Red Gorge was. It was the only place name I knew in that part of Australia. So I came on here. Now I have a job with the mining company and I am very comfortably provided for." She paused a moment and then added, " Thank you for your inquiry, Mr. Lawrence."

He rustled his papers with one hand.

" Is your sister comfortably provided for, Miss Burns?"

" Yes, thank you. She started at school yesterday. We are to have a State cottage shortly."

Gilbert Lawrence moved his gaze to Mr. Morton. Mr. Morton coughed.

" Won't you both sit down," he said as if remembering that for the moment Angela was not so much an employee as a connection of one of the company's powerful partners.

" No thank you," said Angela gravely to Mr. Morton. She turned again to Gilbert Lawrence, who had turned away again. She could see how powerful were his shoulders and that in profile his face had something of the hawk quality of an Indian chief.

" I'm grateful that Mr. Lawrence has been so kind as to inquire after our welfare but I wouldn't like to take up his time." She glanced again at her employer. " Or yours, Mr. Morton," she added apologetically.

Unexpectedly Gilbert Lawrence, who was about the stillest person she had ever seen, made an abrupt movement of straightening his powerful shoulders and turning once again towards her.

" I wouldn't like to keep you from your work, Miss Burns," he said with unexpected shortness. " I'm afraid I must return to Naroo Downs as soon as possible. I have visitors there. But I would be grateful if you would let me know if you need anything. I shall be at your disposal if you call on me."

This last remark made Angela blink. She couldn't imagine Gilbert Lawrence being at the disposal of anyone on earth. His whole bearing, his every word denied such a proposition. And it was odd, surely, that he should make such a suggestion.

" I don't think we shall want for anything, Mr. Lawrence, but it is very kind of you to offer."

" Not at all," he replied conventionally.

And he didn't mean it either, thought Angela. She felt so angry with him that she put out her hand to terminate the interview.

" Thank you very much for calling, Mr. Lawrence. I would like to say good-bye now and go back to my work, if you will excuse me."

" Certainly." He shook hands with her again, and again this slightly hurt her own small hand.

" Will you excuse me, please, Mr. Morton?" she asked, turning to the manager.

" Yes, if you wish it, Miss Burns. But I think we ought to sit down. I might get Miss Wells to make us some tea."

" No thank you," said Angela politely. " I have work to do. I would rather get on with it if you will forgive me."

Mr. Morton looked at Gilbert Lawrence inquiringly.

" I think we should let Miss Burns go, if that is what she wishes," said Gilbert Lawrence. " I have assured her that I will be of any assistance to her if she is in difficulties."

Angela blushed again but this time from sheer frustrated pride. Mr. Gilbert Lawrence, she knew, would be the last person she would ask. And why should she be in any difficulties?

With a pang, she remembered Nellie. Supposing Nellie didn't grow strong in health here in Red Gorge? Supposing she even fell seriously ill?

"I'll cross that bridge when I come to it," thought Angela. She offered Gilbert Lawrence a polite smile, then said, "Thank you, Mr. Morton," again to the manager and walked quietly out of the room. She shut the glass door behind her and was careful not to look back through the glass walls as she went to her own room.

Kevin Richards put his head in the door. Angela was sitting at her table, hands in front of her, staring into space.

"Did you hate him very much?" said Kevin with a smile.

"Yes," said Angela. "About as much as I could."

"Good," said Kevin with satisfaction. "That clears him off my stock route." Then his grin deepened. "They all hate him at first, you know; then they try breaking their necks to get a smile from him."

"Who?" asked Angela dazedly.

"The girls, of course. Who else?"

"Not me," said Angela fiercely. "I'd as soon try to crack a brick wall."

"You don't have to try," Kevin reassured her. "He's out of competition. The beautiful, the divine and the designing Stella Winton is staying out at Naroo Downs."

"I don't know who Stella Winton is," said Angela, suddenly weary and deflated, "but I'm not willing to believe any woman would want to be loved by that . . . that . . . granite statue."

"That's how we men think," said Kevin with mock sorrow. "But it's not the way the girls act . . . not after they've seen him the second or third time anyway."

"I won't ever see him a second time so we won't have to bother about any third time," said Angela.

She looked at Kevin with a sudden warming gratitude. How helpful and kind and friendly *he* was compared with the other man. Her spirits brightened. It was very nice to have Kevin Richards for a good friend. And after so short an acquaintance too.

She smiled at him.

"Good," he said, welcoming it with one of his own. "Now the moon's come out over the desert."

He pulled his head back from the doorway and went off in the direction of his own room.

Fortunately for Angela the removal to Mrs. Sharman's

boarding-house that evening took her mind from Gilbert Lawrence and his frigid acceptance of her presence in Red Gorge.

The packing was already done and when Angela returned to the hotel after work there was only the business of collecting Nellie, gathering together their belongings, hiring a taxi and saying good-bye to Mrs. Smith.

"I can't thank you enough for your kindness," Angela said.

"Don't mention a word of it," said Mrs. Smith guardedly. If Angela had had time to think she would have noticed that Mrs. Smith was exceptionally thoughtful. Bill Smiley, the truck driver who had brought Angela and Nellie to Red Gorge, had mentioned to more than one acquaintance in Red Gorge that his unusual passenger was reputed, in Carnlow, to be in Red Gorge to marry Gilbert Lawrence. Three days had been long enough for the intelligence to seep through to Mrs. Smith's ears as well as to those of other people in Red Gorge.

When Gilbert Lawrence had come in over the roof-tops that afternoon Mrs. Smith had great expectations of something developing. She was a little puzzled at Angela's silence on the visit . . . for already all Red Gorge had known that Gilly Lawrence had gone down to the mine office to meet Angela Burns. All Red Gorge was also puzzled as to why Angela had taken a job there. Surely there was no need for the girl who was going to marry Gilbert Lawrence of Naroo Downs to take a job anywhere? Or was it all only a yarn anyway?

As Angela was in ignorance of what was in everybody's mind and as she was fully occupied in arranging for the change from the hotel to the boarding-house she did not notice the oblique looks, the scarcely veiled curiosity and, in Mrs. Smith, a hint of motherly concern.

"Well, if there's any big events in the future," said Mrs. Smith, seeing the two girls into the taxi, "you'll be back here again for sure, if only for celebrating. I'll be seeing you."

Angela supposed this might be a local way of suggesting she might one day get promotion in the mine office, or have some other such good fortune.

"Oh, yes," she said gladly. "I'll be seeing you before long, I'm sure, Mrs. Smith. There's sure to be occasions for celebrating."

She wondered why Mrs. Smith looked knowing and why there was even a suggestion of a wink in that kind lady's eye.

"I won't say good-bye," Angela said.

"Of course not. No one ever says 'good-bye' in Red Gorge. They generally say 'see you later.'"

Mrs. Smith was disappointed because Angela did not tell her what had taken place in that interview with Gilbert Lawrence at the mine office. Well, she thought, young Mr. Kevin Richards would be in for dinner to-night, that's for sure. She might get something out of him. Gilly Lawrence turning up will certainly put a mote in that young fellow's eye. Mrs. Smith had seen very quickly just how Mr. Richards was taking to the pretty stranger.

Ah, well, that was the luck of the game! There weren't many who could hold a lead over Gilly Lawrence in the marriage stakes.

That reminded Mrs. Smith it was Race Week only a fortnight hence and she hadn't yet booked space on the DC freight plane for food stores. She'd go right in and ring the M.M.A. office now.

Nellie was silent as they drove in the taxi down Emu Flat to Mrs. Sharman's boarding-house.

Inside she could not conceal her disappointment that the rooms of Mrs. Sharman's house did not compare with the modern comfort of the hotel.

"It's hot," she said. "Angela, I feel dreadfully hot. Isn't there any air-conditioning here?"

"No, I'm afraid not," said Angela, busily unpacking the cases while Nellie sat dangling her feet on the best of the two beds. It was the bed by the window and had a pink candlewick coverlet. Nellie had immediately said, "I bags the pink bed by the window."

"Very well," Angela said, not so much giving in to Nellie's every whim as knowing that the fresh air pouring in that window would be good for Nellie.

Now, however, when Nellie showed every sign of discomfiture over the simple unadornment of their room she decided she must be firm with her young sister.

"It is not for long," she said. "Soon we'll have our own little house. And I believe Mrs. Sharman is a very good cook and they have excellent meals here."

"I don't want anything to eat," said Nellie.

"Listen, Nellie, you unpack your own case and see how pretty you can make the dressing-table with those lovely pink cloths you embroidered in England. You did them so beautifully and you won a needlework prize with them. They'll match the coverlet on your bed."

"I don't like them any more," said Nellie. "I'd rather have the kind you can buy in shops."

Angela straightened her tired shoulders and looked at her younger sister. She had had added to a long day's work, the embarrassment of that interview with Gilbert Lawrence and the business of departure from the hotel.

If only Nellie would be happy. Usually her needlework, which really was a matter of pride, could bring an air of satisfaction to Nellie. People had always wondered and marvelled that so young a girl could do such fine stitching. She had won a prize on the ship coming out from England, in competition with adults too.

But now her eyes were downcast. Angela stood above her opened case and looked at her younger sister.

Nellie was not so pale as she had been on their arrival in Red Gorge. Indeed, her face was suffused with a pink glow that although it made her look younger dispelled Angela's fears that Nellie was not well.

How hard it was, Angela thought, to judge when Nellie was exhausted or just childishly playing up. She would have to be firm with Nellie for Nellie's own sake. Life is too difficult for spoilt darlings to find happiness easily, Angela thought.

"Nellie," she said peremptorily, "get off that bed now and unpack your case. After that you can have a shower and we'll go in to dinner. You'll feel better if you *do* something."

"I don't want . . ." began Nellie.

"Do as I ask, please, Nellie," said Angela with a stubborn light in her own eye.

It was Angela who sat down on the other bed suddenly. She felt dreadfully tired and the glimpse she caught of her own face in the wardrobe showed it was white and strained. She wished she hadn't seen that reflection. It caused her heart to drop a little.

Just then she heard the droning of that small plane and her eyes went involuntarily to the window. But this window was facing west. Gilbert Lawrence should be flying that Cessna over the roof-tops eastward to Naroo Downs.

Again she felt that same pang of loneliness, almost of bereftness, she had felt on the first night in Red Gorge when she had seen the red and green winking lights disappearing between the stars over the mountains to the east.

It was an inexcusable as well as an irrational feeling. Angela once again put it down to over-tiredness.

Even as she sat silent, a pile of her own underclothes on her lap, the drone of the Cessna grew louder and a minute later it crossed the square of window light. It flew between the house and the sun which was declining in its last minutes down at the bottom of the western plain. The small plane's shadow flitted across the patch of light on the floor.

"Why," she said, half to herself and half to Nellie, "he's flying west. He can't be going home after all."

"He? Who?" said Nellie without much interest.

"Gilbert Lawrence. Naroo Downs is to the *east* of Red Gorge."

"He came into the hotel this afternoon after I got home from school," said Nellie, tracing a pattern on the carpet with the toe of her shoe. "He asked Mrs. Smith for me but I hid behind the palms and pretended I hadn't come home from school yet."

Angela turned her eyes away from the window to Nellie.

"Why did you do that?" she asked. "It was only a courtesy call. It would have been polite to meet him."

"There were some ladies in the lounge and they started making a fuss of him." Nellie's voice assumed the imitative tones of mockery. "Oh, there you are, Gilly, *darling*! Do come and tell us if this positively earth-shaking yarn going round Red Gorge is true? Gilly, you have no idea how absolutely *floored* we all are."

Angela put her bundle of folded clothes down on the bed and getting up walked to the window. She stood looking out over the immense plain that stretched right away to the sunset. Across that plain was a red track that led to Carnlow . . . the way she and Nellie had come. Along it stockmen were now droving a mob of bullocks towards the town. Over them hung a red-brown dust cloud.

"And what was this earth-shaking yarn?" she asked Nellie without turning round. She wished her voice would sound natural and that it was a natural question to ask.

Nellie's voice went on, imitating the ladies. "Are you going to get married, Gilly? Is it true you're going to marry that pretty . . ."

Nellie's voice stopped short. She suddenly remembered that it was she herself who had boasted about her sister marrying Gilbert Lawrence. Angela had forbidden her ever to mention the subject. *Fairy-tale stuff meant for little children to enjoy*, Angela had said. Nellie suddenly realised the enormity of her exaggeration and that Angela would not only be furious but it might now make Angela look most dreadfully foolish in Red Gorge.

There was a long silence, and at last Angela, still looking out of the window to the place where the plane had since disappeared into the fire-red sky of the sunset, spoke again.

"Whom did they say he was going to marry?" she asked idly.

"Well . . ." said Nellie, thinking furiously. "Oh, I know, some beautiful lady who is just visiting. Someone we don't know, Angela. Besides, it doesn't matter. He doesn't even carry a stock-whip and Emmy, the maid, told me he drove people with the stock-whips. He didn't have spurs on his heels either, though they were sort of funny boots . . . like riding boots only a bit different. They had elastic sides and the heels were a bit high. Emmy said they were cattlemen's boots and they wear the heels like that because when they rope a bullock the heels catch in the ground, and it's like a brake. It pulls up the bullock. He just gets in the plane like that and goes straight back and gets out of the plane on to a horse again. Emmy said so."

"Emmy chatters too much," said Angela. Then seeming to pull herself together again she turned round and went back to her unpacking.

"It would be someone called Stella Winton," she said in a matter-of-fact voice. "She is staying out at Naroo Downs and Kevin Richards told me she was beautiful and . . ." She paused. "Well, beautiful. And a great friend of Gilbert Lawrence's."

"Yes, that's her," said Nellie, almost sighing with relief. Any name would do so long as Angela didn't know what she, Nellie, had said and done about her own sister's intentions.

Nellie, exhausted by the effort she had had to make to evade Angela's questions, threw herself backwards on to the pillow, and spread her arms outwards on either side of her. Her feet still dangled over the side of the bed.

"Oh, I want to go to sleep," she said. "I don't want to unpack. I don't want any dinner."

"Please get up at once, Nellie," said Angela, "and unpack, have a bath, and go to dinner."

"I don't want . . ."

"If I hear that again," said Angela, suddenly and unusually angry, "I won't let you go swimming to-morrow. I won't let you go swimming for a week. Now get up at once."

Wearily Nellie dragged herself from her bed and began to struggle with the catches of her case. Angela did not go to her assistance for she feared that Nellie's air of exhaustion was for the purpose of winning unnecessary sympathy. Nevertheless Angela glanced surreptitiously at her sister more than once. But Nellie looked *well.* That *colour* in her cheeks, and the bright eyes! Why, Nellie hadn't looked so well in years.

"I've got a headache," Nellie complained.

"So have I," said Angela in her most matter-of-fact voice. "But bath, dinner, and bed, with an aspirin will fix that." With great determination she ignored all further complaints from her young sister.

As Mrs. Sharman's other two boarders, one an engineer and one a technical assistant, worked with the evening shift at the mine, Angela and Nellie were the only two who sat down to dinner in the small but spotlessly clean dining-room.

A beautiful meal of roast beef was put before them, but true to her word Nellie only toyed with the meal. She even declined the dessert, lemon sponge and custard, which was usually a favourite. Angela was so cross with Nellie for possibly hurting Mrs. Sharman's feelings that she readily agreed to Nellie's suggestion that she had better go to bed.

"Yes, do that," said Angela. "A good night's rest will make you feel better in the morning. There's nothing wrong with you, you know, Nellie. I fear you are just playing up, and it is very naughty of you."

Nellie did not answer but with a resigned air took an aspirin with a glass of water and put herself to bed.

Angela, herself tired almost to the point of exhaustion, sat on the veranda and watched the lights going on over the small town. Soon her attention wandered to the immensely starry sky again.

She wondered why Gilbert Lawrence flew west instead of east, and she remembered again with absolute clarity the image of those red and green winking lights forging a sky trail away out through the stars to the nothingness that lay beyond the mountains.

They were not very far away, those mountains, yet to Angela they were as distant as a mystery and a dream. Beyond them she might have travelled, if Aunt Kara had lived.

CHAPTER FIVE

When Angela retired for the night she found Nellie stretched on her back, the covers thrown off, and fast asleep. The colour on her cheeks had deepened to roses and the flush of sleep on her forehead again proclaimed to Angela that her sister was in the best of health.

"I suppose she was tired," Angela thought as she got undressed, and she wished she hadn't spoken so sharply earlier. She did not once reflect she too was tired, almost beyond support. It had been a full and a trying day and difficulties still lay ahead. She would have to meet Gilbert Lawrence from time to time. She would have to find the means of furnishing, other than the mere necessities provided, the little house when one fell vacant. And she would have to tussle again with Nellie when they made yet another change.

Meantime she had to find time, between working hours, to go to the school occasionally and take an interest in Nellie's affairs. The swimming for instance. She should have gone already to see how Nellie got on with the other children at the pool.

Tired, but not yet entirely discouraged, Angela fell asleep.

In the early morning hours it was Nellie's frail, frightened voice that called her back to wakefulness.

"Angela . . . Angela . . . I'm sick. My head hurts. I want a drink of water . . ."

There was no mistaking the urgent fear of that young voice this time. Angela sprang out of bed and ran across the room to her sister's bed. Nellie, eyes closed, her face creased with distress, was tossing restlessly on her bed. The cheeks that had last night seemed to glow with health were a bright feverish red. Angela put her hand on Nellie's forehead and nearly cried out with the heat she felt there. She crossed the room hurriedly and fumbled in her miniature medical chest for the thermometer.

"A drink, Angela. A drink . . ." cried Nellie.

"One moment, darling. I must take your temperature first, so that I get it right, you know."

The thermometer, when Angela removed it from Nellie's mouth, read at one hundred and four degrees. With the greatest self-control Angela said nothing but after shaking it down put it back carefully in its case. She then gave Nellie some water to drink by sips. After a little moan or two Nellie seemed to fall asleep again.

Angela threw on her dressing-gown and ran out into the hallway where she had seen the telephone stand the night before. The doctor's name and number had been pencilled on the cover of the telephone book by Mrs. Sharman and Angela hastily dialled the number.

It was the doctor's sleepy voice that answered.

"I'm so very sorry to call you early," Angela said. "But I'm worried. You see . . I'm to blame . . . Yes, a high fever . . . One hundred and four . . . Oh, thank you so much . . . Yes, I'll go and sponge her now while you're coming . . ."

She put the receiver down and ran quickly back to the bedroom. A minute later Mrs. Sharman, also in a dressing-gown, appeared in the doorway.

"I heard the phone," she said. Then looking down at Nellie added, "Oh, the poor wee thing. I didn't like the look of that colour last night. Much too bright. You can manage, can you, miss? Well, I'll go and get dressed so I can let the doctor in and maybe give you a cup of tea to help you along. Great Scot! It's only five o'clock. The poor doctor won't like getting up at this hour for anything less than a baby."

"She is a baby," said Angela on the verge of tears. All the same she kept herself in hand enough to use the sponge tenderly on Nellie's inflamed skin.

Angela had not had time to dress herself by the time the doctor arrived but she was totally unconscious of her own appearance in a blue dressing-gown over which the doctor looked at a white face and anxious confused eyes.

"It was my fault," said Angela brokenly. "She was ill last night, and I wouldn't listen to her."

"Well, never mind," said the doctor in an even, experienced voice. "We all make these mistakes in life, and there aren't any plagues or epidemics around just now so I don't think we'll have much trouble in finding what ails the young lady. Now we'll just run over the patient with the stethoscope . . ."

While the doctor examined Nellie, Angela stood beside Mrs. Sharman on the other side of the bed. Her hands were clasped together and only by the greatest effort could she keep the tears from her eyes. Anxiety and remorse for her own heartlessness on the previous evening fought a battle for her heart.

"Lift her up, please," the doctor said at length. "I want to have a look at the back of her neck. And the back of her legs, too."

There he found the same seared flesh that was so noticeable on Nellie's face and arms.

"Thought so," said the doctor. He helped Angela lay Nellie gently on the bed. Nellie cried out with pain at the touch of her body on the bed.

"What is it? Please, Doctor?" begged Angela.

"Don't panic, young lady," he said, folding his stethoscope and putting it in his pocket. "Over-exposure to the sun. What we call a 'touch of the sun.' A rather severe touch this time. Has she been sun-baking after swimming, do you know?"

"Well . . . perhaps she has. I didn't ask. I didn't really know what she did after she had her swim."

"But you asked, surely? In this climate you only take heavy doses of the sun *after* your skin has become well inured to its effects. Her skin, and yours too for that matter, is far too delicate for drastic exposure."

"Well, you see . . ." said Angela.

Her hands dropped to her sides. How did she tell the doctor she had been so anxious to get a job she hadn't waited to induct Nellie into the ways of a new climate? How does anyone go to work and at the same time look after a young girl who is rash and not particularly strong?

How could she have forgotten so completely the dilemma that had brought them out to Australia? How to look after Nellie and earn the living at the same time! Here it was again, exactly as it had been at home. There was nothing different except that there it had been not enough sun and warmth for Nellie's tendency to cold, and here it was too much warmth and sun for the same constitution.

"You're working down at the mine office?" asked the doctor, watching Angela through half-closed eyes. "Oh, yes, I know all about it. Like everyone else I know everything that goes on in Red Gorge. Now tell me, do you have to go down there and work? Can't you stay home and look after your young sister?"

"Oh, I could stay home for a few days . . . I'm sure."

"A few days? This young lady is going to be a couple of weeks getting over this. She's almost got second degree burns in some places. Do you have to go to work?"

"Yes," said Angela again in a low voice. "But I will stay

home as much as possible. Perhaps the mine can give me part-time work."

"What about Naroo Downs? Aren't you the young lady who was to go out to Mrs. Anstey at Naroo Downs?"

"Well . . . you see . . . I've only seen Mr. Lawrence yesterday. And I'd rather work in Red Gorge."

"Nonsense," snorted the doctor. "This young lady's health comes before any inclinations to be a career woman. I'll speak to Gilly Lawrence about it."

He was moving away towards the door as he spoke. Angela came round the bed.

"Oh, no. Please, Doctor Irvine." Then she remembered Nellie who was beginning to toss herself restlessly and each move was accompanied with a cry. "What shall I give Nellie? Will you give me a prescription?"

"No. I'm putting her in hospital. The ambulance will be around as soon after nine o'clock as possible. You couldn't possibly treat that child adequately here. Your mind would only be half on the business. I'm going to get a hot drink from Mrs. Sharman and I'll give her a powder. Keep giving her sips of water till the ambulance comes."

"To the hospital?" echoed Angela.

"Yes, to the hospital, young lady. I presume, amongst other things, you have to get on with that career of yours down at the mine office." Seeing the stricken look on Angela's face he relented. "She needs proper, trained attention for a few days," he said in a kinder voice. "Don't be too alarmed. She is not going to die. Nothing like it. She just needs care. We'll give it to her down there."

Angela went back to Nellie's bed and sat on the edge of it.

"Oh, Nellie," she said brokenly. "I'm so sorry. Somehow I don't seem to manage very well after all." But Nellie in her semi-delirium did not hear her.

Two days later, Angela, punching buttons and moving levers on the calculator heard Gilbert Lawrence coming over the roof-tops again. Already she was accustomed to every sound in Red Gorge. She knew when the mine truck passed down the street or when it was the airline truck. She knew when the DC mail plane was coming in by the first faint sound of its twin engines. She knew when the doctor passed or the mine manager or the Smiths from the hotel. She knew the different sounds of each make of car without being able to name the makes. She knew when she heard the crack of stock-whips and men's voices with their "Hoo . . . Hoo . . . Hoo . . ." that bullocks were being driven through the town. She didn't have to look up to know there'd be a dust haze everywhere because a mob of bullocks had passed by. And she knew at once the sound of the Cessna and that it was coming in from the west and not the east.

What, she wondered had *he* been doing in Carnlow. There was only spinifex desert, Carnlow, and the great roll of the Indian Ocean to the west of Red Gorge.

She had been an hour late for work on the day Nellie had been put into hospital but she had faithfully worked on an hour after everyone but the caretaker had left the mine office. She had also gone up to the hospital in her lunch-hour and again after that extra hour's work in the evening. She had only had time for iced milk and a biscuit at lunch-time and had missed her dinner altogether in the evening. She had had to suffice with a cup of tea and a sandwich in the one restaurant Red Gorge boasted.

Nellie had been half asleep, half delirious all the previous day. At lunch-time to-day she had seemed cooler and more rested. There was now no sign of delirium. Angela had been so thankful for the change she had forgotten to have the glass of milk and biscuit at lunch-time. She had walked back to the mine office full of dreams of how she could work harder, even overtime, for she could see there was a great lag in the work and knew Mr. Morton would welcome some willingness to work overtime on her part.

As soon as she had some money together she would take Nellie for a holiday down south.

So much had happened to Angela in the space of eight days that time had become meaningless. She had been in Red Gorge, it seemed, half a lifetime. She had had a job for a week and already she was dreaming of taking Nellie for a holiday down south.

When she said this to Janette Wells, the receptionist looked at her oddly.

"Why don't you take her to Naroo Downs? Lots of towns people go out there to visit or to stay. It's on the upper tableland, you know. The heat is drier and the nights are cool. After all, you do know Mr. Lawrence."

"What do you mean, the upper tableland?" Angela asked.

"Well, we're on higher ground than the coast here so it's called the lower tableland. Then when you go up that scarp over there that looks like mountains, you're on another plain, about a thousand feet higher. It's a much better climate than here."

Angela looked at Janette in astonishment.

"You mean those blue mountains over there are not mountains at all?"

Janette laughed.

"No. That's the shelf of the tableland. All the same, when you're out there it's lovely. That's where all the gorges are. You can see the asbestos, peacock blue it is, and hundreds of coloured minerals shining on the walls of the gorges."

"And up on that tableland is Naroo Downs?"

Janette stared at Angela. Like everyone else she had heard the rumour of Angela's connection with Gilbert Lawrence and she couldn't understand the other girl's surprise. Of course, with her young sister being so ill in hospital, Angela hadn't had time to go to Naroo Downs yet. All the same Gilly Lawrence had been in town three days ago and surely he had told Angela something about his station and the surrounding country!

Janette had been particularly nice to Angela since she had heard the rumour of Angela's possible marriage to the owner of Naroo Downs.

Kevin Richards in his teasing manner had accused Janette of sulking now she had lost all chance of the great catch and she in turn had accused him of sulking now that his beautiful English daisy might be out of his reach. She had been quick to notice the small frown, and a sudden bleak look in his eyes.

He likes her, Janette thought. *He really likes her*. Nevertheless Angela was so serious, so kind in her little daily deeds of goodwill, and so polite to everyone that Janette could not find it in her heart to let her jealousy turn to rancour. And if Angela really was going to marry Gilbert Lawrence she would have a tough enough time cracking *that* nut. No one could begrudge her a little admiration and attention in the meantime.

Kevin Richards did pay Angela attention too.

Each night, after dinner, he walked up to Mrs. Sharman's and sat in the starlight on the veranda talking to Angela. All Red Gorge, including Janette, knew that too. All Red Gorge was conjecturing what Gilbert Lawrence would make of it, when he knew.

Needless to say that dragonfly, droning in over the roof-tops, was heard by more than Angela and once again there was a meeting of eyes here and there and much conjecturing as to what would happen *now*.

Janette Wells, like Angela, heard it and she dropped her hands from the typewriter and watched its shadow first on the roof-tops and then on the red open spaces of ground as it came in to land on the airfield.

A minute later the big DC mail plane took off noisily almost as if that little plane had nipped in like a mosquito stinging a giant insect. Janette smiled ruefully at the analogy. Something in the air told her that Gilbert Lawrence coming back into Red Gorge so soon meant business and there was a sting in his coming. Even the DC had taken off in fright.

It was then three o'clock in the afternoon.

At four Angela received a hand-delivered note. It was written on the Red Gorge Hotel stationery and it was short and to the point.

> "May I call on you at the mine office after hours this afternoon? I suggest ten minutes past five. Your colleagues will have left by then.
>
> Yours faithfully,
>
> GILBERT LAWRENCE."

Angela read the note but this time an action of Gilbert Lawrence's did not stir her pulses. Too much had happened in four days. Too much real anxiety, too many valid concrete worries occupied her mind.

She folded the note, put it in her handbag and went back to the calculating machine. One thing was certain, she had plenty of work to occupy her until ten minutes past five and she no longer feared a further meeting with the station owner from the upper tableland. She actually felt calmer than she had since she had woken up on the first morning of Nellie's illness. And she had completely forgotten the doctor's warning that he would speak to Gilly Lawrence himself about these two girls who had originally intended going to Naroo Downs.

At fifteen minutes to five when all the girls went to the washroom to remove the stains of an afternoon's work and to groom their appearances for the homeward walk, Angela went too. She had no intention of deceiving the girls into believing she was leaving the office. She went partly because it was now routine and partly because, as she was expecting a visitor, it was a good time to wash and brush and spruce. One thing she had delighted in in Red Gorge was that no girl or woman was ever seen abroad without that specially cool and groomed appearance. She thought the girls of Red Gorge were the freshest, most bathed-looking she had ever seen. Since everyone had to take about three showers a day to keep the body temperatures reasonable, she supposed they couldn't help looking like this. But it pleased and enchanted her as much as the simple colourful cotton frocks that everyone wore.

"Are you coming now?" Janette asked on the point of departure.

"I've a little work to finish," Angela said. "Then I'll walk up to the hospital."

As Kevin Richards could be seen through the glass wall, still at his desk, Janette had misgivings, but the open candour of Angela's face mollified her misgivings.

"Well, good-bye. Hope little sister is better than ever. See you in the morning."

As she pulled the main office door closed behind her she reflected that after all two people couldn't do or say much in privacy in a house made of glass. Even from the street outside anyone could see right through the main office to the rear wall of the mine office.

Angela went back to her room and her table. Kevin Richards, seeing her, first tapped on the glass and then came round through the front office.

"What goes on?" he said. "Did I overload you, or do you just like working for the fun of it?"

"No. Mr. Lawrence is coming to see me. As he is a partner in the mine I suppose he has the authority to come here after hours?"

"Gilly Lawrence comes and goes as he likes," said Kevin, hands in pockets and walking round Angela's table. She followed him with her eyes.

"Do you mind?" she asked.

"Wouldn't matter if I did," said Kevin unsmiling. He came to a stop in front of Angela's table. He put both hands palm down on the table and leaned across it. His head was less than two feet away from her head.

"What goes on, Sweet Angela?" he said. "Are you going to marry His Nibs?"

Angela returned his gaze with astonishment.

"Marry him?" she said. "Why should I marry him?"

"Give me one good reason why you shouldn't? He's rich, he's honest, he's good-looking . . . so the ladies say; and you'd be Queen of Red Gorge and its environs for about a thousand square miles. Why shouldn't you marry him?"

Very quietly Angela said:

"Are you quite sane, Mr. Richards?"

"No. Only in love. In one short dazzling week I've fallen in love. Guess with whom?"

Angela's eyes met his own eyes and there she read his sincerity. A gentle flush stole gradually up her cheeks. She felt oddly moved. A tiny glow warmed her heart.

"That was a very nice thing to say," she said gently.

Kevin put out his hand.

"Well, now you know," he said. "So let's shake hands on it. And don't say 'yes' to Gilly Lawrence until you've consulted me. I can hear the beggar's footsteps coming down the street right now."

Outside, the ten minutes past five hush lay on the town. The only sound was that of heavy measured purposeful footsteps coming down the street. Angela did not heed them as she put out her own hand and left it in Kevin's hand. She couldn't find words to express her feelings. She didn't quite know what her feelings were but she was deeply touched. Then she said the only concrete thing that came into her head.

"Two wives," she said. Her hand was still in his. "Remember? There are two of us. Me and Nellie."

"We'd be awful poor but awful happy," Kevin grinned. If she had left her hand there another second he would have leaned forward and kissed her, in spite of those footsteps which were already in the entrance of the mine office.

A key turned in the lock and the door opened. The footsteps came on.

Angela sighed, and withdrew her hand.

"I might have to take Nellie away from here, Kevin," she said. "Would you ask me about ten years hence?"

"Twenty, if you like. But you're too pretty, too sweet, and, by golly, too courageous to last out that long . . ."

Angela smiled.

"You too, Kevin. I mean not pretty, but, well other things. Awfully nice."

CHAPTER SIX

The footsteps and the shadow were in her own office doorway, and unwillingly Angela took her eyes away from Kevin's face and looked beyond him to Gilbert Lawrence standing outside the glass door of her office. Kevin straightened himself and slowly turned round.

"Put out the red carpet and bow three times," he said sideways through the corner of his mouth to Angela. "Well, here he is. But don't forget I asked you first."

Angela stood up.

"Come in please," she said.

He opened the door and came a few steps into the office.

"I hope I am not intruding," he said.

He was as powerfully good-looking as ever, his eyes were as unsmiling, his arrogance as unnerving. Well, not quite so unnerving for much had happened to Angela in the few days since she had last seen him and the few minutes she had just had with Kevin had touched and warmed her so that her face was softened and her eyes quite steady and even friendly as she looked at the tall, powerful man across the room. As, on these momentous occasions, one notices and afterwards remembers the irrelevant things, Angela noticed his boots.

They were as Nellie had described. They were a cattleman's riding-boots but there were no spurs. In spite of the thin coating of red dust which they must have gathered on his way down from the hotel Angela could see the fine-grained soft leather under the tan polish. They fitted his feet like gloves. The heel must have been an inch and a half high.

Angela had a mental image of a man braking himself against the pull of a roped bullock, and those heels churning up the red earth like a miniature pair of bulldozers.

All this had passed unthinkingly through Angela's head, yet not half a minute had passed.

"Please come in," she said again.

"I'm just going," said Kevin. "You been out west, Gilly?" he asked politely. "That plane of yours does nothing but go and come in the wrong direction these days."

"To Carnlow," Gilbert Lawrence assented. He watched Kevin Richards walk to the door with the kind of expression in his eyes that said he found only a modicum of interest in anything the young man had to say.

As Kevin went to the doorway Angela did get a strong impression of his youth. He was not as easy in Gilbert Lawrence's presence as he was elsewhere, in spite of the fact he called the other man "Gilly." Perhaps everyone did that in Red Gorge.

Angela felt vaguely uneasy because Gilbert Lawrence made everyone near him appear puny, even lacking personality. She remembered how Mr. Morton had coughed and seemed uncomfortable on the day of his former visit.

"'Bye, Angela. See you later," said Kevin from the doorway.

Gilbert Lawrence closed the door after him. He came over to the table behind which Angela was now standing.

"Do you mind if I sit down?" he said. "And please be seated yourself, Miss Burns." He seemed to cogitate a minute and then he raised his eyes from the cigarette he had taken from a packet and looked directly at Angela. "I think I had better correct that to 'Angela.' Please sit down, Angela. I have a lot to say. To begin with, you can forget that young man."

For all the world Angela might have been receiving a visit from the Security on an espionage charge. That was exactly how she felt. He was the aggressor in this impending conversation, she the defendant. A strange atmosphere had pervaded the office with the going of Kevin Richards and the sitting down of Gilbert Lawrence.

He lit his cigarette, drew on it and expelled the smoke upwards in a blue shaft that dissolved itself in the rising air of the air-conditioned room. He watched the wreath of smoke become nothing, and in a fascinated way so did Angela. Why was she ordered to forget Kevin Richards? She soon knew.

"I have come to make a proposal of marriage to you, Angela," Gilbert Lawrence said slowly. His eyes came away from the nothingness of the cigarette smoke and met Angela's startled ones. "A proposal I don't propose to allow you to refuse," he added even more slowly. There was a cold sting in each word.

"I beg your pardon," stammered Angela.

"I think that's about in order," he said dryly. There was a silence. "You owe me an apology, but I'm afraid it is too late to accept it."

"I don't think I quite understand you, Mr. Lawrence."

"Gilbert Lawrence," he corrected. "Commonly called

'Gilly' by all and sundry north of Perth and south of Darwin. You might as well join in with the ruck."

"I still don't understand you . . . er . . . Gilbert." With a slight sense of shock she realised she had obeyed him. She had called him by his Christian name.

He drew on his cigarette again.

"When I came into Red Gorge last Tuesday . . . that is four days ago . . . I was greeted by the mention of the fact that I had come in to collect my bride-to-be, Miss Angela Burns. I checked this piece of unusual information on the grounds there might be some innocent misconception as to the reason for your coming to Australia in general and Red Gorge in particular. I was informed it was a matter of common knowledge in Carnlow. I came down here that day to make the acquaintance of this lady I was supposed to be on the point of marrying but you failed to mention the matter to me, Miss Burns. That is . . . *Angela.*"

When he had first begun to speak, Angela had been staggered, then embarrassed but before he had finished she was cold with anger.

"Go on, please, Mr. Lawrence. I mean Gilbert. You are being very interesting."

"No. It is you who are an interesting personality, Angela. On the surface you are a very engaging person. Quite charming, in fact. Underneath just a little too ambitious. Or were you merely foolish and trying to be impressive when you made those statements about our future relationship during your trip up the coast?"

Angela went quite white.

"I still don't understand you, I'm afraid." She was sitting bolt upright in her chair, her hands clenched in her lap until the knuckles were white.

He drew on the cigarette again and once again watched, as if he had infinite time and infinite patience, the dissolving of the smoke cloud into the ether of the room. In the long silence Angela did not take her eyes from his face. It was cold, implacable, but it did not dismay her, or thaw her sense of frozen anger.

"To recapitulate," he said, bringing his eyes back to her face. If her anger was cold his eyes were icier still. "During the seven-day trip up the coast to Carnlow you announced you were travelling to Red Gorge in order to marry Gilbert Lawrence of Naroo Downs. Myself, in fact. The statement was commonly accepted by the passengers, all of whom are more or less known to me. It was commonly accepted in Carnlow where I am known to everyone. It was highly credible, as why else would you be coming . . . a stranger from another country . . . to Red Gorge? Oh, yes, I know my aunt had invited you. But meantime you and I had not met, Angela. The visit, after you and I had made some contact, *yes*. But the statement of marriage intentions? Was that really necessary to establish your position once you had arrived?"

Angela was speechless. She could hardly find her voice, much less something to say. At length she spoke and it was between white lips.

"Would you mind leaving, Mr. Lawrence? Yes, I know you have an interest in this mine and a right to be in the office. But not my office until after I hand in my resignation."

"I haven't the slightest intention of leaving," he said. "You have nothing about which to be anxious at the moment." There was a slightly cynical smile on his lips. It was the first time Angela had seen him smile at all. "We live in glass houses in Red Gorge, as you have probably noticed."

"I did not suppose I had anything to fear from you, Mr. Lawrence. Here or elsewhere," said Angela. The stiffness had seeped out of her and with it the anger died quietly away. What else could happen to her now? What further misfortune would befall? Pack up, move on, find somewhere else to go? Find another job? And meantime Nellie was ill in the hospital!

Did anything this man had to say matter so very much after all?

He stretched an arm forward and stubbed out the cigarette on the ash-tray on her table. He then leaned back in his chair and folded his arms.

"I see you begin to admit the rudimentary facts of my story," he said, misreading the sudden look of vanquishment in Angela's face and manner.

Her eyelids had drooped momentarily over her eyes but she now looked up at him again.

"Who told you all . . . all this?" she asked.

"Everyone. I even took four days off to go to Carnlow. A man in my position does not allow himself to appear a bounder in the eyes of his own particular public without checking the facts, you know."

He waited for Angela to say something but she remained silent, her eyes dark.

"In Carnlow," he went on, "I waited an extra day on the

ship's return trip. She only went as far as Hedland this time. *Miss Burns . . .*" he said sarcastically. "*Miss Burns . . .* mark you, made these statements herself on board ship. To the stewardess, of all people. And when the story was repeated she made no attempt to deny it. It was the most fascinating piece of after-dinner bar gossip from a hundred miles out of Fremantle to Hedland."

"I'm surprised anyone thinks it so important," said Angela with a touch of returned spirit.

"You are surprised it is important? In this country men occasionally steal one another's cattle; they occasionally jump one another's mining lease; they bet beyond their means on race-horses, and on occasions they drink overmuch beer. They've been known to shoot one another and, far enough outback and far back in history, they've been known to silence spearing black fellows with rifle-shot and later a large bonfire." He paused to let his words sink in. Not once did he take his eyes from Angela's face. "But no man . . . I repeat, *no man* . . . north of latitude twenty-six allows his name to be mentioned unchivalrously with a woman's name in the bar of a ship or a hotel without taking immediate action. It is the unwritten law of the country. A custom. You find it odd?"

"I see," said Angela slowly. "And you are taking action how? Do I get shot? And does a large bonfire follow?"

"No. You continue with the fiction. You marry me . . . whether you like it or not. No one north of twenty-six is ever going to say that Gilly Lawrence made a fool of any woman. Or, for that matter, that any woman made a fool of Gilly Lawrence."

Angela smiled wryly.

"In the world of affairs, the things that people say of Gilly Lawrence must be very important," she said.

"That was your reasoning I suppose when you discussed my future with the stewardess on the ship coming up the coast?" he said coldly.

"I didn't reason anything, Mr. Lawrence. I did not discuss you with the stewardess at all. Your name was never mentioned to anyone except . . ." Angela stopped dead.

"Yes? Except who?" he asked.

Nellie! Nellie and her romantic idea that Angela would marry a rich station owner! Nellie and her propensity for gossiping with the stewardess and then with Emmy the housemaid in the hotel! Nellie with her terrible disappointment that there was no Aunt Kara to meet them, coupled with an imagination that had learned to run riot in the bosom companionship of Kate and Nora Thomason back there at home.

Nellie, lying sick and weak in the hospital and with neither of them any prospect of where to put their heads once they left Red Gorge!

Nellie, whom the doctor said should go and live up in the more rarefied atmosphere of Naroo Downs on the upper tableland!

Angela, whose eyes had moved away from Gilbert Lawrence and who had been staring at the glass wall through which she could see the world darkening outside and hear the occasional sound of a passing car or footstep, now looked again at the man sitting at the side of her table.

Nellie, in her childish innocence, had done this! And Nellie, who was not strong, had to be looked after by somebody. Nellie had to have a home . . . a future . . . happiness . . . education.

There was Kevin Richards, Angela thought sadly. But how long would his love last in the face of keeping two women. It wouldn't be so very long before Nellie was a woman and needing all the entertainment and happy occasions of a young woman on the doorstep of real adult life.

Angela never once in all her young life had thought she too was entitled to these considerations. She thought only of her responsibility to a delicate sister, and the last two days had been filled with remorse and a sense of inadequacy that she had not known that on this occasion Nellie had been very ill indeed. She had even been harsh with her.

"You are very silent, *Angela*," Gilbert Lawrence said.

Angela brushed her hand over her eyes as if to cast away the images that had been filling them.

"You did not finish your last sentence," he reminded her.

"It is of no importance," Angela said. "Please go on, Mr. Lawrence . . . I mean Gilbert. What was it you were saying?"

"So the matter of a possible marriage between us *was* mentioned between you and someone else?" he persisted.

Angela nodded with a touch of weariness in the movement of her head.

"It was mentioned," she said. "But not quite that way. It's of no consequence."

Gilbert Lawrence took out another cigarette.

"By the way, do you smoke?" he asked.

Angela shook her head.

"At least we've got down to the facts of the situation," he went on, putting a cigarette in his mouth. He inclined his head forward a little as he struck a match and lit the cigarette.

Angela could see the white parting at the side of his black hair. When he straightened up she noticed again the silver threads above his temples. Men with very black hair go grey over the temples, she remembered. She wondered how old he was, and what were the things she had heard about him? Rich probably, and powerful obviously. An honourable man? Well, he would hardly be here on this strange errand if he didn't have a quixotic sense of honour. Perhaps it was true that all Australians on their cattle baronies maintained this code of conduct where women were concerned.

Or was it simply agressive vanity on his part? No one talked about Gilly Lawrence except in the terms he dictated. That, Angela suspected was more the root of the matter than anything else.

But what a price to pay for it! Find himself tied for life to someone who might turn out a complete wash-out as a wife!

Angela started. Perhaps he didn't mean a life sentence!

"What . . . what was it you were saying?" she said. "What was it you proposed, Mr. Lawrence?"

"*Gilbert,*" he reminded her. "For an ambitious woman you are inclined to forget your cues."

"Very well, then," she said. "Gilbert."

"The most obvious method of silencing the kind of talk that has got Red Gorge, as well as Carnlow, by the ears."

"What . . . just what do you mean by marriage?"

"I . . ." said Gilbert Lawrence, once again watching a spiral of cigarette smoke dissolve into nothing. "*I* am the one who dictates the terms of this marriage. We simply announce the date of marriage. I come in from Naroo on that date and we get married."

"And then?"

"You return to Naroo Downs with me. You can stay there as long as you like. It's big enough. I only ask you not to get in my way and that your young sister does not get under my feet. When you are tired of it, you may go. You should be perfectly safe to do so as you will be able to claim marital coldness on my part and the laws of the land will see to it I pay you a maintenance . . . adequate to *my* position, not yours . . . for the rest of your life. You should be reasonably comfortably off. A very good piece of business, I would say."

Angela leaned back in her chair, and closed her eyes. Never would she forgive him.

There was a long silence.

"Well?" said Gilbert Lawrence and then added cynically, "I hope you have noticed . . . I'm sure you have . . . I am also providing a home for Nellie."

A home for Nellie. Angela's anger died hard but she began to think of Nellie. Janette Wells's words rang in her ears. The doctor's words rang in her ears. The upper tableland! The heat was drier and therefore more bearable. The nights were cool, even chill.

For Nellie there would be horses to ride, a home, security, stability. What were the alternatives? If she refused this proposal she would have to resign her post here in the mine. She would have to gather up Nellie and their few possessions and fade away out of Red Gorge. She would leave behind a bad impression and a scar on Gilbert Lawrence's honour like an abrasive sore. Perhaps it was true she would damage him in the estimation of the people of his own countryside.

Then having left Red Gorge . . . what? Where?

For herself, alone, she would make out. But for Nellie, there was nothing. There was not enough money or anything like it, to take them back to England.

How odd, Angela thought, that out of a cloudless day, following hard on those few sweet moments with Kevin Richards, this frightful cloud storm should burst! Why hadn't she had a premonition?

She opened her eyes because she suddenly suspected that Gilbert Lawrence was silent because he was quite certain her answer to this proposal was a foregone conclusion. He, the law-giver, wouldn't permit any other answer.

"Very well," she said quietly. "When do we get married?"

His eyes came back from space and met hers. The expression in them was one of sardonic amusement.

"Fourteen days from to-day, I suggest. That will give you enough time to sort out your belongings and bring your sister to the right frame of mind about the matter. Furthermore, I would be pleased if you would look your best at the marriage ceremony. Not a trailing dress. It's hardly suitable in Red Gorge. Something reticent. A becoming hat . . . perhaps . . ."

Angela remained unexpectedly unhurt. Nothing very much could hurt her ever again. She only prayed she wouldn't get angry with him that way again. It was pointless and only she herself suffered. Nothing and no words would hurt this man. He was made of flint.

" Very well," she said quietly.

He stood up, at the same time stubbing out his cigarette beside the butt of his first one in the ash-tray.

" I will see Mr. MacDonald, the rector, about it now. The reception can be small and at the hotel. Mrs. Smith will arrange that. Perhaps you will be good enough to have dinner with me at the hotel to-night. We might make the announcement then. Will your sister join us?"

" No," said Angela. " She is otherwise occupied."

He raised one eyebrow.

" Too occupied to meet her future brother-in-law?"

" She is in hospital. A patient."

He was on his way to the door and he paused, then turned round.

" What is the matter with her?" he asked curiously.

" Sunstroke," said Angela. She waited while he digested this and then added, " She is constitutionally delicate. And that, and that only, is the reason why I am marrying you . . . Gilbert."

There was a prolonged silence. Angela too was on her feet now.

" You won't believe it, of course. You will still think I'm an ambitious, designing woman. Perhaps, after all, I am that, but it is for reasons other than those you think. Good evening . . . Gilbert. I am going to the hospital now but I will come to the hotel later. Will seven o'clock be suitable?"

She thought of Kevin Richards sitting at that other table at the end of the hotel dining-room. In imagination she could see him turn round; she could read the surprised look on his face and anticipate the shadow there when he learned the reason for that rather solemn dinner party that was taking place at the other end of the room.

Gilbert Lawrence's manner changed. He became a shade more human.

" If you are going to the hospital now perhaps I could get the car from the garage. I keep one here in Red Gorge. I will drive you up. I might speak to Irvine, the doctor."

" No thank you," said Angela, not without bitterness. " Nellie is not yet fit enough to receive visitors. Besides, she is disappointed in you. You do not carry a stock-whip."

It was clear that Gilbert Lawrence knew quite well how

people spoke of him and what the reference to the stock-whip meant. He flushed with anger under his dark, sun-weathered skin.

"Very well," he said. "I will make her acquaintance later. If you will excuse me now, I have things to do."

Angela had not moved from her place behind the table. She nodded. She had no words left, and she was amazed at her own capacity to say the cruel thing.

But he dealt in cruelty, surely, she thought. He, of all people, should understand that language.

Would he ever know that he had taken her pride and broken it across his knee? Or did he know these things, and care nothing!

At least all would be well for Nellie for the next few months. Perhaps with care and tactfulness she, Angela, could prolong the security into a year.

She must remember not to get in his way, or let Nellie get under his feet. Those were his words. And she must remember to curb those bitter words before they were uttered. Tact! Please God, a large dose of tact for both herself and Nellie might bring them through this experience safe and unharmed.

Odd, Angela thought, as she put her hat on her head, said good night to the caretaker, who had just come in, and went out through the door: "I have a feeling, no, a certainty, one would be *safe* with him. No harm will befall us. But neither will happiness. Not for me, anyway. Perhaps for Nellie. She need never know . . ."

It was thinking of the health-giving climate of the upper tableland that brought a smile into Angela's eyes as she went into the hospital bedroom to see Nellie. Horses to ride! Dogs to befriend! Security! *Health.* And all for Nellie. Angela's smile deepened.

Two hours later, Angela, very charmingly dressed in the one good "special occasion" dress she had allowed herself for the trip out on the ocean liner, arrived at the Red Gorge Hotel for her dinner engagement with Gilbert Lawrence.

The dress was of Spanish satin made with a simple round neck and a flared skirt that fell in soft folds to four inches below her knees. The charm of the dress lay in its simplicity and the pattern of rich golden roses on an ivory background. With it went her one good pair of delicate black suède court shoes, her three-quarter length white gloves, a little black handbag to match her shoes and a tiny hoop of black satin roses which she wore across the back of her head.

It had not been an expensive rig-out. Angela was far too conscientious about how she spent her small hoard of capital money but she had guessed rightly there might be more than one occasion on the ship . . . "the Captain's dinner" at the end of the voyage, for instance . . . when even Nellie would want her sister, as well as herself, to pass muster in a galaxy of well-dressed women. Angela had made the dress herself and it had justified her belief that the loveliness of the design on the ivory satin would carry the day. She only had to make it simply . . . and carefully. The same principle had gone into the making of Nellie's one good "special occasion" dress. It had been a pale blue linen which Nellie, with her talent for needlework, had embroidered herself.

Now Angela wore what Nellie called her "dress with the golden roses." She loved the touch of her dress against her fingers, and the luxurious frou-frou of her taffeta petticoat under the satin of the skirt. It all gave her confidence. Angela's head was quite high as she went through the double glass doors of the Red Gorge Hotel into the big hall which was also the main reception lounge.

Gilbert Lawrence, dressed now in tropical whites, rose from a deep arm-chair at her entry. Angela felt it *was* an entry. In her mind's eye, she could see herself as her slender-heeled black shoes tapped their way across the polished floor, then on to the deep red carpet. That image pleased her. She was without vanity but she knew her dress was lovely and that it made her feel rich, like the rich fabric, and worthy of this man's colossal idea of his importance in the district. If he was marrying her for the look of the thing, then she too would play her part and pay attention to the look of herself.

Angela smiled as he pressed a button above the table for a steward and then moved out an arm-chair from the table for her.

That's surprised him! She was still thinking of her dress. *I know I look nice. I feel nice.*

There had been a tiny flicker in his eyes when Angela first came in but there was still no smile. Angela had seen that flicker and that was why her smile came more readily. She was determined to behave as naturally as possible, and to give no sign that there was anything unusual about their relationship. The one thing she was afraid of was meeting Kevin Richards's eyes when he learned why she was there in the hotel.

" Do you like a sherry or a cocktail, Angela?" Gilbert Lawrence asked. He had not resumed his own seat but stood towering above the table, looking down at her with an expressionless face.

His first question caused Angela's confidence, even in the dress of golden roses, to tremble on its base. She had never had sherry, or a cocktail, and she didn't know which of the two would sound more sophisticated. She didn't even know what they looked like, or how one drank them.

Either would do, surely? He wouldn't have given her the choice if either had been wrong, she thought.

Cocktail was a familiar word in books, films, and even TV, so Angela said, " Cocktail, thank you," and was of course immediately stunned by the next question.

" Have you any preference? Do you like Italian vermouth and gin?"

Angela gave up trying.

" I haven't very much experience of cocktails. Would you please order for me . . . Gilbert." His name came out after a brief hesitation. She wished she could keep on calling him " Mr. Lawrence " . . . even after their marriage. Somehow it suited him better.

" Don't ever be afraid to consult your host, or the drinks steward, if you are in doubt," he said. " Even sophisticated drinkers are not above consulting a steward on vintages."

Angela flushed. He had directly told her she had much to learn in her new role, and that he knew it. As she looked down at one slim clad knee crossed over the other, the gold in her roses lost something of their bloom.

At that moment the steward came to the table.

" Yes, sir?"

" Three gins with Italian vermouth, olives not cherries, thank you. Miss Winton will be here by the time you bring them."

" Yes, sir, certainly, sir." The steward moved the ash-tray on the table by an inch. He neatly placed three small d'oyleys, one in front of Angela, one in front of Gilbert and one on the table immediately in front of the third chair which was drawn up at the table.

Angela stared at that vacant chair with fascinated eyes. *Miss Winton.* That was the person Kevin Richards had described as " the beautiful and designing Stella Winton." Janette Wells had told Angela all about it. But wasn't she supposed to be out visiting at Naroo Downs? Had Gilbert brought her into Red

Gorge with him? Perhaps even taken her on that Carnlow trip with him?

Why was she with him at all, if he was going to propose to Angela Burns as a matter of face-saving chivalry?

Angela was thankful she had been looking down at the moment when Gilbert had made his announcement to the steward. She was bewildered and knew he would have read it in her eyes if he had been looking into them.

As if he wanted to look into her eyes anyway!

On this thought Angela gained courage and looked up. Gilbert had moved to his own chair and was on the point of sitting down when the sound of someone approaching caused him to look towards the palms where they stood in their huge pots at the entrance side of the room.

They were light footsteps and Angela knew it was a woman coming towards them. She had her own back to the newcomer so she did not look round, instead she looked up at Gilbert Lawrence who had again risen to his full height. His face, she noticed, did ease the severity of its lines. There was almost a smile on his mouth—Gilbert's version of a smile. His eyes were certainly welcoming. They had lost their expression of cold remoteness.

Angela had a curious feeling down the back of her spine. Only with the greatest control could she prevent herself turning round and staring. Good manners, poise, if there was such a thing, demanded that she wait until those footsteps had brought their owner right up to the table.

"Oh, there you are, Gilly!" It was a high clear assured voice, not unpleasant. Indeed there was a hint of amusement in the clear tones.

Angela did turn a little in her chair now. She watched Stella Winton approach the table with eyes both fascinated and awed. Coming across the room towards them was one of the most beautiful women Angela had ever seen.

She was tall and slim, her hair was a flaxen blonde, her eyes were as blue as the Arctic ice and her golden-tanned skin was as smooth and natural as any Swedish beauty's. Her brows, unlike her hair, were dark, making a clear definition of her forehead, her straight chiselled nose and the grooved sockets that held the blue eyes. Her mouth, which seemed a natural red colour, was the least noticeable feature about her but only because everything else was so striking.

To complete the illusion of an Arctic princess she was dressed in a slim-fitting dress of white sharkskin, its lovely texture making Angela feel her own beautiful dress was only a sham. On Stella Winton's feet were a pair of smooth, glove-fitting off-white shoes whose toes and heels would have made the Italian tapers look clumsy.

Even if she hadn't smiled, Stella Winton would have been breathtaking. She was poised, she was pleasant, she was beautiful. What was much more important, she took Gilbert Lawrence and his stern dignity with the casualness of one who is long acquainted, and a member of the inner circle.

"Ah," she said as she came up to the table. "So this is Angela Burns."

She stood looking down at Angela, smiling readily, absolutely secure in the knowledge of her own striking, perfectly groomed appearance. Deep in the smiling eyes Angela read, for a fleeting moment, curiosity, a quick appraisal, the final pigeon-holing.

"Miss Winton—Angela," Gilbert said formally. "This is my fiancée, Stella."

Stella held out a hand, the finger-nails of which were the same striking red as her mouth and the bead handbag which dangled from strings on her left wrist.

Angela offered her own hand and shyly said, "How do you do, Miss Winton?"

Stella Winton laughed.

"How formal we all are," she said. "Gilbert, we need a sledge-hammer to break the ice. What have you ordered to drink, darling?"

Darling.

Angela blinked. She could say nothing because the conversational ball had not been tossed in her direction.

"Your usual cocktail," Gilbert said, drawing out the third chair for her.

He remained standing beside it a minute as he took out his cigarette case and offered her a cigarette then lit it for her. Stella drew in deeply and then slowly expelled a long shaft of smoke through which she looked at Angela with amusement.

During this little pantomime Angela had not once taken her eyes from Stella. She was as fascinated as a child at a puppet-show, except that deep in her heart was a sudden and awful misgiving.

This little play that she and Gilbert were to act out? Dear heavens, it was not going to be as blatantly absurd as Stella Winton's presence seemed to make possible? *No* . . . with that, she, Angela Burns, could not go through. Not if Stella Winton was to have a part in the farce.

Just how much of a fool was she being made of by these two? What had they to gain?

But then Gilbert Lawrence had said she, Angela, had made a fool of him! She had made the world of north-west Australia believe that Gilbert Lawrence and Aunt Kara had brought her out from England to marry Gilbert.

Now they were going to punish her. They were going to make her go through with it, right up to the altar steps, perhaps. Then what? Would he go on with it from there?

Vaguely, in spite of her fears, Angela knew he would. There was something about Gilbert Lawrence that told her that that would not be his particular way of making a fool of her . . . leaving her waiting at the church door.

On the contrary she made a small guess that he expected her to do as she was told by him. She had to look and be the part of the girl who was going to marry Gilbert Lawrence. She had seen that tiny flicker of approval in his eyes when she had walked in.

He was looking at Stella Winton now with one eyebrow raised. He was waiting for *her* verdict.

The steward brought the cocktails and set them neatly on their mats before each person. Gilbert signed a chit and the steward departed. Angela lifted the little stick with the olive on it from the cocktail glass and looked at it.

"Don't you like olives?" said Stella. There was a laugh in that clear voice. She leaned forward and took the olive stick from Angela's hand. "I do," she said, and her laugh was clear, amused and friendly. "I always eat everyone else's olives. Gilly, darling . . . you don't want yours, do you?" The last few words were not so clear because Stella had already put Angela's olive in her mouth and she was now discarding the stick in the ash-tray.

She was nice. Really friendly and nice, yet it made Angela's heart drop a little. How could one ever compete with someone like Stella Winton who was beautiful and *nice*. She had everything.

CHAPTER SEVEN

That dinner passed very simply and easily. Stella managed everything. Kevin Richards did not come in, and everyone in the hotel from the staff upwards seemed to take Angela's engagement to Gilbert Lawrence for granted.

At first this puzzled Angela but when she remembered the stories that had been going around and realised they had been going around for days, she understood why there was no surprise anywhere.

At the dinner-table Gilbert sat with Angela on his right hand and Stella on his left. Stella, her elbows nonchalantly yet somehow gracefully on the table, took charge of the conversation. She set herself out to attract Angela. From frozen silence Angela found herself thawing in Stella's lively company. Stella Winton would be much nearer thirty than twenty, Angela thought. That, perhaps, accounted for her poise, and for the right which she assumed to herself to control the scene.

This is, if anyone else could dominate a scene when Gilbert Lawrence was present. Except for odd assents, a few words here and there, he was a very silent man. He rarely smiled, only doing so once or twice at some quip or quick rejoinder of Stella's. Then it was Gilbert Lawrence's version of a smile. It was the merest relaxation of his stern mouth, a faint amused softening of the steely colour of his eyes. Yet this silent giant of a man seemed to dominate the whole room.

Eyes at other tables were frequently turned to their table and Angela sensed this would always be the case when the great Gilbert Lawrence and the beautiful Stella Winton were present. Her few days in the mine office had already told her that Gilbert Lawrence held the lives of many people in and around the town in the hollow of his hand.

A man wanted a job, and if Gilbert Lawrence wanted him to get one he had only to speak to the foreman out at the mines or to Mr. Morton in the office. A young girl had reached the school leaving age and if her mother wanted to place her as a domestic at the hospital or in the hotel she sought out Gilbert Lawrence.

The policeman had his doubts about someone in the town and he had a few words with Gilbert Lawrence before he ran the doubtful character out of town.

The stockmen riding in for a Saturday spree from the outside cattle stations made too much disturbance, and Gilbert Lawrence knew about it on Monday morning, even if he had not left Naroo Downs.

Yes, he was very much the king of Red Gorge and no man would willingly have crossed him unless he was leaving the district for good.

This had been the kind of legend that Angela's unwilling ears had picked up in the mine office. Though she had rightly guessed that much of the legend was indeed fable she realised, watching the impression he made on other people in the hotel, which was a club and a home as much as a hotel, that there was enough truth in it to make Red Gorge a one-man-town.

And she was to marry him.

She had so much to keep her wits about her at this momentous dinner that she hadn't time to think about it now. All her mind had to be concentrated on the business of getting through the evening as smoothly as possible and with her pride intact.

When she had time to think about it, she would think of Nellie. Poor Nellie lying up there in that hospital bed with the outer skin already peeling from her burns and leaving ugly red patches of raw flesh.

Nellie could never—not for years anyway—be trusted to look after herself or to do the wise thing.

Yes, Angela would marry Gilly Lawrence, save his stiff-necked pride for him and bring Nellie safely to a home where she would be secure and well looked after. Angela could then stay home from work to bring her up properly.

Every time her heart sank, and it did as she watched and listened to the scintillating Stella Winton or caught a glimpse of the human iceberg beside her, she only had to say "*Nellie*" to herself to raise the beating of her heart to a more normal pace.

When the dinner was over and as they walked into the lounge Mrs. Smith sent a steward with a message inviting Angela into her office for a few minutes.

"Well, you're a one, you are," said Mrs. Smith when Angela answered the invitation in person. She put an affectionate arm around Angela's shoulders.

Mrs. Smith was mother to all lonely people in Red Gorge and no one minded her taking the privileges of her position.

"Keeping that to yourself all the time," she said, referring to the engagement. "Never mind, dear, I understand more than you think. Mrs. Anstey arranged it all, didn't she, and you wanted a breathing space to look him over first? You should have come to me. I'd have told you what a gold mine you're getting in the owner of Naroo Downs."

She saw the quick almost wounded look in Angela's eyes and hastily added as she dropped her arm:

"I didn't mean *money*, dear, when I talked about gold mines. I mean he's a good man. Really good. Silent and hard to get to know. And he walks by himself. Suffers no one to be intimate, if you know what I mean. But he does good."

She nodded at Angela.

"He does a lot of good nobody knows anything about. But I know. We get all kinds of people in out-back hotels and we learn a lot. I know whose hand is behind it when a bit of good is done round this place. Not exactly a friendly man . . ."

"But he is," Angela found herself saying in Gilbert's defence. After all she had to put on the front of loyalty. She was his fiancée, wasn't she? She went on quickly, "We've had a lovely dinner party with Miss Winton. She is very, very friendly . . ."

"Oh, *her*!" said Mrs. Smith. She turned away to her desk and, leaning over it, began to leaf through a diary. "Now, let me see. Thursday week, Mr. Lawrence said. And we're not going to have a big reception. Just half a dozen of the nobs in. Mr. Morton, and the rector'll be two. Then there's young Nellie. You'd better let me know who else, dear, so I won't go dropping any bricks with the people who aren't invited. There'll be a bit of heart scalding about that, I can tell you."

"Oh, I hope not," said Angela anxiously. "I will have to get the names from . . . Gilbert. You see, I don't really know anyone yet."

Mrs. Smith straightened herself and looked through the glass window of her office, past the array of palms to where Gilbert and Stella Winton were sitting at the same table they had occupied in the lounge before dinner. Stella was leaning back in her chair, one arm thrown over the back, the other hand waving a cigarette in the air as she illustrated some point she was making with Gilbert. He was watching her face intently, and she was smiling back at him as she talked.

"Well, there's her," said Mrs. Smith, tapping her teeth with her pencil. "Wonder if he's going to ask her. If he does there'll be half a dozen others . . ."

"Miss Winton said she would be in Perth for the next two weeks," Angela said.

"Just as well, too," snorted Mrs. Smith.

What Stella Winton had actually said at the dinner-table when the subject of the wedding had come up was, "I'm going to Perth to get away from your wedding, Gilbert darling. You won't mind, will you, Angela? It would be like cutting off my right hand to stand in a church and see Gilly married to some-one else."

She had laughed quite gaily and Angela had not quite believed her. She had been joking. Yet as she ceased speaking Stella had looked down and toyed with a piece of fruit on her plate. When she had looked up and smiled at Angela again there had been something questing in her glance. Angela, who knew about calculators and had been trained in an IBM office, had thought that for a second Stella's eyes looked the cold blue of an adding machine. She had been adding something up about Angela. What?

Then Stella had laughed, and talked about everything else under the sun except weddings. She had been very charming and once again Angela had liked her.

After dinner they had had coffee in the lounge and Mrs. Smith had sent the message inviting Angela into her office. Angela had gone because, as long as she lived, she would never forget Mrs. Smith's kindness when she and Nellie had arrived, lone waifs, in Red Gorge.

Now, standing in the office, Angela watched Mrs. Smith's eyes cloud as she looked through the office window at Stella Winton and tapped her teeth with a pencil.

Angela could not forbear asking the all-crucial question.

"Do you like her, Mrs. Smith?"

"Who, me?" asked Mrs. Smith, looking back quickly at her young guest. "Of course I like her. Everyone likes Miss Winton. And it takes a lot to be liked, to be downright popular, in fact, when you've got everything Miss Winton's got. Owns Winderup, that's the station next to Naroo Downs. Money, brains, beauty and the shrewdest head north of the Leper Line. And that includes Mr. Lawrence too. You watch out, young lady. When Miss Stella Winton is at her most popular, and being most friendly, she's up to something. I could make half a guess, so could the whole town, at what she's been up to out at Naroo Downs this last week or two. Ah, well, it remains to be seen."

Mrs. Smith was talking in conundrums and Angela felt it would be undignified and not very wise to probe further. But there was a little stab of misgiving in her heart. If Stella Winton wished to marry Gilbert Lawrence herself, why was she being so friendly to Angela? She had actually, in a subtle way, helped Angela to get through that dinner with dignity. Was it possible she knew why Gilbert Lawrence was doing what he was doing? She knew him so well, that was clear from the way she talked to him, she might well have gauged the meaning of all his actions.

"She gets her own way in the end," Mrs. Smith was saying. "She's got patience, that's why. You know what, dear, we'd all be rich people if we had patience. Me? I can't be bothered buying into stocks that have got a long term to wait for capital improvement. I like a good smart speculation. Like buying oil shares one day before the oil boom starts."

Again Mrs. Smith was speaking a language Angela did not quite understand.

"I think perhaps I'd better go back and join them," Angela said. "Thank you very much, Mrs. Smith, for the lovely dinner to-night."

"That's nothing to what I'll order up for your wedding, dear. And it won't be so hard a thing either. Race Week the week after and I've a good order coming in by the freight plane. Full of specials it is too. We'll have a crowd of people in here. Place will be full. You'd better ask Mr. Lawrence if you're going to stay for Race Week. I'll need to book. He always does come in, you know."

"Yes, I'll ask him. I'm afraid we haven't got round to talking about all the details yet. Mrs. Smith, before I go, may I write a little note to Kevin Richards? He comes in for breakfast, doesn't he? Would you please give it to him. It's awfully important he gets it before he goes down to the mine office . . ."

"That's all right, my dear." Mrs. Smith was pushing a piece of writing paper forward on the desk as she spoke. She took an envelope from a pigeon-hole and handed Angela a fountain-pen.

Somewhat unhappily Angela met Mrs. Smith's eyes.

"I understand," Mrs. Smith said. Then she shrugged her shoulders. "These things happen in life. I know. I've lived long enough and seen enough to know these things happen in life." She shook her head dolefully and then putting more heart into her voice said, "Now, you go ahead and write your note. I'll give it to him myself. And not a word to anyone."

"Oh, it's not like that . . ." stammered Angela.

"Now don't you fib to me, young lady. Young Kevin Richards is in love with you and if Gilly Lawrence hadn't smartly come into Red Gorge in the nick of time you'd have been in love with him. Now get on with it while I jot down the menu for breakfast."

Angela wrote her note, folded the paper and put it in the envelope. She tucked the flap of the envelope inside the opening.

"Lick it down, lick it down," said Mrs. Smith almost testily. "I might leave it around and who knows who'd look inside. I might even take a look myself I'm that sad about the poor fellow."

"Oh, please, Mrs. Smith," Angela begged. "It's not like that . . ."

"No more fibs," said Mrs. Smith, taking the letter and gently pushing Angela towards the door. "Run along with you now and prise your man loose from that blonde siren or you'll lose out on both of 'em. Such a thing as falling between two stools, you know."

But she smiled as she spoke and Angela knew she didn't mean what she said. At least she *hoped* she didn't mean what she said.

As she went back towards the table in the lounge Gilbert rose from his seat. All his movements were slow yet decisive. They had an air of the inexorable about them. As he rose slowly from his chair he looked as if all the power in the world would not have been sufficient to prevent him.

"The car is outside, Angela," he said. "I think I'd better take you home now. Stella tells me she is going to bed. We'll be leaving first thing in the morning for Naroo Downs so I won't see you until the end of the week. I'll be in town again then."

"You, and Stella, are both going back to Naroo Downs?" Angela asked, and then bit her lip. With that question she had really given herself away. Stella laughed.

"Oh, I'm not going to run away with him," she said. "He's got a housekeeper and half a dozen other bodyguards out there. It's just a case of my car being there and I'm overlanding to Winderup. I couldn't leave my very latest thing in Bentleys gathering dust at Naroo, you know. By the way, Gilly, did you tell Angela about Hopkins and Smart being out at Naroo? What are you going to do with them while you're honeymooning?"

"Send them in here for Race Week," said Gilbert. "They might as well learn what out-back life is like when it's play-time."

"They certainly see what work-time is like when they're out your way," laughed Stella again. She stood up in a single graceful movement. "Oh, well, I'll to bed. I'll see you in the morning, Gilly." She turned to Angela and held out her hand. There was nothing but friendship in her eyes as she smiled. "I've loved meeting you, Angela. I think you're sweet. I ought to say 'Happy days' but . . ." She turned her eyes round in an amusing way to Gilbert. "I imagine being married to you, old thing, might be a bit grim. Still . . ." She looked back at Angela and smiled again. "I've got a feeling you'll get your just rewards." Her eyes were both kind and fun-making and Angela couldn't bring herself to believe that Stella Winton knew just what those "just rewards" were in Gilbert Lawrence's estimation. A punishment for having made a public use of his name.

In silence Gilbert held first one glass door and then the other open for Angela as they went out. A large dust-covered touring car was drawn up outside the hotel. A shadowy man loomed up out of the shadows.

"I didn't know you were coming in, or I'd have cleaned it up, Mr. Lawrence," he said apologetically. "But she's right for oil and petrol. Tyres okay, too."

"That's all right, thank you, Evans," Gilbert said. Angela was surprised that his voice was pleasant and friendly. He was obviously talking to an employee yet his voice had lost the cold severity to which she was already becoming accustomed. "I'll leave it outside here to-night when I get back. You might put it away first thing in the morning."

"Okay, Mr. Lawrence, I'll do that."

He held the door open for Angela. When she got in she said, "Thank you."

"That's okay, miss. Anything for the lady what's goin' to marry Mr. Lawrence."

"All right, Evans, good night," Gilbert said as he started up the car.

"Good night to you, Mr. Lawrence." He sounded as if it had been a pleasure to wait up to see that Gilbert got safely into his own car, and that it had been a pleasure to wish him good night.

It was a small incident but it made Angela want to turn her head a little and look at the man sitting silently driving the car, beside her. All night she had been avoiding looking at him. By not seeing him she didn't have to worry about what he was thinking or what he would be like when she had to share a house with him; or a *homestead*, as she had already learned was the name of the owner's residence on a station. Now she felt curious about him. She wanted to see what the man Evans saw in him that must be so different from what she, Angela, had seen in him down at the mine office.

There was only the moonlight to help her as once off the main street of Red Gorge there were no lights, except in sparsely spread houses. The moonlight, flickering between tree shadows, on his face seemed to make it colder and more remote than ever.

"Who are Hopkins and Smart that Miss Winton spoke of as being out at Naroo?" she asked by way of breaking an uneasy silence.

"Two business-men interested in buying up an option on the manganese on the north boundary of Naroo. One of them is a geologist and they're making a survey of the patch." His voice was noncommittal and not very informative. After a minute's silence he added, "I'll get rid of them for Race Week but after that they're likely to be with us another week or two. There'll be others. The place is heavy with a dozen different kinds of minerals."

"Is that why you're both a mining man and a cattleman?"

"I'm a cattleman who happens to have a lot of valuable minerals lying about on his lease," he answered somewhat shortly.

Angela felt silenced. He glanced at her sideways.

"I'm afraid you'll find Naroo Downs a busy place at present. I have a lot of people staying from time to time. I want to get rid of this business of geologists and mine promotors wandering over the run, and be left in peace. So I'm getting it all over in one shot. Then the cattle and I'll be left to one another for a year or two. I hope."

"Two more, such as Nellie and myself, won't make so much difference just now?" Angela couldn't help saying. Moreover, she felt entitled to bring the conversation, some time or other, to a personal basis. After all he was marrying her.

"No. So long as you keep out of my way. I think I mentioned that before."

Angela winced. His short rejoinder had had the effect of a blow. He was making her clearly understand exactly what her relationship was to be. And he was unforgiving.

"Yes, you did mention it, and I'll be very careful about that." She paused. "Shall I arrange for Nellie to meet you when you come in at the end of the week?"

"That child will be in bed for at least another week. I've already spoken to Doctor Irvine about her. He hasn't much of an opinion of your capacity for taking care of your sister, you know."

"Thank you," said Angela. "I'm sure his opinion is valuable."

"It is," said Gilbert swinging the car around the bend to run down Emu Flat. "It confirmed my own opinion that there was only one thing to do with the pair of you. Take you out to Naroo Downs."

"Did you have to marry me to do that?" asked Angela with a touch of bitterness in her voice.

"Yes," he replied shortly. "Since that was what the rest of the country from Carnlow to the Territory border was expecting." He braked sharply outside Mrs. Sharman's boarding-house. He sat, his hands resting on the steering-wheel, and for the moment made no attempt to move. Angela did not move either since she expected him to say something more. He made a short sharp sound as if he gritted his teeth. "Well, it's what Aunt Kara wanted," he added.

He turned to Angela. His face was a dark shadow, but the moon, low on the skyline, shone straight through the wide windows of the car on to Angela's face. It was very white and just a little drawn. Perhaps something in it touched some softer spot in his heart or perhaps he too perceived that both of them had been caught in the fine web of Aunt Kara's plans.

"If you can find some healthy occupation at Naroo Downs, I don't think you'll be too unhappy," he said. "And it will make a new person of your sister. You can forget what I said about keeping out of my way all the time." Angela got the impression that the swift half smile that sometimes relaxed his stern expression had passed across his face. "I promise not to carry a stock-whip in your immediate vicinity."

Angela's soft heart was immediately filled with remorse for her cruel reminder to him that people spoke of him as "driving men with stock-whips." The behaviour of Gilbert to that man Evans outside the hotel to-night had given the lie to that particular legend about how he treated his men.

"I'm sorry I ever mentioned stock-whips," Angela said.

"Don't be sorry," he replied. "If we do get to know one

another, I'll show you how to use one. But only to make cracking sounds in the air."

He got out of the car, walked around it and opened the door for her. She wondered, as she got out, if she held out her hand . . . or whether she merely said " good night " and then walked away.

Gilbert opened Mrs. Sharman's gate and stood so far back, as Angela entered, that handshaking was out of the question.

" Thank you," she said. " It has been an interesting evening."

He walked the few paces with her to the foot of the veranda steps. Angela ran quickly up the steps.

" Thank you," she murmured again. " It was a beautiful dinner," then quickly went inside.

Because of the hot humid air all doors and windows were open and she did not have to pause on the doorstep. Inside her bedroom she stood listening a minute before she turned on her light. She heard his footsteps walk quietly and firmly away.

Was he thinking of Aunt Kara's wish? Or had the comparison between herself and Stella Winton been too marked?

She crossed the room and drew the curtains and then went back to the doorway and switched on the light.

She stood in front of the mirror and looked at herself. She had had a long evening full of strain and her face did indeed look pale. Stella Winton's face had been a smooth golden tan and full of vivacity and health.

" But if I were married to him . . . and was out there with him," Angela thought, " perhaps I could find some way to . . . to . . . to, well what? Just bring him a little human warmth."

She slipped out of her clothes, hanging up her " dress with the golden roses " in the diminutive wardrobe. She washed, and cleaned her teeth and brushed her hair. She crept between the sheets, first throwing back the covers because in this climate they were never anything more than a decoration. She punched her pillow into a comfortable shape.

" Well, I mean to try," she said with the last punch. Then she put her head down on her pillow and said her little prayer . . .

" Thank God for finding Nellie and me a good home. I mean to deserve it."

It did not occur to Angela that there had been a marked change in her own attitude to Gilbert Lawrence, and to her future life at Naroo Downs. Her life had been a life of service and now it was second nature to her. Her last waking thoughts on that memorable night were to be grateful for her lot in life and a resolution to do something to make Gilbert Lawrence's life comfortable, even happy. She did not realise that unconsciously his remoteness and aloneness had touched her with compassion.

CHAPTER EIGHT

Angela continued working at the mine office until the day before her wedding. She felt guilty in letting Mr. Morton down by leaving so soon after her appointment but the mine manager took it philosophically.

"We never can keep the young ladies," he said glumly. "If you hadn't made up your mind to marry Gilbert Lawrence, it would have been someone else. There aren't enough women to go round."

"Could I spend my remaining time showing someone how to use a Comptometer and a calculating machine? Of course they couldn't become expert at it without practice but they could at least do the elementary calculations."

"There aren't any females in Red Gorge looking for a job," he said pessimistically.

"What about a man? Why shouldn't you train a young clerk?"

Mr. Morton looked at Angela as if she had taken leave of her senses.

"They regard it as women's work."

"Not if they thought it was a first lead into keeping the books and finally the accounts. You have to bring your book-keepers and the accountant up here from the south, don't you, Mr. Morton?"

He looked at her with an expressionless face for some time, but Angela could see he was nibbling at the idea.

"Mention it to Mr. Richards. There's young Dacres. He's only a stripling. His father has been bothering me about what kind of a future there is for him in the clerical work here. I was expecting him to leave any moment. Shifting sands, that's what the mine population is up here in the north."

Angela mentioned the matter to Kevin Richards and that very afternoon Simon Dacres, an eighteen-year-old clerk, moved into Angela's office with her. The beautiful brain machines had a fascination for him and it took Angela all her time not to let him get to work with a screwdriver to find out how the "brain" ticked.

Kevin had received her note from Mrs. Smith's hand but he had already heard the news. When Angela came to work on the morning following the dinner party with Gilbert and Stella Winton, Kevin Richards was already in the office, his head bent over his table. Angela was early so that Janette Wells and the two typists and Mr. Morton's secretary had not yet arrived. Kevin did not lift his head as Angela entered the main door. She felt sure he knew whose foosteps they were crossing the floor.

She took off her hat and then crossed her room to the plate glass wall separating it from Kevin's room. She leaned her forehead on the glass and looked at him. He lifted his head and for a minute remained seated, looking back. Then he got up, walked round the table and came to the glass wall. He slid back the pane of glass and revealed a small window. It meant they could hear one another speak.

"Why did you do it?" he asked, looking at her with eyes that were both angry and sad.

She found it hard to answer him.

"Didn't I tell you to consult me first, Angee?"

The little nickname, which he had never used before, brought a lump to her throat. It was tender and reproachful and somehow told her how kind and nice Kevin Richards might have been if he had been the chosen one instead of Gilbert Lawrence.

Of course she could not tell him the truth, partly out of loyalty to Gilbert Lawrence and partly because she knew that Kevin Richards would come out fighting against such an artificial way of disposing of her life. She couldn't afford to have that happen. There were complications enough, as it was. She had to make Kevin think less well of her. In that way the hurt, if his affection for her was real and deep, would be more bearable. In fact it would help him to forget her. His love could turn to dislike and that would be the kindest thing to do to it.

"You gave me the idea yourself, Kevin," she said, banishing the tender look that had been in her own eyes as she had looked at his down-bent head through the glass wall. "Why shouldn't I marry him? As you said, he's rich, and powerful. I'll be queen of the whole district."

"You're not that kind of girl, Angela, so don't fool me. The whole thing was a fixed-up idea by that crazy sentimental old aunt of his. And he never said 'No' to her and I don't suppose your people on the other side of the world did either." He paused while his gaze went over her face as if seeking for the truth, and then came back to her eyes. "But you're shrewder than I thought. You meant to look him over first, didn't you? Just to make sure? For a quiet demure little thing there aren't any weak spots in your make-up, are there, Angela?"

She shook her head.

"No," she said in a low voice.

"And, of course, you had to do something about young Nellie?"

Angela nodded.

"Yes," she said in the same low voice.

"You think you've used your head the same way as you use a calculating machine? You just punch all the right buttons and the right answers come out?"

"Yes," Angela said.

Kevin Richards put his finger up and pointed it through the glass at Angela. It left a smudge on the wall where it touched, and his fingertip was flattened and white. Angela was too ashamed to take her eyes away from it and look into Kevin Richards's eyes.

"Well, let me tell you," he said, "no machine can *think* in spite of what the technologists say. Nor has it any real warm human blood in its veins." He took his finger away and put his hands in his pockets. He rocked gently backwards and forwards on his heels. "You may think, young Angela, that you have the same precision in judgment as that blue steel machine on your desk but I'm telling you sadly but surely, that that's what you're marrying. Gilly Lawrence hasn't got a heart, and maybe you'll miss that pulsating piece of human organism much more than you think when you find yourself married to a calculating machine. One that happens to wear a coating of ice at that."

Angela pursed her mouth a little and held her head higher.

"You are speaking of my fiancé," she said with an attempt at hauteur that was entirely foreign to her nature.

Kevin gave a sarcastic laugh.

"The queen of Red Gorge already? Come, Angela, it takes a little more training for the post than you think. You have a lock of hair astray over your right temple, and your shoes gathered a fair covering of red dust on your way down from Mrs. Sharman's boarding-house this morning."

Angela flushed. In short Kevin had, in a bitter fashion, told her she was making the pantry-maid to duchess circuit in Red Gorge and she wasn't misleading him by her haughty reminder that Gilbert Lawrence was her fiancé.

Kevin was hurt, and he sought to hurt back.

It was better that way. That way he would hate her.

How the interview would have ended she was never to know because at that moment the outer doors of the office opened and Janette Wells and the two typists came in together. The glass walls of the office precluded any attempt to continue this embarrassing conversation.

Angela turned away and went back to her table. Her heart felt sore and there were unshed tears at the back of her eyes. She stood behind her table but had to look down as if sorting out papers to hide her distress from the other girls. It was then that Mr. Morton came in and Angela went straight to his office to hand in her resignation and make her offer to try and teach someone the first principles of using the machines.

Angela had never willingly hurt anyone in her life, and never before had anyone deliberately set out to hurt her.

How many people in Red Gorge, she wondered, would add up her progress from the boarding-house on Emu Flat to Naroo Downs the way Kevin had implied? How many would see her as a baby-faced but astute adventuress?

Of course! That was what Gilbert Lawrence had seen in her. He was making her pay the price. He was marrying her . . . and see how she liked it!

It was with a heavy heart that Angela put in a day's work that day.

Nellie was the one who was delighted.

As she recovered first from her fever and finally from her sunburn the nurses in the hospital filled her ears with all the charms of station life. There would be horses to ride, that had been enough, had the nurses only known, but they went on to further descriptions of things to do on a station. Swimming in the creek, bush picnics on the ranges, cattle musters, homestead parties when the buyers came in to buy the cattle, wild flowers to pick after the rains . . .

"Oh, Angela," Nellie cried in delight. "We'll be rich! Won't it be wonderful!"

How to stop Nellie thinking and talking this way was quite a problem.

"People who only marry for riches are always very unhappy people, Nellie."

"But you're not that much in love with him already, are you, Angela?"

"Of course I am. Head over heels. Why not? Every girl in Red Gorge is that way, not to mention all the other station owners' daughters round about."

"Golly," said Nellie, awed at Angela's swift fall into love. "Do you think I could find someone with a station all to himself as quickly as that? You know, I always thought you'd marry Gilbert Lawrence. Ever since Aunt Kara's letters. You must have meant it all the time yourself, Angela. Why didn't you tell me?"

"Oh, Nellie!" Angela said. She was sitting by Nellie's bed in the hospital and she suddenly leaned forward and put her head down on the side of the bed. For a few minutes the only sound in the room was Angela's racking sobs.

"But Angela," said Nellie aghast. "Whatever is the matter?"

Angela lifted her head, wiped her eyes and blew her nose.

"Nothing," she said. "It's just that I'm so happy. People often cry when they're happy."

It was then, sitting there by a bed in a hospital room, that Angela made up her mind that come what may she would be happy. The only alternative was desperate loneliness and heartbreak. She must be happy or die. She didn't want to die so she would have to be happy. She would make herself happy . . . in spite of everything.

"Let's talk about all the lovely things we'll do, Nellie," she said brightly. "Let's tick off on our fingers all the nice things about getting married. There's the wedding dress to begin with. Well, I'm going to wear that white linen dress I've never worn, and you're to embroider something round the short sleeves for me. And what do you think about the neckline? Would there be time for something, perhaps roses appliquéd on? It's too plain as it is, isn't it?"

"I always said it was plain for a round neck, Angela. I could do that ever so quickly. And I could put a little flower, say a rosebud, on the buttons too. They're linen-covered, aren't they?"

"Nellie, you are a darling. Thank you ever so much. Now have you any idea about a hat? For some reason or other Gilbert seemed to think the hat was more important than the dress."

"They've only got sun hats up at the shop," said Nellie glumly. "And all we've got is a big straw and a little hat each."

They sat in silence for a few minutes and ruminated on the subject of big and little straw hats.

"I don't think either would look very nice with a white linen dress," said Nellie, even more glumly. "They're plain. And, you know what, Angela, they were a bit cheap, weren't they? I mean, they don't look like nice expensive hats."

"Perhaps we could do something to them. The little hats, I mean. The one for you and the other for me. Daisies round the brim . . ."

"Can't have daisies," said Nellie. "We're having roses on the dress. White roses . . . the same colour as the dress. You ought to have a different colour on the hat. Pink ribbon . . . do you think?" She shook her head. "No. I don't think ribbon's fashionable. In the magazines people were wearing roses everywhere. All over the crown of the hat . . ."

Angela's eyes met Nellie's in the excitement of a new idea.

"They've got roses, strings of tiny little roses up at the shop. We could pull them off the wire . . ."

Nellie nearly crowed.

"I know what we'll do, Angela. We'll take the crowns right off. Just cut them off. Then we'll put a net crown on. And we'll sew roses all over the net. Then a tiny little circle of them just on the edge of the brim. It is only a tiny brim, and the straw is really fine."

"Pink roses on mine and blue forget-me-nots on yours, Nellie," said Angela, delighted. "They've got blue forget-me-nots in little bunches up at the shop. They are on the same counter as the roses and the handkerchiefs and gloves."

"And a nice long pair of white nylon gloves. Can we afford them, Angela? They have to be plain."

"Absolutely, they have to be plain. And we can afford them. It's a must. We'll have to . . ."

"And it won't matter if we can't. Gilbert Lawrence is rich and things like that won't matter any more, will they?"

Alas, they had come full circle back to that unhappy subject . . . Nellie's awe and delight in Gilbert Lawrence's reputed wealth.

"He's probably wealthy in sheep and cattle and mining shares, and hasn't got a bean in the bank," said Angela, still in a bright voice. "Kevin Richards up at the office told me most station owners are like that. They run on credit. Then when the wool clip is auctioned, or the cattle buyers come, they have a grand and glorious pay-off, a grand and glorious spree, then go back to being penniless until the next season. Kevin told me he worked as a book-keeper on a station that had nearly a million acres before he got the job in the mine office. He said he never saw money, not even a penny, until the pay-off at the end of the season."

"What did he do without money?" asked Nellie, round-eyed.

"There's nothing to spend it on, on a station, he said. Anything you want you get at the station store and it's docked when the pay-off comes at the end of the season."

Nellie was still digesting this when the nurse came in to tell Angela she must go now because it was the hour for Nellie's salt bath. The salt bath, Nellie had informed Angela with the superior air of one who shares medical secrets, was the most important part of the sunburn cure.

"I'll bring the dress and the hats when I come up to-morrow," Angela said from the doorway. "And your sewing basket."

"Get me two more skeins of white embroidery cotton," Nellie commanded. "And make sure my thimble's there. And don't forget the roses and the forget-me-nots before the shop closes . . ."

"My, my!" said the nurse with raised eyebrows at Angela. "There seems to be something more than a salt bath in the cure to-day."

"There is," said Angela gaily. "There's a wedding in the air."

She walked away from the hospital with a light tread. Every girl loves a wedding and Angela Burns was no different from any other girl. She had given this wedding a build-up to help Nellie and indirectly help herself.

There was going to be a wedding and it might as well be a nice one. If there was going to be a bride and a bridesmaid in the family, then they'd be lovely ones. Gilbert Lawrence, and people like Stella Winton, didn't know what people like Angela and Nellie Burns could do with a couple of sewing needles between them and a couple of bunches of flower trimmings bought in a draper's shop.

In fact, if Angela Burns was going to be queen of Red Gorge for one day, then she was going to be a nice queen. She would have long white gloves, and the pearl ear-rings that had been her mother's. Her hair would be shampooed and set and her finger-nails would be lacquered a nice pale, pale pink. Not blood red, like Stella Winton's. And she would hold up her head, with its crown of roses, and she would *smile.*

That would surprise Gilbert Lawrence!

After it was all over she needn't look at him again. She just had to keep out of his way. She would buy a text-book and a practice book on shorthand. Out at the station she would teach herself and Nellie shorthand. That would get them ready for their next job, after they had stayed on Naroo Downs long enough to satisfy Gilbert's pride and restore Nellie to health.

Why, the whole world was in front of Angela Burns. Except that she would have changed her name.

Oh, well, she would have to get used to that, just as she must remember to do something for Gilbert Lawrence, something unobtrusive but effective that would leave him a happier man for the experience. That would repay him the injury Nellie had done to his idea of chivalrous conduct. And it would pay for their board and lodging. He would never know, of course, but she, Angela, would know. It would satisfy her own idea of chivalry.

For there is such a thing as chivalry, even in women, thought Angela Burns as she mounted the steps of Mrs. Sharman's veranda and met the world of the boarding-house with a smile.

She was going to be married. She might as well have some of the fun of it too. And certainly Nellie must enjoy it. It would give Nellie something to which she could look forward, and take her mind off the pain of her sickness and the dull deadly heat of Emu Flat and Red Gorge.

At the end of the week Gilbert Lawrence came into town, flying over the roof-tops as usual so that everyone knew he was there.

"He's come in to see his girl," everyone said with a wink and a nod and a smile.

This impending marriage of Gilbert Lawrence's was a very titillating piece of news. To the people of Red Gorge he had something of the aura of royalty and everyone was agog to know what sort of a wedding it would be. Who would be asked? Would it be townsfolk or would it be station folk? He was being married two days before Race Week began and already station owners from as far as five hundred miles north, east and south would be coming in. A special trip had been chartered with one of the coastal ships to bring horses down from Wyndham and Derby and up from Geraldton. It was rumoured a man was bringing a stranger horse across the overland stock route. It had won every race in the Northern Territory. There was a double flight schedule for the M.M.A. planes coming into Red Gorge.

The heat was a calamity forgotten. People were too busy making new dresses or, in the case of the men, having their hundred-bale hats dry-cleaned ready for the burster at the end of the following week.

One could always say one was having a new dress made for the races, then one didn't look a fool if one wasn't invited to Gilly Lawrence's wedding. The burning question of the hour had nothing to do with the shade temperature outside. It was . . . who is going to be asked to the wedding?

Meantime quite unconscious of the furore in the town, Angela went quietly backwards and forwards to the mine office; and backwards and forwards between the hospital and Mrs. Sharman's house on Emu Flat.

Nellie, by the end of the week, had graduated to being an arm-chair case. In the evening she was allowed to receive her visitors on the hospital veranda. And Nellie had a great many visitors. Mrs. Sharman and the fellow boarders came. The girls from the High School came. Mrs. Smith from the hotel came. The doctor's wife and the mine manager's wife called. Moreover, her sister was going to marry Gilly Lawrence.

And what did little sister think of her sister getting married?

Nellie pulled her needles and threads in and out of her embroidery and told everyone with great delight what she thought of the wedding.

" Of course Angela was always going to marry Gilbert Lawrence. Aunt Kara and my mother fixed it up years ago. Yes, years ago, even though Angela was only a little girl. It was all arranged, like they do with foreign royalty in Europe."

So much attention was paid to Nellie, everyone was so kind, she had already accepted the status of royalty for Angela and herself as a natural right.

" Of course it will be a big wedding. Gilbert Lawrence is awfully rich, you know, though he runs on credit for most of the time. Pays for everything he gets with bales of wool, you know. Everybody will be asked . . ." She would turn her eyes on her current visitor and say, " You'll get an invitation next week. I'll tell my future brother-in-law not to forget your name."

Some of Nellie's visitors tried not to look askance at this intimation they might only get an invitation because of the intervention of this young girl. They had to swallow hard and say, "Well, that's nice of you, Nellie. But you see, Gilly Lawrence is a very quiet man. He might decide at the last minute just to make it a handful of friends."

In those cases Nellie eyed her beautifully embroidered roses on Angela's linen dress, or she would think of the roses and forget-me-nots on two pretty little straw hats, and she would shake her head vigorously. These efforts were not going to be wasted on a "few" people.

"It's going to be a lovely big wedding. Angela says so. It's always the bride who decides, you know."

Then while the conversation was being delicately turned aside Nellie would give herself temporarily up to the dream of sweeping up the aisle of the church, looking so utterly charming that no one, not even Gilbert Lawrence, would have time to notice anyone but the bridesmaid. The best man—Nellie hoped he would be tall and handsome—would give a little gasp and turn deathly pale. Hours later he would hold a glass of champagne in one hand and her own drooping bouquet in the other and in a deep tremulous voice say . . . "*Nellie.*" She, of course, would treat him coldly, but after a year or two she would forgive him (what for, she hadn't yet decided) and would marry him and would live rich and happy and the envy of Red Gorge for ever after.

She would take a honeymoon to England in order to show him off to Kate and Nora Thomason. She would even invite them out to Australia to get a station owner or two for themselves.

Nellie always appeared just a little dazed from her day-dreaming by the time Angela arrived to see her later in the evening.

"Darling, you seem tired," Angela said on one evening.

"Not tired," said Nellie with a wan and weary note in her voice. "Just exhausted."

"Exhausted? But what with? The doctor and the nurses say you are nearly ready to come home . . . if you promise to stay out of the sun . . ."

"With all the visitors," said Nellie with a sigh. "It's rather a bore being important in Red Gorge, isn't it, Angela?"

"Nellie," said Angela with a touch of anxiety in her voice, "what have you been saying to all your visitors? And who were they?"

"Oh, everybody who's anybody," said Nellie, bored. "There wasn't really anything to talk about except the wedding. Of course I told them it would be a big wedding. You'll have to see they're all invited. After all, they've brought me fruit, and home-made cakes, and scented bath soap all wrapped up in silver paper."

"Nellie!" said Angela exasperated. "I forbid you to talk about the wedding to anybody. It's Gilbert's wedding. I haven't any idea whom he wishes to invite. Perhaps nobody at all . . ."

Nellie ceased to be bored and opened her eyes wide.

"It's not his wedding. It's your wedding, Angela. It's for you to say."

Angela had to catch her breath to prevent herself saying something sharp. There was a short silence in which Nellie looked at her with hurt, puzzled eyes. Angela remembered that an illusion of a happy love marriage had to be maintained with Nellie.

"Listen, dear," she said quietly. "Gilbert knows people in Red Gorge. I don't. I must take his advice on this matter. Now I beg you don't talk about the wedding to anybody. Not even to the nurses. After I've seen Gilbert on Saturday I'll tell you all about it."

"And am I going to see him?"

"Of course. He will come to see you."

Angela closed her eyes and uttered a little prayer that Gilbert would do just that. He attached so much importance to appearances, he surely would not cause comment by ignoring his bride's sister!

It was on Saturday morning that Gilbert flew in. Angela had gone down to the mine office to put in some extra hours and she heard the sound of the small plane as it flew across the mountain ridge to the east. She went to the office window and watched it come in over the roof-tops.

It was impossible for her to tell what her feelings were, or even if she had any feelings at all. She had been mostly happy during the last week because she had had to work hard in the office and the time had passed quickly. Moreover, her Comptometer pupil was an apt one and she had a feeling he would be very useful to the office. Also Mr. Morton, and even Kevin Richards, the latter a little grudgingly, had shown they were very impressed with her thorough way of teaching Simon Dacres. She felt they were pleased with her and this fact helped to mitigate the disappointment that she was only holding the job for so short a time. She would leave with a good record. There would be no ill-will felt towards her.

Yet, as she watched the single-engined plane appear, to glide in low over the town, there was a touch of sadness somewhere deep in her heart. She tried to put her finger on it, to locate it, and know its cause.

She had completely adjusted herself to the idea of marrying Gilbert Lawrence. The marriage held no fears for her, because as a marriage it held no hopes.

Kevin Richards's forewarning that marrying Gilbert Lawrence was like marrying a calculating machine held no terrors for Angela. The one thing she couldn't explain to Kevin was that she was not marrying Gilbert for love or for a lifetime. His coldness would not dry up any wells of love in herself. There weren't any there to dry up.

Perhaps that was what made her feel a little sad.

Here was a man, flying his own plane in over the roof-tops to meet her. He was tall, handsome and a man of considerable prestige and substance, yet it meant nothing, absolutely nothing to her.

Yes, that was the pity of it. The pity of it, and the waste.

Angela sighed and went back to her table. She spent some time tidying up the papers there, then locked her drawers and went to the wash-room to comb her hair, put fresh lipstick on her mouth and put on her straw hat . . . the large one. Thinking of it, and the glamorous future in store for the small hat, she smiled.

It's funny what happens to some orphans in the world, she thought. In the first instance she meant the little straw hat but a second later she had seen the analogy in her own fate.

As she went back through the main office she looked through the glass pane into Kevin Richards's room, and once again she sighed. Kevin had been extremely official and distant after that early morning talk they had had through the glass wall. Angela had helped to keep it that way but somehow that too made her a little sad. She wondered if she was very much to blame for having made him unhappy. And what would it have been like to be happy with Kevin . . . Perhaps later! But that was perfidy, she must lock away such a thought from her mind for ever.

She walked out the main door and pulled it shut behind her. She stepped out of the air-conditioned building into the blinding midday heat of the street, to find Kevin Richards waiting for her. He had propped his shoulders against the veranda post of the next building and he now straightened himself and moved across the path to Angela's side.

"I was waiting for you," he said.

"Yes, I thought perhaps you were," said Angela honestly.

"I don't suppose Gilly Lawrence'll take a gun to me if I walk up the hill with you . . ."

"I don't suppose so, either," said Angela but all the same she didn't think it advisable, for both their sakes. One didn't know how to say so without hurting Kevin's feelings.

Kevin fell into step beside her and they walked on a little way in silence.

"Supposing we go in and have a cool drink," Kevin said as they drew abreast the open door of the restaurant. A purr of cool air was gyrating outside the doors by means of punkahs which for a moment tempted Angela.

"I don't think we had better," she said ruefully. "I've got to get home. You see, they sent Nellie home from the hospital this morning. Then I have to have a bath and change. I think Gilbert might be expecting to see me."

"Might be expecting . . ." Kevin echoed her words half angrily, half sarcastically. "Listen, Angela, what goes on? There's something phoney about this whole thing. You've met him twice. I know that for a fact. He hasn't been in touch with you since he went back to Naroo last Saturday. I know that too. He can't because the line from Naroo is relayed through Milga Station and Enmore. Enmore relays to Red Gorge through the mine office. It's got our biggest mine on its lease. And there hasn't been a call through from Enmore except mining business for a week."

"One couldn't do anything very private in Red Gorge, if one wanted to," said Angela lightly.

"Certainly not make love calls by telephone," said Kevin.

"Then perhaps that is why Gilbert has not called," said Angela evenly. She looked up at Kevin with cloudless eyes.

He stopped and Angela had perforce to stop, too, otherwise the few people about would have known they were quarrelling.

"You might be marrying him for his money, Angela," he said accusingly. "But what is he marrying you for?"

That was indeed a poser. She could hardly justify Gilbert's choice by saying she was beautiful or charming or rich. What could she say of herself that would make the marriage look right in other people's eyes?

"You haven't any answer, have you?" said Kevin. "Well, I'll give you one. It's to put up some kind of buffer state between Naroo Downs and Winderup. Stella Winton is about the one person in this part of the world who is more than a match for Gilly Lawrence and he knows it. With a wife out there, then Stella's under a bit of a handicap. You, or any other girl who'd pass muster, what's the odds? It was that, or marry Stella Winton herself. And she's about the only girl in the world who . . . Dash it all! What's the good? You'll find out all about Stella in plenty of time."

Kevin paused. Angela turned and walked on and a minute later Kevin was beside her, keeping step, intent on walking all the way to Emu Flat with her.

He was angry and bitter and he made no attempt to hide it. What had he been going to say about Stella? Why had he stopped? She couldn't possibly ask him. Angela let him go on talking to himself. He was thinking aloud and Angela knew it. It added verisimilitude to what he was saying. There was a dilemma here, in Kevin's mind, and in an unconscious kind of a way he was exposing it to Angela's view. He was not so much telling her things, as revealing his own thoughts. And they happened to be honest thoughts even though they were spiking themselves on a painful subject.

She could say nothing because she knew nothing of the relationship between Stella Winton and Gilbert.

That dinner party! There had been something in Stella's manner. The friendliness was genuine, but there was a doubt, a glint of some hard appraisal deep in those Arctic blue eyes. There had been a purpose barely revealed and quickly hidden in the manner in which Stella had first looked at Angela and then had set herself out to please the young girl and help her get over the embarrassments of a first dinner party.

Could that be it?

Of the two of them, Stella and Angela, very cleverly and very subtly Angela had appeared the inferior, Stella the superior.

The little strand of sadness that had been in Angela's heart all the morning seemed to loop itself into a hard knot.

"Kevin," she said resolutely, "let's talk about something else . . ."

A car gathering both momentum and dust streaked down the wide red road. It loomed up from behind, passed them, and was gone in less than a minute.

"That," said Kevin furiously, "was your fiancé, Gilbert Lawrence. Driving himself in from the airstrip and breaking every road regulation in the place." The quality of his voice altered and he added sardonically, "Just give me one good reason why he didn't stop to pick you up, Angela?"

"I think she was sitting in the front seat with him," said Angela in a low voice.

She wondered why she felt defeated, and that Kevin Richards had gained some momentous victory over her. He had indirectly called Stella Winton one good reason why Gilbert should pass her in his car and one reason would suffice.

CHAPTER NINE

In the end the whole town was invited to the wedding of Angela Burns to Gilbert Lawrence.

On the Saturday preceding his wedding Gilbert hadn't been in Red Gorge very long when he knew that many people expected to be invited.

Stella Winton was the first to discover this. She was having a drink in the lounge after Gilbert had gone to his room to bath and change and Mrs. Smith came towards her.

"Where's that man?" Mrs. Smith said rather testily. "He really must tell me what he's going to do about this wedding. I've half the ladies in Red Gorge telling me young Nellie Burns is issuing invitations right and left. There's going to be both muddle and heart-burning unless we straighten it out."

Stella Winton, her knees crossed and one elegantly-shod foot waving in the air, laughed.

"Oh, Mrs. Smith," she said, "you mustn't begrudge those two pretty youngsters their bit of fun. What's a wedding without a crowd?"

"Wait till Mr. Lawrence hears you calling his bride a 'pretty youngster,' Miss Winton. He won't like that."

Stella laughed again.

"I've already told him," she said. "Several times. Well? She is pretty, isn't she?"

"Yes. And a very nice girl into the bargain."

"Of course she is. I'm all on her side for having a big wedding. I shall tell Gilly so."

"So long as he tells me so . . . I'll be happy. I've got to know how many to feed."

Mrs. Smith walked away in the direction of her office, grumbling. Stella Winton looked amused as her light-blue eyes followed Mrs. Smith's irate figure.

When Gilbert came into the lounge she called him over.

"I know you're off to call on Angela," she said. "But before you go I'd better warn you. The pair of them, Angela and her sister, have asked half the town to the wedding. I'm wondering how you're going to sort out the weeds from the tares, Gilly. Those girls wouldn't have any idea who is who, and who is not who, in Red Gorge." Her laugh was a little mocking. "I'm beginning to be sorry I won't be here for it. I think there might be some fun."

Gilbert stood by her chair, silent, his eyes unamused. He signalled the steward to bring him across his usual drink. The steward was already carrying it in anticipation and Gilbert drank it standing up.

"The solution is more simple than you think, Stella. The weeds and the tares will both be there."

Stella watched him through curious eyes as he took out a cigarette. He did not have to offer her one as she was already smoking.

"You made up your mind on that in a flash," she said.

"I do sometimes, you know."

She leaned forward and stubbed out her cigarette in the tray on the table. She looked up and there was no laugh in her eyes. They were suddenly a little hard, a little calculating.

"Then why do we have to drag out this other business? Gilly, it's time you and I came to terms."

He looked at his watch.

"If you don't mind, I have a call to make. And you, I believe have a mail plane to catch."

The provocative smile came back into Stella's eyes.

"Both busy people, aren't we? Well, thanks for the lift into Red Gorge. I'll see you after the wedding."

"Yes," said Gilbert. "After the wedding."

Gilbert's car was outside waiting for him and he drove down Emu Flat to Mrs. Sharman's house.

Angela, sitting with Nellie behind the creepers on the side veranda, watched him get out of his car, open the gate and walk up the path towards the steps.

For the life of her she couldn't analyse her own feelings. She had forgotten what a striking figure he was. Even the cold aloof expression of his face seemed to add something attractive to him this evening.

Mrs. Sharman and the engineer from the mine were also on the veranda as Gilbert came up the steps and it was quite clear they were going to stay and meet the man of the moment.

Angela as she made the introductions had an unexpected feeling of pride. But then who wouldn't? She was introducing to these people, who already knew him by sight and hearsay, the man she was going to marry. And no girl anywhere could have produced anyone as striking and even awe-inspiring as this man.

"Well, Nellie?" Gilbert said, looking down at the younger girl. "You are better, I hear? Well enough, I understand, to take a key part in a large wedding?"

Mrs. Sharman said with a flap of excitement:

"Oh, Mr. Lawrence, are we to have a big wedding? How *lovely.*"

Gilbert transferred his grey eyes from Nellie to Angela.

"I understand that is what Angela would like," he said without looking at Mrs. Sharman.

Angela drew in a breath, then slowly she expelled it. She knew what had happened. Nellie and her visitors at the hospital!

"It would be very nice," Angela said quietly. She wished those grey eyes would show some human feeling. Would he hold all Nellie's weaknesses as an account against Angela?

"It shall be as you have already expressed a wish," he said evenly. "I shan't discriminate between anybody in the town. I shall arrange for the hall to be hired and the whole town can come."

"That's mighty big of you, Mr. Lawrence," the engineer said.

"Great," breathed Mrs. Sharman in a voice of awed excitement. "It will be like Christmas, or Anzac Day."

"Quite," said Gilbert. He had not taken his eyes from Angela. They held her gaze relentlessly. "Is that what you wish, Angela?"

She found her voice.

"Thank you, that is very kind of you," she said quietly.

Nellie had for a few minutes been overawed by the visions of her dreams coming true.

"Oh, Gilbert," she said, making sure that Mrs. Sharman and the engineer registered just how close a relationship she could claim to this distinguished man. "Are you taking Angela out to dinner? Am I invited, too?"

"No, Nellie," he said, turning to her again. "When I take you out to dinner I will send you a gilt-edged invitation. In the meantime Angela and I have rather a lot to say to one another." He looked at Angela. "Are you ready?" he inquired politely. "If so, I think we might go now."

Angela went inside to pick up a light stole and when she came out Gilbert was standing by the steps. Mrs. Sharman and the fellow guest had gone inside. Nellie had lapsed into a thoughtful silence as she contemplated the iceberg who was shortly to become her brother-in-law.

To her surprise, in spite of his frigid manner, Nellie decided she liked him. She settled back to enjoy a reverie in which he was destined to play quite an important and heroic part.

When Angela came out on to the veranda Gilbert stood aside with a perfunctory kind of good manners and then politely took her elbow as they descended the steps and went down the path to the gate. As he opened the car door his eyes met hers again with a quick flickering look.

"If there is anything else you want, Angela," he said quietly and coldly, "besides marriage and a big wedding you had better let me know first this time, instead of last. It would be simpler in the long run."

Angela remained silent as she got into the car and he carefully, quietly and firmly closed the car door after her.

She watched him as he walked round the bonnet of the car to get into the driver's seat.

What could she say? That Nellie had done it? Cast on Nellie's shoulders all their joint sins of omission and commission?

From loyalty to her young sister she said nothing.

As they drove back towards the town the hum of the mail plane could be heard and a minute later it rose up from the airfield beyond the houses like a giant grey and silver bird. Angela, glancing sideways at Gilbert, saw his frowning eyes leave the road and watch the plane climbing away towards the southern sky.

"Taking off into the wind," he said casually, as if conversation must be made.

"Is Miss Winton on the plane?" Angela asked and then was surprised that she wanted to know.

"Yes. She's gone south on business matters. I flew her in this afternoon."

"I saw you. I mean, I saw you driving her to the hotel."

"Oh, did you?" He seemed surprised. "I'm afraid I didn't see you. I would have stopped. Were you walking home from the office alone?"

The question was polite and casual and sounded as if he had no real interest in her answer. It stung Angela to a rare show of spirit.

"No. I was with Kevin Richards. It was near the restaurant, and we were debating whether we would go and have a cool drink or not."

His head turned to her. It was getting dark now and she could not see the expression on his face.

"I told you to forget that young man," he said abruptly.

"Why?" asked Angela surprised.

"Because you're marrying me," he said shortly. "My wife will not have a shadow of admirers in the offing."

Angela knew he was angry when he had first spoken to her on the veranda but this was beyond the bounds of kindness or reason.

"I don't think you know quite the kind of person I am . . ." she began.

He swung the car into the main street and pulled it up beside the kerb outside the hotel.

"I think I do," he said.

"What kind of a person am I?" she asked quietly.

He had opened his door but not yet left the car. He turned to look at her as he spoke.

"A young girl . . . just a little foolish. Unfortunately her foolishness leads her, and other people, into embarrassing situations. When you are married to me, they can be avoided. We will be at Naroo Downs. In the meantime I ask you to express your wishes to me *first*. It would be helpful to know to what I am committed before the event. Not after it. I think I said that a few minutes ago."

Angela put out her hand and touched his arm.

"Don't you think we'd better call this marriage off?" she said. "Somehow I think we are going to make one another unhappy . . ."

"What? With the whole town invited?" he said almost bitterly. "I should say the fact that the marriage will go on is very safely insured. Red Gorge is not only my home; it, like Naroo Downs, is my livelihood. A man like myself, Angela, does not make a fool of himself before any town, let alone before his own town."

"You would rather sacrifice happiness?"

"I am perfectly happy when left to myself, and my own devices. That can be arranged once you and Nellie are safely at Naroo Downs. Now shall we go inside? I think dinner will be served."

Angela never knew how she got through that particular dinner. It would have been a nightmare except for the fact there were a number of Gilbert Lawrence's acquaintances dining in the hotel that night. A party formed in the lounge and Angela found herself thankfully left to one or two of the quieter women who were both chatty and kind to her.

When Gilbert drove her home at the end of a long evening, he once again escorted her to the door, once again standing away from her so there was no question of her even shaking hands.

"I will be returning to Naroo to-morrow," he said. "To-day's visit was merely to make final arrangements and, of course, to keep up appearances. Stella had to catch the mail plane, too. I will be in first thing on Thursday morning but I don't think we should meet before the church service." There was a pause before he went on. "I understand there is some kind of superstition about that sort of thing . . ."

"I am not superstitious, if you are not," Angela said.

"No, but the townsfolk are. A mining community is always superstitious. We have others to consider." There was unexpectedly a note of sardonic amusement in his voice.

"I think we owe it to them . . ." he went on, "that they, at least, shall enjoy a wedding."

"I'm glad you think that way," said Angela quietly. "Now if you'll excuse me I think I'll go inside."

"Of course," he said politely and perfunctorily. "I'm sorry I have delayed you."

Angela felt when she went inside that she took a gale from the south pole with her.

Several times in the ensuing four days she thought of packing up and running away. But how? Where to?

When she was most panicky she thought of Nellie.

Nellie was in the seventh heaven of delight. She was sewing and packing and planning and talking. Life had taken on a new radiance for her because she was going to live on a big station. And before that great adventure she was going to be a bridesmaid at a wedding in which the whole town would take part. She had the true colour of health in her cheeks now and her eyes sparkled as Angela had not seen them in years.

The town was agog with excitement because of the "big wedding" and the following Race Week. Wherever Angela went that excitement touched her. People smiled and stopped to speak to her. They wished her well and they sent her presents. The miners raised their hats and waved to her, the children in the domestic science class at the school made and iced a four-tier wedding cake that made everyone who saw it gasp with admiration. The stockmen from the nearby stations, Enmore, Milga and Winderup, began riding in as early as Tuesday.

No, Angela could not run away. She was imprisoned and confined by what she owed in expectations to a whole town-load of people. The kindness, jollity and general goodwill disarmed her.

She would have to stay and face the music.

The one person in the town whom she dreaded but would have liked to see was Kevin Richards and he was the one person she did not see. Where he was or what doing she did not know, and she could not bring herself to ask. At the last minute she hoped he would not be at the wedding.

CHAPTER TEN

The wedding day dawned fine and hot like any other day in Red Gorge.

Mrs. Sharman insisted on bringing Angela's breakfast to her in bed, but long before that Angela had been awake, listening for the sound of a small plane, like a singing wasp droning in over the roof-tops.

Suppose he didn't come? Ah, what a relief that would be! But would it? If he changed his mind and didn't come would she be able to retain her job at the mine? And would she be able to live with the townsfolk after such a débacle?

He did come, however. Half-way through her breakfast she heard the plane. She leaned back against the pillows and closed her eyes. The oddest thing of all was that with the sound of that single engine in the air she felt relief.

He had come. She would be all right.

It was extraordinary she should feel that when for four days she had fought off a frenzied compulsion to flee!

Years of worry and even hardship had sat heavy on Angela's shoulders and intuitively she knew now they were over. Gilbert Lawrence might dislike, even distrust her, but he would take care of Nellie. He would never deviate from a hard road of honour. His cold stern pride would dictate that to him. At long, long last Nellie was safe.

It was a wonderful wedding. The town people voted it so. It was a wedding worthy of the big man of a small town.

The hall was laid out in long trestle-tables with white cloths. They were loaded with food brought up from the south and managed and arranged by Mrs. Smith. No wedding down in the fertile south had more. Gilbert Lawrence had it all brought up by plane. There was iced albacore, sucking pigs, cold roast turkeys and devilled chicken wings. There were salads, greens, red and white. There were mountains of fruit on huge platters like an Arabian Nights dream. There was trifle and fruit salad and melon, all accompanied by cream and ice-cream. There were sandwiches and cakes and, crowning it all, the four-tier wedding cake. The wonder of all this was that it went on all day. Outside, under the shade of a group of gum trees, there were ginger beer and kegs of beer for the stockmen and miners who were too shy to do more than make brief fleet foraging tours into the hall.

In the afternoon the children had pony races and the stockmen staged a mock rodeo.

By this time, however, Gilbert and Angela were married. There had only been a handful in the small church. Mr. Morton had given Angela away and a Mr. Sullivan, the owner of Enmore Station, had acted as best man for Gilbert. Mr. Morton was a Justice of the Peace so he was able to give Angela —technically a minor—statutory permission to marry.

Nellie was slightly disappointed in this choice of Mr. Sullivan as, though he was tall, he was not as handsome as Gilbert. Moreover, he had a wife of his own. However, there were two younger sons to support Mr. Sullivan and to these Nellie addressed her attentions. If anybody had had time to notice the bridesmaid instead of the bride they would have noted that these two younger Sullivan sons . . . both in their late teens . . . also addressed their attentions to Nellie. Her frail prettiness was at its best in the gay linen dress. The forget-me-nots on the little straw hat turned her eyes into a blue that matched their own.

Nevertheless it was Angela on whom eyes rested most of the time. The white linen dress was charming. Its simple bodice and rounded neck had been beautifully embroidered by Nellie, and the skirt fell away in soft folds that were very graceful.

The hat with the crown of little pink roses was enchanting and the excitement, or perhaps it was ordeal, had brought into Angela's cheeks roses that matched in colour those on her hat.

It was, indeed, her warm glowing complexion that drew most of the admiration. Some people's eyes almost seemed to speak for them . . . "Now we know why Gilly Lawrence married the little English girl. She is lovely."

Gilbert Lawrence was tall, stern and immaculate in a light sand-coloured tropical suit. He smiled rarely but often enough for people to think he was happy. At any rate he was proud and they interpreted that as being proud of his lovely bride.

Walking down the short aisle of the church on Gilbert's arm, Angela could hardly believe this was happening to her. She felt neither unhappy nor afraid, because the atmosphere of happiness and excitement enveloped her as it did everyone else.

There was certainly something in being married to a man who all but owned the town. It was a general holiday and everyone made the most of it.

Angela knew that Stella Winton would not be there so she did not look for her but every now and again her eyes strayed around the people in the hall, looking for Kevin. Each time when she did this, and there was no sign of him, she felt relief. Immediately afterwards she felt regret.

She did not want Kevin to see her married to someone else, yet his absence made her heart sore. It filled her with regret. He was the one person in Red Gorge who had really won something of her love. Yet he was absent.

Would others in the town notice it?

Though Gilbert stood or sat beside her she could not bring herself to turn and look at him. That was a farce she could not play out in the church or before these people so firmly believing in their happiness.

In the church she had promised to love, honour and cherish. She found no difficulty in that. She did honour Gilbert as a stern but honourable man. There were different kinds of love and different degrees of love. Duty and loyalty were kinds of love and she would give both those affections to him, so long as he in their married status demanded them.

In the mid-afternoon Nellie left by car with Mr. Sullivan of Enmore Station, together with his wife and the two sons who had accompanied the party. Nellie, it had been arranged, was to stay the week-end at Enmore and she would then be motored overland to Naroo Downs. Nellie was delighted. She found herself the centre of interest and had no vapours about leaving

Angela to enjoy her "honeymoon" alone with Gilbert. Angela, when Gilbert had told her the arrangements, had feared this but Nellie's heart was for the moment engrossed with those two young men from Enmore.

Gilbert had also added that "this was a suitable arrangement for the look of the thing." Once again bowing to the tyrant Prestige! Gilbert had certain standards of public performance and nothing would ever make him deviate from them. Appearances would be kept up to the very end.

He would fly Angela himself in the small singing Cessna that he used as other men would use a taxi.

Angela, after accepting the gift of a few motherly tears from Mrs. Smith, many handshakes and not a few kisses, flew away over the roof-tops with her husband.

Only then, high in the sky over the escarpment that had so looked like mountains from the town of Red Gorge, did Angela really look at her husband.

She was still in her white linen wedding dress; the hat with the crown of pink roses lay on the seat behind her. Gilbert, again for the look of the thing, had helped her into the tiny seat beside the pilot's place. Side by side they had to complete the fiction, and fly away on their honeymoon as if it was the most natural thing in the world to do. It made the townsfolk, not to mention the rollicking stockmen in town for the fun, happy. In that respect it made Angela happy too.

When they flew over the escarpment Angela saw that what lay below them was a vast, almost treeless, plain with red earth, like irregular maps, lying between the nests of spinifex and clumps of mulga. She turned her head a little and looked at Gilbert.

"It went off all right," she offered by way of the first effort at conversation. "I hope you are quite happy about it, Gilbert."

"Quite." A slight smile appeared on his lips. "I hope *you* are quite happy about it," he said. "After all, it was your wedding."

She knew what he meant but she remained silent. She had said she was going to marry him . . . that was what rumour had carried to his ears . . . and she had married him. Now she had better be happy about it.

"Does it take us long to get to Naroo?" she asked.

"One hour. And please call it Naroo Downs. I detest names cut short."

"Yet people call you Gilly . . ." she ventured.

"That's different," he replied.

"Why is it different?" she asked. She wanted to keep some warmth of conversation alive between them, but instinctively she expected a rebuff each time she spoke.

"That is what Aunt Kara called me. People copied her."

"Aunt Kara!" said Angela softly. "What was she like, Gilbert? Did you love her?"

He was silent and she saw that his mouth had tightened into a thin line. Then unexpectedly the rigidity seemed to go out of him and he relaxed back in the pilot's seat. His hands eased on the half-wheel.

"Yes, I loved her," he said, then added a minute later, "she was a very strong-minded woman. She always got her own way."

"Did she? In what way?" Angela asked gently. She sensed she might be probing the one place where his heart was soft.

He turned his head and looked at her. The grey eyes were no different from any other time. The marriage ceremony had not altered the expression in them.

"As an immediate example," he said with a touch of irony in his voice, "you might consider us sitting here enjoying the first few hours of married bliss. It is exactly what Aunt Kara intended."

"But . . ."

"You're going to tell me she didn't have anything to do with it? Oh, yes, she did. She implanted the seed in your mother's heart and probably in your own. She certainly tilled some very solid ground with me. That is undoubtedly why you took it for granted when you arrived in Australia and it certainly contributed largely to my decision to settle the business and stop the conjecture once and for all."

"I still don't understand, Gilbert, why she wanted us, you and me, to marry. She only knew me as a child . . ."

"Very simple," Gilbert said. "You *were* a child. That was exactly it. As I said before, she was a woman with a will of her own. A kind, loyal and loving woman. But she wasn't going to have anyone but one of her own choosing on Naroo Downs. She was so anxious to keep particular persons from intruding there . . . persons who might have been a match in will-power for Aunt Kara . . . that she dreamed up a gentle little rosy-cheeked girl from thousands of miles away who would be such a stranger in this very lonely country she would have to turn to Aunt Kara for everything. That way, indirectly, Aunt Kara would continue her reign," said Gilbert, glancing at Angela.

"You don't speak as if you really did love her, Gilbert."

"I did. She had her foibles and that was one of them. I let her dream her dreams because at the time I wasn't considering marrying anybody. Aunt Kara saw to it that nobody got near enough to marry me."

"But you have neighbours . . ."

"Oh, yes. I have *now*. The invasion is on, you might say. Manganese—on my cattle run—and my neighbour's cattle run."

Stella Winton! Kevin had said Stella Winton lived on the neighbouring station, Winderup. Aunt Kara had tried to prevent Stella and Gilbert being too much to one another. Why was that? Angela wondered.

She leaned forward and wrapped her arms around her knees.

"You know, Gilbert," she said lightly. "You don't seem the kind of person, to me, that is, who would not marry whom he pleases."

"Exactly. It suited me to allow Aunt Kara her foibles. I would have combated them when I wanted to if necessary. But . . ."

"Yes, but?"

He glanced at her once again. His eyes were sardonic.

"You intervened in person. Shall we leave it at that?"

"Is it too late for me to say I'm sorry?" said Angela.

"Much too late. Besides, somebody had to look after the pair of you. Inevitably it was myself. We will not raise this matter again." He abruptly changed the subject. "If you look down through that side window you'll see Enmore homestead. That fine black line east of it is Naroo boundary. Winderup lies to the north. We are nearly there."

Angela was so effectively silenced that all she could now do was look at the red earth beneath and the scatter that was the homestead and outbuildings of Enmore.

Half an hour later, Gilbert brought the plane down on to a short runway and taxied it up to the door of a galvanised iron hangar that looked more like a huge silver shed than a place to house an aeroplane.

"Why is the shed silver?" Angela asked in wonder.

"To throw back the heat. I like to keep the hangar locked because of inquisitive black boys. The heat in it can become intense enough to dry out oil and expand parts of the bodywork. I have the roof insulated and the outside painted with silver oxide."

Gilbert explained this as he taxied to the hangar and in the manner of one who is giving brief information to an inquisitive and not-so-bright student.

He helped Angela alight from the plane. She stood in the last light of the sun and watched him as he slid open the huge doors and then pushed the plane inside as if it wasn't anything more than a toy. He put blocks under its wheels, tested the ventilation grilles in the shed and then came outside again. He shut the doors and locked them with a padlock. The key he put in the side pocket of his coat.

Angela was standing by her two cases. Gilbert picked up the cases and they began to walk towards the homestead garden. He said nothing but Angela noticed how his eyes roved around the area as if checking that all was well. There was not a soul in sight. The station was like a deserted village.

Down the roadway past the homestead garden she could see other buildings . . . all with their doors shut. Behind the homestead a great windmill stood. Its vanes were still and silent. As they went through the garden gate the deep shadows of the wide veranda were inviting but the front door was shut. The only sound was that of sunset insects clicking their legs together in their evening song. The whole place was utterly still; warm, kindly, but still.

"Is there no one . . .?" Angela began.

The front door was not locked and Gilbert turned a handle to open it. He looked down at Angela as he did so.

"They've all gone to the wedding," he said. Then added dryly, "There was a wedding, you know."

He stood aside for Angela to enter. There was a brightly polished passage leading straight down the middle of the house. There were several doorways on either side. Angela stood inside the front door, slightly diffident, while Gilbert brought in the cases. He opened the first door on the right-hand side and motioned Angela to enter.

It was a large square bedroom, furnished with good solid old-fashioned furniture. There were fresh chintz curtains to the front and side windows and a freshly laundered pink candlewick cover on the big bed that stood in the middle of the room, its headboard against the back wall. There was a big dark wardrobe against the far side wall and opposite on the near side was a dressing-table with a centre mirror and two wing mirrors. There was a chair on either side of the bed and a small table beside one of the chairs. The floor was highly polished . . . as the passage had been . . . and there were three carpet mats, one at the foot of the bed and the other two on either side of it. It was a room that was set about with furniture in a perfectly balanced pattern like a mechanical drawing. It was large, comfortable and airy, but belonged to nobody.

"The guest-room," said Gilbert briefly, putting Angela's cases down against the wall under the front window. He straightened up and turned to her. "Yours," he added.

"I see," said Angela slowly, looking round the room.

From the carpet mats on the floor she lifted her eyes to meet Gilbert's. He was looking at her with a slightly curious expression in his eyes but with his mouth closed in that tight clamped line she had begun to find familiar.

He couldn't have said it more clearly and more definitely. She was a "guest." The lady up in the front room who was making a short visit.

"Thank you," she said, walking to the bed and putting her hat and handbag on it. "It is very comfortable. I'm sure I will like it."

He went to the door.

"The bathroom is at the end of the passage on the right-hand side. There is another bathroom on the veranda on the other side but I generally use that. The dining-room is the third door down on the left-hand side. You go through the dining-room to the side veranda which leads to the kitchen. I'll go and put some tea on."

"Is there no one to help you, Gilbert?" Angela asked. "Perhaps I could . . ."

"Thank you, I'll manage. You might like to find your way about the house. The whole of this side can be considered yours. There is a small writing-room next to you which Nellie might use for her studies. Next to that is a bedroom suitable for her. Last is a larger living-room which is used if we entertain. Beyond that the linen room and then the bathroom. You are not likely to get lost. It is a house with rooms one behind the other on both sides of the passage until you come to the back wall."

"Thank you," said Angela. "I would like to explore."

"I reserve the left-hand side of the house for my own use, except for the small dining-room," he said abruptly. He meant, "Don't explore in my domain," and Angela knew it.

"I see," said Angela.

"Now, if you'll excuse me I'll put that tea on."

She stood quite still and listened to his footsteps going down the polished floor of the passage and then fading a little as he turned into the room he had said was the dining-room and through which one went to get to the kitchen.

Then once again she looked around the room. *Her* room, the *guest* room. There were no pictures on the walls, no ornaments. It was spotlessly clean, but airless. Angela went to the front window and threw it up. A life-giving draught of fresh air poured in. She turned to the side windows which were french doors and opened them. They gave on to a side veranda which was wired in against insects. On this veranda were tiers of pot plants on wooden stands, hundreds of them. The air was heavy with sweet-smelling ferns and flowers.

"Oh!" said Angela, stepping out on to the veranda. Her relief was so great that tears came into her eyes. "How lovely!"

She walked from one shelf of pot plants to another, looking with gratitude at the many varied ferns, the cyclamens, the geraniums, the African violets. She drew in deeply of the air that was warm with moisture and growing life.

"Beautiful flowers," she said. "Somehow I don't feel so alone now."

She picked up one small pot with a tiny red bell flower growing in it and carried it back into the room. She put it on the dressing-table and then moved the wing mirrors so that the flower's reflection could be seen from every part of the room. She felt she had a companion, someone . . . something to love.

"Redbella," she said. "I don't know what your real name is, but you're Redbella to me. And please don't mind my talking to you. I've got to talk to someone."

Angela went down to the bathroom where she found fresh towels and after she had washed and changed her dress, brushed her hair and put a little lipstick on her mouth she went in search of the kitchen.

She felt better, more confident. All on account of Redbella. The house was not as empty of people as Gilbert thought. Flowers were people.

The kitchen was a long room with a big wooden fire-range at the end of it. Gilbert had the fire alight and as Angela came in he was opening the refrigerator door in search of milk.

"Let me begin my duties by making the tea, please, Gilbert?" Angela asked gently.

"You don't have any duties," he said. "I have a housekeeper, Mrs. Cummins. Like the rest of them, she is in Red Gorge but will be back on Monday. She has left everything prepared . . ."

He drew out of the refrigerator a large plate that was covered with greaseproof paper and when he lifted the paper there was beautifully set out on it some cold chicken and salads. He put this on the square table in the centre of the room and returned to the frig. to take out milk and another plate that held cream puffs and sponge cakes.

"Please, Gilbert," Angela pleaded. "I can't stand here doing nothing."

"Then please sit down," he said shortly.

She was silent a minute.

"If you insist on getting the tea," she said at length, "perhaps I can look around in the meantime. Is that the kitchen garden one sees from the veranda?"

"Yes. Go and look around by all means. I don't advise you to touch anything, however. Mrs. Cummins always consults Jackie the kitchen gardener."

Angela went to the veranda and stood looking at the garden. She was just outside the kitchen door.

"How will the garden be watered while they're all away, Gilbert?" she asked. She was determined they would not sit down together . . . indeed pass this interminable long weekend together . . . in silence and enforced idleness. Somehow she would make him talk to her.

"The black boys have not gone into Red Gorge. They're probably preparing their corroboree down at the creek. Jackie will put in an appearance in time to bring up the milk, and water the garden."

"Corroboree?"

"Yes. They have their own way of celebrating the 'Boss's' wedding, you know."

Angela turned back into the kitchen and Gilbert was in the act of lifting the loaded tray to carry it out. He looked up at her over the tray. "Their custom is to celebrate the nuptial night," he said shortly.

Angela flushed, but as her back was to the light Gilbert would not have seen it. She followed him out on to the veranda and then through the door into the small dining-room. Gilbert put the tray on the table, set about the knives and forks and placed the dish of chicken and salad with the serving forks before his own place at the head of the table. He put the teapot and hot-water jug beside Angela's place. The cups and saucers were already set there.

"You may pour the tea," he said, as if offering largesse to the ill-deserving poor.

He held her chair for her while she sat down and then went to his own place. He proceeded to serve her without consulting her as to her wishes.

"Do you like your tea now? Or afterwards, Gilbert?"

"Now, and I like it strong with very little milk, thank you."

Angela poured his tea for him, then they ate in silence. Angela felt she could make no further efforts and Gilbert was determined not to make any efforts at all. Except for the touch of their knives and forks on the plates, the clink of china on china, there was not a sound in all the house or in the garden around. They might have been alone on the earth.

Towards the end of their meal Gilbert looked up at Angela. He was toying with a piece of bread by his plate.

"You are not afraid to stay alone with me for the next two or three days?" he asked. His grey eyes held inquiry, that was all.

Angela looked at him steadily. "No," she said firmly. "That is one thing I am not afraid of."

Her firm answer surprised him.

"Oh!" he said. "That, at least, is . . ."

"Satisfactory? Please don't worry, Gilbert. I haven't any intention, or any wish, to be anything more than what you have already indicated. A guest. In my case a most unobtrusive and undemanding guest, I hope."

He looked at her for a few moments as if he was seeing her for the first time.

"As long as you understand . . ." he began.

"I understand perfectly," Angela said.

When they had finished the meal Angela did not wait for Gilbert to say "yea" or "nay." She rose from her place and began to gather the dishes together. As she piled the dishes on the tray Gilbert said:

"I will carry that out for you."

In the kitchen Angela put the dishes in the sink and Gilbert put the remnants of the meal back in the frig. There were hot and cold water taps over the sink and Angela quickly began washing the few dishes. When she put them in the rack Gilbert took them down, dried them and put them away. He did everything with a deftness that made Angela think that in spite of the housekeeper he was not unused to finding his way round the kitchen. She dared not ask him any questions, however. She had tried that on the flight out from Red Gorge and all she had got was a little information and a great deal of cold rebuff. He was the most silent and uncommunicative man she had ever met. Or was this state of affairs because of herself?

Once her arm brushed his and she went on feeling the place on her arm where it had touched his as if it had left a mark there. *The place where Gilbert touched me*, she said to herself, trying to wring a little amusement out of her own silly reaction.

His silence made her think he wasn't aware of her presence, that his thoughts were miles away and that he was going through the motions of doing things in the kitchen but was unaware of them. He had asked no questions about herself or Nellie, or her home. He was either totally or deliberately indifferent. She was merely the girl that Aunt Kara had deposited in his home, and Nellie was merely the added appendage.

Yet Angela knew every move he made. She knew when he was behind her, at her side, over by the cupboard.

Suddenly, sadly, she thought how different it would have been if it had been Kevin Richards and not Gilbert Lawrence. They would have talked and laughed, and occasionally kissed...

She shook her head.

Such thoughts she must banish. She must not think of them again. She was married. Even in her thoughts she must be faithful to her husband, so long as he was her husband.

When they had finished it was dark outside.

"I'll put the light on in the passage for you," Gilbert said. "If you don't mind we will sit out on the front veranda for a while. The black boys will expect it."

"You mean, to watch their corroboree?"

"From the distance of the veranda, yes. They do not invite white people to their corroboree, but as it is in our honour they will expect us to take note of the fact that it is going on."

Gilbert preceded her up the passage, went out on to the veranda and set two comfortable chairs on either side of a small round table. Angela sat down and looked out at the darkling sky and the stars shining through like lamps. There was no moon and everything outside was warm, still, silent and smelling pungently of the dried grasses and red earth.

Gilbert went inside again and brought out a tray of drinks, some cigarettes and an ash-tray. He sat down in the chair on the other side of the table.

Angela leaned back. The quietness was peaceful, she thought.

"Will they come up to see us?" she asked, meaning the natives.

"No. But they'll know we're here. You'll hear them presently. It's quite a din."

"How long will it last?"

"All night. But they won't expect us to wait that long. They'll have sung us to bed long before they are ready to go."

"I see," said Angela. She did see. The natives thought the "Boss" had brought home a bride with whom he was happy, and that the day would end as all wedding days, even those of the natives, should end, the bride and bridegroom going to bed and the wedding guests carrying on with the fun.

Gilbert helped himself to a whisky and Angela to a fruit drink. He lit a cigarette. Even in the dark, shadowed veranda, the glow of his cigarette and the light from the brilliant stars showed Angela where he sat, leaning back in his chair, his long legs stretched out before him, his silence wrapping him around like a cloak.

Down by the creek she saw the camp-fires spring up like huge winking lights among the low mulga trees. Presently the chanting and the long hooting sound of the didgeridoo could be heard. Black shadows gyrated about before the fire-light and in and out the trees.

Little did they know how abortive were their attempts to "sing" happiness to the married couple up there on the home-stead veranda! It seemed an ingratitude to them not to be happy.

Angela began to feel very tired. It had been a long exacting day. The rhythmic chanting of the natives down by the river had a soporific effect. It was dark on the veranda, it did not seem a discourtesy to anybody, not even the friendly brightly shining stars, for Angela to close her eyes. Gilbert, armoured in his silence, would never know.

Her lids drooped over her eyes.

Presently she stirred to make herself more comfortable. Half asleep she turned sideways and curled up in her chair.

Gilbert spoke to her but she did not hear. She had passed out of the cloudland of a not-very-happy marriage into a happier dream-world that was peopled with tiny flowers all called Redbella. She was walking in a garden of flowers and ferns and they seemed to lean forward as she passed, to caress her arms. Always, where the flowers touched, was that feeling on her right arm where Gilbert's arm had touched her in the kitchen. But in her dream it was flowers, and their soft delicate touch made her happy.

"Angela!"

"Mm . . . mm?"

"I think you had better wake up. We should retire now." He was standing over her, touching her shoulder.

Angela uncurled slowly.

"Yes?" she said vaguely. "Where am I?"

"Here," he said peremptorily. "On Naroo Downs veranda. I think you had better go to bed, Angela."

"Yes, of course. I'm so sorry . . ."

She stood up rather awkwardly for she was still not quite awake. He put out his hand to steady her. Dazed and sleepy, Angela leaned against him.

"I think you had better wake up, Angela," he said. There was a sudden uneven note in his voice. It brought Angela completely to her senses.

"I'm sorry," she said. "I'm awfully sorry . . ."

Her ears strained to hear his voice again. If they were both unhappy couldn't they do something about it? They were here —alone in this great homestead. Couldn't they be friends?

It was a crazy thought, born of over-tiredness and dreams of a garden where flowers touched and caressed and made happy . . .

He did not speak.

"I'm sorry," Angela repeated, and then as if to explain her stupidity added, "I was thinking of someone else."

Whatever made her say that? How crazy can a person be when she's half asleep and talks to a flower called Redbella?

He turned and walked away abruptly. When he had switched on her bedroom light she heard his footsteps going resolutely down the passage. He had not said "Good night."

She did not see him again until morning.

CHAPTER ELEVEN

That week-end was the strangest passage of time Angela could imagine. Yet she was not unhappy.

The silence all around and the emptiness of the homestead were peace-making. For a very long time Angela had been under the strain of anxiety. Now she felt a release from it all. Gilbert Lawrence might be cold and remote, yet he had provided for herself and Nellie this sanctuary of security. For that she owed him a debt and presently, when she had accustomed herself to the new surroundings she would try to find some indirect way of repaying him.

During the following three days, before Mrs. Cummins and

some of the staff of Naroo Downs returned, Angela had quickly discovered a way of getting to the kitchen before Gilbert. She raided Mrs. Cummins's larder to produce something both unobtrusive and tasty for their meals. By lunch-time, on the day after the marriage, Gilbert had, by silent acquiescence, shown he did not disapprove of Angela's activities. He vacated the kitchen, without comment, in favour of the stables and engine house.

On Saturday Angela took herself on a tour of discovery amongst the outbuildings . . . the bullock yards, the sheep race, the wool shed, the men's quarters.

She did not go inside any of the buildings, contenting herself in discovering where they were and what they were.

She managed to capture the elusive Jackie's attention when he came early to the house with milk and to set the reticulation plant working in the garden.

At first with awkward shyness but finally with many smiles and much friendliness Jackie explained in his pidgin English how the solar hot water system operated.

"Them two alla same big black boards altogether catch that fella sun. Water in dem pipes all-over black boards. They get pretty darn hot, missus. That fella sun blistering hot, I tell you plenty."

Angela had been mystified as to where the continuous hot water in the bathroom and kitchen had come from. Now she knew. It was a solar hot water system. The sun did it all.

Each night just before they dined Gilbert came in, showered and changed from his outdoor clothes, and invited Angela to sit on the front veranda by the small round table before they went to the dining-room. This required a little ingenuity about timing the cooking but with the help of a giant oven in that giant cooking range Angela achieved it.

Gilbert was obviously tired when he came in at that hour so Angela carefully avoided plying him with the hundred and one questions that were burning for release in her mind. She let him sit there silently smoking his cigarette and sipping his appetiser. Now and again he spoke to her, telling her briefly of something he had been doing during the day.

"The station will be out of routine until after Race Week in Red Gorge," he said. "A few of the men will wander back before next week-end and there's always much to do around the homestead. Several hundred thousand pounds' worth of machinery to be gone over."

"Is that what you have been doing to-day?"

“Yes. Greasing up in the engine-room.”

Again there was a long silence, and again it was Gilbert who broke it.

“If you feel the heat, Angela, there's a swimming-pool in the creek. Go east of the natives' camps. They have the down-stream water.”

“Where does the creek come from, Gilbert? It all seems flat plain to me.”

“Out of the ground,” he said shortly. “The geologists tell me it is an off-shoot of an underground river.”

Angela was very interested but she dared not interrupt him. She waited hopefully for him to go on. After a few minutes he spoke again.

“The geologist . . . a fellow called Smart . . . will be in here next week when Hopkins comes back. Hopkins has been here since the beginning of the month.” He paused, then added, “I got rid of them all in order to get married in peace.”

“It is peaceful here, at this hour,” Angela said hopefully.

Again there was silence.

“I imagine Stella will be over from Winderup,” Gilbert added. There was an odd hard note in his voice.

“Is it necessary to prepare bedrooms?” Angela asked tentatively.

“Mrs. Cummins will attend to that. If Stella comes she will have the front room opposite you. Hopkins uses a small room off the office next to me. Smart will go down with the store-keeper. The storekeeper has a cottage, and is a bachelor.”

“Do you often have a house full of people?”

“No. This is for the purpose of business conference. I will be glad when I'm shot of the whole manganese question. Then the cattle and I can get on with our own interests.”

Angela, sitting quietly, watched the flights of cockatoos going over to the trees along the creek bed. As the sun died hard against a blazing sky, she tried to piece together what these snippets of information meant.

This was Saturday night and in thirty-six hours she had sensed a gradual easing of tension in Gilbert. Leaning back in his chair he was almost relaxed. She thought he was a man who liked peace from the intruding outside world and that he was finding it now . . . unexpectedly. He had had to stage this honeymoon week-end for the “look of it” and he was finding it restful.

Perhaps this was one way in which she could repay him for the security and release from worry that he had given to herself and Nellie. She must be very quiet, keep out of his way, have everything orderly and smooth running for him.

Angela prayed very hard that she would get on with Mrs. Cummins and that Nellie too would be quiet and considerate when she came.

On Monday morning, two days later, there was a telephone call relayed through another station from Enmore to say that Mrs. Cummins had arrived there and she would be motored across to Naroo Downs with Nellie. They expected to reach the homestead at sundown. There was a second relay which was a pressing invitation from people in Red Gorge for Gilbert and Angela to fly in for the finish of Race Week.

As the calls were relays Angela did not have an opportunity to speak to Nellie nor could she reply on Gilbert's behalf to the invitation to return to Red Gorge.

He had taken some lunch in his saddle-bag and gone out on horse-back for the day. He had not said where he was going but Angela's heart was softened a little when she noticed Jackie working round the homestead gardens.

"You work here all day always, Jackie?" she asked.

"Sometime," he said. "When Boss go away I look after Mis' Cummins. To-day Boss say 'You look after that fella my missus, Jackie. Don't you go anyplace garden. My missus call you if she want.'"

The black boy's interpretation of what Gilbert had said warmed Angela's heart. She knew that Jackie's words had not been exactly Gilbert's words . . . he had probably told Jackie curtly to stay within earshot of the homestead . . . but nevertheless the intention had been there. He had not left her entirely alone.

This piece of news she confided to the red flower on her dressing-table as she changed her dress after a bath in the late afternoon. Until the telephone relays she had busied herself with the fernery outside her bedroom door. After the calls she had conducted a real raid on Mrs. Cummins's larder. There would have to be an evening meal for quite a number of people to-night. In addition to Nellie and Mrs. Cummins there would be the driver from Enmore.

"We're not doing too badly, Redbella," she confided to the little red flower. "On Thursday night he was angry and he disliked me. On Friday he was just quiet. On Saturday he spoke to me . . . ten times . . . without my first asking questions. Yesterday he spoke to me twelve times and once he said quite six sentences in one speech. To-day he left Jackie to look after me."

When Gilbert came in shortly after four o'clock Angela gave him the messages. To the invitation to go to Red Gorge he replied curtly:

"Certainly not. What do they think I am? I've had the first three days of peace in five years and they want me to go in and join that raucous thirsting gang in Red Gorge."

A little bird lifted its head in Angela's heart. He had *liked* his three days' peace. Redbella the flower seemed to nod her head in approval too. It did not occur to Angela that Gilbert might have consulted her wishes. She knew she was here on sufferance, and perhaps temporarily. She did not expect him to do anything for her. All she wanted to do was something for him. She had a big debt to pay.

"I've cooked a lot of food," she told him. "You see, there'll be Nellie . . . and Mrs. Cummins . . . and a driver . . ."

They were standing on the side veranda that led to the kitchen. Gilbert was thwacking his riding-boots with his furled stock-whip. There was a red rim where his hat had cut a swathe on his forehead. He looked dusty and tired.

"Yes, *Nellie* . . ." he said. "I suppose the child has to be fed." He turned to go towards his own bathroom at the other end of the veranda. "Mrs. Cummins prefers to take her meals alone. It's more convenient to both of us. The driver will eat and sleep down at the quarters."

He had not asked her how she had spent the day. He had not commented on her freshly bathed and ironed look. He had hardly looked at her at all. There had been a fleeting glance as he stepped up on the veranda from the gravel square and then he had turned and looked out over Jackie's garden and thwacked his boots with his stock-whip while he spoke. Then he walked away.

Angela went into the kitchen.

Yet he had said he didn't want to go to Red Gorge . . . because it was *peaceful* here. Well, that was something, anyway.

Nellie's arrival was tumultuous. Angela in between her feelings of relief and excitement at seeing Nellie so well and happy was having anxious moments as to how Gilbert was taking this.

"Oh, it's *gorgeous* at Enmore," cried Nellie, hugging Angela. "Is it like that here? I went for a ride. Sam and Bob both took me. I can't make up my mind which I like best. I think

I'll just play them along . . . Angela, have I really got a room to myself? Oh, how scrumptious! Mrs. Cummins is awfully nice and said I can make scones on a wood-fire. I did at Enmore . . ."

Angela did not notice Nellie's lack of interest in how she herself had got on since they were last together.

Gilbert stood leaning his back against the railings of the veranda and watched the greetings between the two sisters. In between Nellie's ravings Angela's eyes kept moving anxiously to Gilbert to see how he was taking all this. He gave no sign. His eyes were veiled and expressionless.

"You haven't spoken to Gilbert, darling," Angela said.

"Oh, Gilly darling," said Nellie, turning impetuously to him, "wasn't it a gorgeous wedding? And you looked absolutely scrumptious. So did Angela, of course. At Enmore they said you were the catch of the north . . ." She stopped and giggled and then looked back at her sister. "Aren't you lucky, Angela?"

Over Nellie's shoulder Angela looked at Gilbert. Their eyes met. On Angela's mouth there was a slightly rueful smile but Gilbert's mouth drew itself into that formidable straight line that had already become familiar.

He said nothing but the sudden half-angry, half-sarcastic expression in his eyes was answer enough.

"Come inside, Nellie, I'll show you your room," Angela said. She turned to Gilbert. "The driver knows where to go?"

"He does," said Gilbert. "He's been here before."

Mrs. Cummins proved a very pleasant and unobtrusive woman. She was tall with fair hair drawn back in a loose knob at the back of her head. Her eyes were dark and friendly. Angela thought she might be a little shy and this was exactly what Angela herself was feeling so there was an immediate bond of sympathy.

"I have prepared a meal, Mrs. Cummins," Angela said. "I do hope you don't mind my invading your kitchen."

"Oh, no, Mrs. Lawrence. It is your kitchen. Please tell me just how you want things to be. I'll do my best, I'm sure."

Angela felt a shock when she was addressed as "Mrs. Lawrence." Is that really me? she wondered.

"I'm not quite sure about how we will serve the evening meal," Angela said uncertainly.

"I generally serve it for Mr. Lawrence in the dining-room," Mrs. Cummins said.

There was an awkward pause in which each sought to say the right thing to make the other happy.

"Yes . . ." Angela said. "Yes . . . of course."

"If you don't mind, Mrs. Lawrence," Mrs. Cummins said apologetically, "I always have my meals at the little table outside the kitchen. I would like to go on . . . please, if you don't mind. You see, Mr. Lawrence is always having so many business visitors these days. And I can't quite cope. I mean I like to be by myself. I do hope you don't mind, Mrs. Lawrence . . ."

"Of course not," said Angela, also anxious to make Mrs. Cummins happy.

The housekeeper was tying an apron about her waist.

"Aren't you tired after your long drive?" Angela asked.

"What, me?" Mrs. Cummins said in surprise. "Oh, no, miss. I mean Mrs. Lawrence. Out here on the plain that's nothing unusual. The young people, like Miss Stella from Winderup, drive twice that distance in a day and then spend all night dancing. Besides, Mr. Lawrence will want his dinner served. He would think I have had quite enough of a holiday as it is. Mr. Lawrence doesn't like people loafing about, you know. Now, if you'll excuse me . . ."

Mrs. Cummins hurried into the kitchen and Angela understood at once that the housekeeper not only wanted to work, she would be very unhappy if she didn't. Also she was undoubtedly the kind of person who worked best alone.

Angela went back to Nellie's room where her younger sister was pulling out all the drawers and opening all the cupboards to investigate her new home.

"Tell me all about Enmore, darling," Angela said, sitting down on the bed.

Nellie began to open her cases and put away things in the cupboards and drawers.

"Oh, you wouldn't understand," she said. "It's quite different from anything you're used to." She stopped and turned to Angela. "They've got a concrete swimming-pool alongside the veranda, and what do you think, Angela? The water is warm. Where do you think it comes from? Up out of the ground. And it's warm when it gets there. I mean, they don't have to do anything to it to make it warm."

"It's the same here," said Angela, nodding her head. "Except in the creek. You can swim in the creek here, Nellie."

Nellie was at her cases again and did not look up.

"Oh, can I? Goody. Angela, when do you think we can

ask the Sullivans over from Enmore? And when can I go over there again? They've asked me to go whenever I like. Are there some horses I can practise on here, first?"

"We must ask Gilbert about that," said Angela. "Nellie, darling, you will remember this is Gilbert's home, won't you? And he likes peace and quiet. Don't get in his way, dear. And I'm sure he will let you ride a horse . . . in time."

"In time?" said Nellie. "I'm going to ride one to-morrow. I'll ask him myself."

"Nellie . . ."

Angela broke off. How could she tell Nellie? How could she even make her understand?

Something in Angela made her feel a little rebellious that she had to tell this young and vivid girl, now so full of healthy happy spirits, that she had to quieten down; had to wait until she was spoken to; that she had to accept with quiet gratitude such largesse as Gilbert Lawrence might care to distribute.

"Wash and change for dinner, darling," was all Angela said as she rose from the bed and went to the door. "And don't be late, will you?"

Dinner was a trying meal. Nellie chatted to both Gilbert and Angela alternately and did not notice the care in Angela's eyes or the fact that Gilbert neither asked questions nor made comments. Angela noticed that often his eyes were on Nellie's face as if in the quiet recesses of his mind he was adding up and conjecturing what his future might be if he had to live cheek by jowl with this voluble magpie.

Angela wondered if, after dinner, she might ask Gilbert if he preferred, now that the "honeymoon" was over, to have his meals by himself. She was conscious of that admonition when Gilbert had laid down the terms of his marriage . . . "Keep out of my way and don't let your young sister Nellie get under my feet."

Angela had the beginnings of a headache wondering how she was going to achieve this.

She remembered the small study room between Nellie's bedroom and her own. They could make it into a private dining-room of their own! She must handle all these delicate matters very carefully.

As they rose from the dining-table Gilbert spoke directly to her.

"I think we'll have our coffee on the veranda, Angela," he said. "Nellie might care to help Mrs. Cummins clear away."

Angela felt a little lift of happiness as he offered this invitation but it looked, for a moment, as if Nellie was going to pout. Gilbert settled that with one look and very few words.

" I like a little privacy in the evening, Nellie," he said. " Angela will join me and your duty is to help Mrs. Cummins. If you regard this as a privilege you won't find it a hardship. I will expect you to do this every evening."

Nellie, astonished, opened her eyes very wide.

" I've never had to work in the house because I'm not very strong," she said.

" Then I'm afraid you will not be strong enough to come out on horse-back with me to-morrow . . . or any other day."

Nellie's mouth closed and then suddenly she gave a little jump for joy and clapped her hands.

" You're going to take me riding? Oh, Gilly, you are a darling. Thank you so much. Yes, I'll clear away and wipe up for Mrs. Cummins . . ."

She stopped short, realising she had made a concession she had never intended to make. Somehow she had to cover up and excuse that weakness. She suddenly looked very coy.

" Of course, I'm really doing it for you two. I'm quite old enough to know that lovers like to sit by themselves on the veranda at night. I won't interrupt. You needn't think I will."

She giggled and then with a toss of her head picked up two or three dishes and went through the door on her way to the kitchen.

Angela turned away and with a quiet dignity went down the long passage to the veranda. She sat down and leaned back in the chair she had already begun to think of as her own.

" I'll never be able to manage this situation," she told the stars. " It is beyond me. Why didn't I foresee? Why didn't I appreciate how lovely it was the last three days? So peaceful, so unworrying . . . with just Gilbert and me."

It was some time before Gilbert joined her and when he came he was carrying the coffee tray.

" I should have thought of that," said Angela.

Gilbert set the tray on the table.

" You can pour it out," he said. " I liked the coffee you poured the last two or three nights."

" I'm so glad," she said eagerly.

With these few words of praise . . .

" Mrs. Cummins will bring it out as a routine," he said, sitting down. " I went to the kitchen to tell her Nellie was expected to help her in the mornings and the evenings. I don't know who was the more surprised, Mrs. Cummins or Nellie."

"I do hope we won't upset Mrs. Cummins. After all, she is necessary to you."

"My orders won't upset Mrs. Cummins," Gilbert said, taking the coffee cup from Angela's hand. "I have a way of seeing they don't upset people. And the sooner Nellie knuckles down the better."

Angela wanted to demur but she didn't quite know how to go about it. At all costs she must have peace between Nellie and Gilbert. Trouble there would be disastrous.

"Nellie is perhaps a little . . ."

"Spoilt," he concluded for her. "Quite. But we'll rectify that in time."

"She is not really very strong," Angela pleaded.

"That is why I intend to take her riding . . . keep her in the fresh air. Give her plenty of exercise. We'll rectify that want of stamina in time, too."

Angela sipped her coffee. She found this conversation such a strain that her hand trembled. She could not, in her mind, get beyond the fact that she and Nellie were impositions here and that he had ruled they were not to be a bother to him.

"Cease worrying about her," Gilbert said, putting his coffee cup down on its saucer. "She is my responsibility from now on, and we'll soon lick her into shape. Is there some more coffee in that pot?"

Lick her into shape? Gilbert was the man whose reputation said he drove his men with stock-whips. Was this what he would do to Nellie? Lick her into shape? Those were hard words. Frightening words.

Angela poured Gilbert's coffee and put a little more in her own cup. She felt she needed it.

There was a long silence and it was Gilbert who broke it with an unexpected remark.

"Now we have our quiet again," he said. "I hoped you were enjoying it too." He lit a cigarette. "I did," he said. "We haven't much to say to one another, Angela . . . but it was rather companionable, I thought."

"I'm so glad," Angela said softly.

Again there was silence but it was only a silence of the world. In some incredible way she felt as if they were both reaching out with their minds, like candle flames blowing towards one another in a varying wind.

Friendship would be enough, Angela thought. Anything other than silent enmity.

Perhaps Gilbert missed Aunt Kara very much.

"Would you like to walk down to the garden fence?" he asked her. "You can't see the Southern Cross from here. The side veranda blocks that part of the heavens."

"Yes, please . . . I would," said Angela.

They got up and Gilbert put his hand under her arm as they went down the steps. Once on the path he dropped his hand.

When they reached the fence he turned round and leaned his back against it.

"Look to the south," Gilbert said. "Those two bright stars over the corner of the roof are the pointers. Now look on them from here and you'll see the Cross."

Angela also leaned her back against the fence.

"Yes," she said at length, "I see it. It was pointed out to us on the ship after we had passed over the Equator."

"You can always find direction from the Cross," said Gilbert. "The direct north lies . . ."

The figure of a young girl came flying down the lighted passage of the homestead which was directly ahead of Gilbert and Angela. Nellie ran through the doorway and on to the veranda.

"Where are you two?" she called. "Oh, there you are . . ."

She jumped down the three steps on to the path below the veranda and ran down the path towards them.

"I've finished, Gilbert," she said. "All dried up and put away. Now what time are we going riding? Have you got a *quiet* horse for me? I mean I can't ride much yet."

"You'll have the horse I give you, Nellie," Gilbert said evenly. "And you'll ride it, quiet or unquiet as the case may be. If you fall off you'll get up and get on again. And you'll do exactly as I tell you . . ."

"But . . ."

"That way I'll make a good horsewoman of you. And there are no 'buts' in the vocabulary of Naroo Downs. Now if you don't mind, the evening hour is private to me. You may join us when I invite you, not otherwise."

Angela stirred but Gilbert put out his hand and caught her elbow, commanding silence.

"You may say good night now, Nellie," he continued. "If you go into the sitting-room you will find the radio set. Mrs. Cummins will show you how to get on to the air yourself. It must be time for the open session and with luck you might be able to talk to Enmore. Good night, Nellie."

"Nellie, darling . . ." Angela began.

But Gilbert, holding her elbow, held her back.

Nellie hovered on the path uneasily before them.

"But . . ."

"*Good night*, Nellie," Gilbert said again.

"Good . . . good night . . ." Nellie began in a reluctant voice. Then she brightened. "But Angela always comes and tucks me in."

"Not to-night. You may say good night to your sister now."

Angela slipped her arm out of Gilbert's reach.

"Nellie . . . do be a darling and do as Gilbert asks . . ."

"*Good night, Nellie*," Gilbert said again. There was no mistaking the foreboding note in his voice. Nellie retreated backwards a few steps.

"Good night," she said with a catch in her voice. Then she turned and fled up the garden path.

Angela turned to Gilbert.

"How *could* you . . .?" she said.

"I could and I did. Very easily," he said. He had not moved from where he leaned against the fence. "If I'm going to have you and Nellie here, Angela, I'm also going to have order. It is better to begin as one intends to go on."

"And how am I to behave in this orderly state of affairs?"

"You will keep to a strict routine the same as Nellie will. The same as I do, as all my staff does."

"But that is inhuman, Gilbert. I thought to-night . . ."

"That the quiet drinking of coffee on the veranda, the short walk to the garden fence, was a pleasant way of putting a period to a long hard-working day? You are right. And that is what we'll do every night. Now, shall we go inside?"

"You are inhuman," Angela breathed.

"Not inhuman," he said. "I am an orderly man who is beset with a lot of extra worries. I deal with each and all of them in order and with a routine."

"And Nellie and I are to become part of the routine?"

"An extra part of the routine," he amended. "But I begin to see we might make a success of it. Shall we go inside?"

Success of what?

In silence Angela turned and retraced her steps towards the veranda. At the foot of the steps Gilbert once more put his hand under her elbow as if politely to assist her mount the steps.

At the entrance to the house he still had his hand there.

"Are you going to your room now, Angela?" he asked.

"Yes . . . yes, I think I will . . ."

"I have work to do in the office," he said.

His hand was still under her elbow. Angela did not feel she had the right to shake it off, though she longed to do so.

His voice altered and there was that curious jagged unhappy note in it.

"Don't judge me harshly, Angela," he said. "I have much to do, and I must do it my way."

"Is there so much to do you have no time for human companionship? A little human love?"

He dropped his hand suddenly.

"That is something you do not understand," he said. "We will not talk about it. Good night, Angela."

He turned and walked away round the veranda. She heard his footsteps turn the corner and presently she knew from the reflected light he had gone into his office. She heard him shut the door.

From anxiety and anger her mood inexplicably changed with the dying away of those footsteps.

He was a man who had walled himself in from something. His orderliness, his routine, was part of that wall. What was the something from which he protected himself so vigilantly?

She herself was richer for she had Nellie. As she turned on the light of her room she saw the little red flower in its pot on her dressing-table.

"And Redbella," she added.

Angela had, the previous day, brought a small watering-can to the side veranda. And now she filled it with water and began lovingly to water all the pot plants. Lastly she attended to Redbella.

With the opening of the door the air was soon filled with the sweet odour of many ferns and tiny modest flowers that sat in their starry darkness with the life-giving moisture misting up from their leaves. Angela had something to cosset with her love. Presently, when she was sure that Gilbert had settled down to his evening's occupation she would steal on tiptoe along to Nellie's room. She would cover Nellie up, if she was sleeping. If she was awake they would have their short heart-to-heart evening talk that would comfort Nellie and help her to bear with Gilbert's sternness.

Half an hour later when Angela went into Nellie's room her sister was lying on the bed in her recently acquired shortie pyjamas which had pink flowers printed all over the soft cotton material. Nellie's arms were outflung on the bed, her eyes were closed and the only sound in the room was her deep rhythmical peaceful breathing. There was a luxurious smile on her lips.

On the chair against the wall were set out blue jeans and a white blouse. Below the chair was a pair of riding-boots, a gift from Enmore store probably.

So much for Gilbert's hard words and her own anxiety!

Nellie had gone to bed with only one thing on her mind and that was a riding lesson to-morrow.

Angela put out the light and tiptoed away. She didn't know whether she felt relieved or just a little sad. Had she herself been a party to this spoiling of Nellie? Was Nellie really spoiled and not merely delicate? How had Gilbert known so quickly?

No, Gilbert was wrong. Nellie happened luckily to be in good health and spirits now, but hadn't the doctor in Red Gorge castigated Angela because she was a "Career" girl instead of staying home to look after her ailing sister?

CHAPTER TWELVE

In the morning Angela, from the veranda, watched Gilbert and Nellie walking their horses away from the stables down towards the track that crossed the creek by a log bridge.

Gilbert had had early breakfast but after Angela and Nellie had had their breakfast at half past seven he had come up from the stables.

Nellie was already dressed in her blouse and jeans and had pulled on the riding-boots.

"Look at them, Angela, aren't they gorgeous?" she had said, showing off the boots to her sister. "They're only little boots and the sides are elastic, but golly, they're comfy . . ."

"Have you borrowed them from Mrs. Sullivan at Enmore, Nellie?"

"No. They have a store on Enmore. People buy things from the station store. Didn't you know, Angela? Really, you don't know anything, do you? I guess you can get things from the store here too. I'll ask Gilly when I go out with him . . ."

This *Gilly* which Angela herself did not dare use filled her with both admiration and envy of Nellie. Oh, to be so young, so thoughtless, so natural! For the first time in her life Angela, who had strained all her resources to help her sister, realised just how fortunate Nellie was.

" I hope you had enough money, dear," she said.

" Golly, no. They cost three pounds because the storekeeper told me, but Mrs. Sullivan said I could have a pair if I could find a pair to fit. You see, I told her we were awfully poor and that we didn't have any money. But I expected Gilly would give you some now you're married."

" *Nellie!*"

Nellie tossed her head. " Oh, don't worry. She was awfully nice about it. She said . . . ' Poor things!' most sorrowfully. Then she said . . . '*That's Mrs. Anstey all over. Brings out those two penniless children and foists them on Gilly.*' When I asked her what ' foists ' means she said she didn't know and anyway it didn't matter so long as a pair of boots would fit me, and I could have them."

They had walked out to the side veranda as Nellie talked. Nellie had barely time to notice the sudden stricken look in Angela's eyes before she heard Gilbert's heavy tread on the gravel path.

" Here he is! Here he is!" she cried. She balanced on the edge of the veranda, watching him come towards them. " Don't ask me if I've done my work, Gilly," she called out. " I've done it all. I've dried up and put away and swept the kitchen floor."

" Good," he said, coming up to the veranda and stepping on to it. He looked at the older girl. " Good morning, Angela," he said and then turned to Nellie. " Now we will go into the kitchen and inspect."

" Oh, I like that . . ." began Nellie indignantly.

" I'm not asking whether you like it or not. Just come with me, please, Nellie, and we'll see if it is done to my satisfaction, not necessarily yours."

Angela fled. She filled the watering-can and feverishly watered her pot plants, unnecessarily this time.

" I wonder if Aunt Kara kept you to love?" she said to the ferns. " Maybe she too longed to love someone, and Gilly Lawrence wouldn't let anyone love him."

She had said the magic name " Gilly " and when she realised it she bit her lip.

Presently, after she heard Gilbert and Nellie cross the veranda and jump down on to the gravel path, she went back to the kitchen veranda to watch them ride away.

What went on down at the stables Angela could neither hear nor see but it was twenty minutes before Gilbert on a great roan horse led, Nellie on a smaller horse, bumping and rattling about in the saddle uneasily, followed. Gilbert did not once turn his head to see how she was getting on.

When they disappeared into the trees down by the creek Angela went into the kitchen. Mrs. Cummins was rolling and turning dough for bread at the big table but as she worked she watched through the window as the riders walked their horses across the creek bridge. She shook her head slightly as Angela came in.

"He's a hard man," she said. Then added after a pause, "But he's a good man. If she does as he tells her she won't come to any harm. But he's got to have his own way."

"Mrs. Cummins," Angela said, setting out the bread tins for her, "someone in Red Gorge told me Aunt Kara was a strong-minded woman. Who won when they . . . I mean my husband and Aunt Kara . . . came up against one another?"

There was a silence as Mrs. Cummins carefully folded the dough.

"They didn't . . ." she said quietly. "They didn't win, and they didn't lose. Well, you see, Mrs. Anstey died. I don't know how it would all have come out had she lived. At all events she wouldn't have Miss Winton from Winderup taking up residence here the way she has these last weeks. It's all beyond me. Mrs. Anstey no sooner gone and Miss Winton all but moves in."

She paused. Angela didn't want her to go on yet she couldn't for the life of her say the one word that would change the subject. What did go on, anyway? Perhaps she would be happier if she knew. She would be able to cope better. Why had Gilbert married herself if Stella Winton had "moved in"?

"All the same, she got her own way in death if not in life," Mrs. Cummins went on, speaking of Aunt Kara. She looked up fleetingly and somewhat shyly at Angela. "She was dead set on his marrying you, miss. That was for certain. She wouldn't have Miss Winton at any price. She meant to make him safe. She meant him to marry a nice girl she knew in England. And now you're here . . . If Mrs. Anstey had lived it might have been a battle. Mr. Lawrence had his own ideas." She stopped. "My tongue runs away with me, Mrs. Lawrence. I'd just like to say I'm awfully glad you're here. I'd like to feel you'll make him happy. He's a hard man, but he's a good man." There was almost a plea in her voice.

"I'd like to think so too," said Angela sincerely. "I mean to try."

All morning she conjectured on the meaning of Mrs. Cummins's words. She had come no nearer to understanding the relationship between Aunt Kara and Gilbert Lawrence. She must not probe Mrs. Cummins any more. It wasn't fair to either Mrs. Cummins or Gilbert. Time would be revealing; and in any event time would dispose of herself as Gilbert's wife. He had said so. In due course she and Nellie could leave. She would be well provided for. Gilbert had said that. For herself she would take nothing. But Nellie? If only they could stay long enough for Nellie to be old enough to take some kind of a job. Then they would both be independent.

In the meantime, for pride's sake, Angela must earn her keep!

With willingness and energy Angela set about spring-cleaning the sitting-room.

At midday when she was shaking a duster from the kitchen veranda she saw Nellie come through the stable doors. The young girl hung on to the stable door for a moment as if she had to support herself. Then she wiped her face with the back of her hand and began to walk towards the homestead. As she walked she reeled. She stopped and put her hands on her back and leaned forward as if she would fall.

Angela dropped the duster and jumping off the veranda ran across the gravel square towards her sister.

"Nellie! Nellie!" she cried.

Nellie lifted her head. Angela looked at her sister with a sick feeling in her own heart. Nellie's face was more than dusty, it was dirty. There were marks on her cheeks that could only be tear stains. Dust and gravel were ground into the knees of her jeans. Her shirt looked as if she had been rolling in the red earth. There was a cut on the back of one hand and the knuckles of the other were scraped.

"I hate him," said Nellie. "*I hate him.*"

Suddenly her temper got the better of her wounds, and she stamped her foot, tears sprang hysterically to her eyes and once again she wiped them with the back of her hand.

"I *hate* him. He's a beast!"

"Nellie, where is he?" breathed Angela. A cold, purposeful rage took possession of her. "We'll leave here, Nellie. We'll walk away if there's no other way."

"He didn't come home with me," sobbed Nellie. "He made me ride home alone. He said the only way to learn to ride a horse is to get on it and keep going till it stops."

Angela stood in a stiff silence. With an effort she thrust

aside her anger in her concern for her sister. She put her arm around Nellie.

"Come along, darling. You're home now. I'll get a bath for you."

By the time they reached the veranda Nellie stopped sobbing in order to groan as she put one foot up and tried to mount the step. Angela helped her.

Mrs. Cummins had seen them coming.

"I put the bath on," she said. "I've put soda in it. A whole pound of soda, and some bubble soap. It works wonders, Miss Nellie . . ."

"Thank you," Angela said with stiff lips and not daring to look at Mrs. Cummins for fear the housekeeper would read in her eyes what was in her heart.

Once in the bathroom Angela helped Nellie remove her clothes. This was accompanied by heart-rending groans from Nellie but Angela was relieved to see there were no bruises on her sister's body; and even the fall that had brought Nellie to the ground on her knees had fortunately not cut them.

"Go away and let me soak," pleaded Nellie. "Just let me soak. Mrs. Sullivan at Enmore said to soak and soak and soak and then the stiffness comes out."

"You were stiff when you rode at Enmore?" Angela asked gently as she folded up Nellie's discarded clothes.

Nellie, deep in the frothy bath, spoke angrily.

"Don't be silly, Angela. You can't start riding without getting stiff. You use all different muscles. Mrs. Sullivan told me. And they haven't been used before, so they're stiff."

"I see," said Angela. "Then it's the stiffness that's making you cry. Not Gilbert."

"Him?" said Nellie indignantly. "I hate him. When I fell off he just sat on his horse and said . . . *Get up, Nellie, and get on again. You're not hurt.* And when I said you've got to help me get on he just said . . . *No one's going to help you on, Nellie, so the sooner you do the better. In exactly twenty seconds I'm going to ride on whether you've mounted or not. So make up your own mind.* And, Angela, he meant it."

"Yes, darling. I think that is something you have to learn about Gilbert. He means what he says. But if he is going to be too hard on you I'm afraid we will have to go away."

"When, Angela? Not before I can learn to ride *properly*? I mean gallop and jump the fences the way he does, and mount his horse on the run . . ."

Angela turned and looked at her sister whose head appeared like a small brown ball above the bubble bath.

"If you hate him . . . if he's so hard on you . . . how can you learn?" she asked.

"Oh, I don't hate him that much," conceded Nellie, splashing bubbles gently with one hand. "Anyhow, I'm not going to let *him* beat me. I'm going to show him I'm not afraid of falling off a horse. And I'm not afraid of him, either. In spite of his beastly stock-whip."

"Nellie! He didn't use a stock-whip!"

"Oh, only to show me how to crack it. But I can't crack it. The lash just drops on the ground. When he cracks it it sounds like a pistol going off."

"I don't think you've had such a bad time after all," said Angela, going to the door. "Please don't frighten me another time, Nellie. I'll bring some clean clothes for you and after that you can have a rest."

She went out of the door and closed it quietly behind her.

Odd, but the picture of Gilbert cracking a stock-whip for Nellie's entertainment had filled her own heart with a sudden envy.

Angela wouldn't mind falling off a horse, and being told to pick herself up *or else*. Angela wouldn't mind watching the magic of making a whip with a twenty-eight foot lash crack if it meant that companionship and that sharing that Nellie had enjoyed to-day—in spite of the spills and the tears.

Gilbert was hard but he was right. Nellie didn't have very much to cry about, after all.

All the afternoon Angela found herself waiting for the sound of his footsteps coming across the gravel square. Several times as the dinner hour approached she found herself going to the dining-room door that led on to the kitchen veranda to look out over the paddock to see if he was coming home.

She supposed all wives did this. For other wives it meant a moment of bliss when one's lover came home at sundown. For herself it was only the coming of another person to whom she happened to be tied, but because she had now lost that tie with Nellie she felt a desperate need to belong, if only in token, to someone else.

If she could make him at ease in his own home, if she gave him that thing he prized most, peace in his house, then he too might find the homecoming each evening had a meaning.

She would have to have someone since she had now lost Nellie. She could pretend that someone was Gilbert. It gave the waiting hours meaning and the approach of sundown substance.

She had indeed lost Nellie.

Each time during the afternoon she had asked her sister some simple question about what she had done at Enmore or this morning during that historic riding lesson, she received an irritable answer from her younger sister.

"Don't be silly, Angela. You couldn't possibly understand. People like Bob and Sam Sullivan at Enmore are my own age. Well, just a few years older. They *understand*. You're too old to understand. As for riding a horse! Well, there isn't that much to it, but you'd never be able to do it. You'd fall off, all the time."

When the open session came on the air Nellie poured out her heart over the transceiver set, first to Mrs. Sullivan and then to Bob and Sam. The riding lesson this morning had by this time become a great adventure and Nellie had shown such staggering prowess on horse-back that "Gilly" had done nothing but praise her. She was stiff? Oh, yes, just a bit. But that was nothing. Angela, of course, had had a fit, but then Angela was so old-fashioned . . .

Angela listened to the young fresh voices coming over the air until the matter of her own old-fashionedness came under discussion and then she picked up her sewing and went out. Mrs. Cummins who, through the open door, had also heard the air conversation, touched Angela's arm as they met in the passage.

"Don't you worry, Mrs. Lawrence," she said in her quiet voice. "I had girlies of my own. Two of them. It's their age. They go through a stage. They don't mean half they say. It's just their way of sprouting their wings, you know. They come out all right in the end."

"Thank you, Mrs. Cummins."

They went through the dining-room in the direction of the kitchen together, away from Nellie and the transceiver set.

"I'd be very glad of your advice," Angela said, looking at the older woman with her serious eyes. "You see, I'm not really a mother, and yet I have to be a mother to Nellie."

"Yes, and you'll have a mother's sore heart every now and again too," said Mrs. Cummins, taking down crockery from the dresser. "But it all comes out right in the end. We mothers do a little suffering and a little laughing, and sometimes shed a few tears. But it all comes right in the end. 'Specially now you've got Mr. Lawrence to help you. You'd be surprised how much notice they take of a man's voice. One word from *him* . . ."

"Yes, I can see that. Thank you very much, Mrs. Cummins. You're very comforting."

"If you don't mind me saying so, Mrs. Lawrence, you stop worrying about young Nellie. She'll do all right. You have a little life yourself. After all, you're a bride. I'd think about my husband if I were you. He is the one who needs your love and attention."

"Yes," Angela said. "Yes." She had begun to help Mrs. Cummins with the crockery without knowing quite what she was doing with it. She was putting the wrong cups in the wrong saucers and the kind gentle words had brought tears to her eyes so she could not see what she was doing.

Mrs. Cummins looked down at Angela's foolish hands and her own heart ached for this young girl. She knew all about that separated life. Mrs. Lawrence hadn't even been inside her husband's room, or the office for that matter. It was as if she was afraid to invade. She had walked quietly about the house doing this and that as if she was trying to do something to fill in time.

Always there was a bleak lost look in those eyes that were meant to be young and gay and happy like that thoughtless young Nellie in there at the radio.

And Mr. Lawrence out there on his horse . . . he was lonely too. Why couldn't these two lonely people get together and do something about it?

Ah, it was the hand of Mrs. Anstey again! Why hadn't Mrs. Anstey been wise enough to know you can't separate two people by force the way she had tried to separate Naroo from Winderup? Sooner or later they dig their toes in. They see virtues in one another they would never have seen before, all because they are determined to do just this . . . because it is forbidden fruit. And Miss Winton had a way with her . . . She hadn't waited until Mr. Lawrence had returned from Mrs. Anstey's funeral to ensconce herself on the front veranda of Naroo Downs. She had been here to receive him when he returned from the south.

"The cups and saucers are ready now, thank you," Mrs. Cummins said in a bright voice. "I am a little late with the dinner to-night so I wonder if you'd mind my asking you for a little help."

"Yes, of course. I'll set the table," said Angela gratefully.

Mrs. Cummins shook her head as Angela went out of the door. Never had she dreamed she would see the day on Naroo Downs when it was she who asked the mistress of the house for help. Shades of Mrs. Anstey!

But then young Mrs. Lawrence needed to help in order to be helped.

Ah, well, he was a hard man, but a good man. If only that Stella Winton would stay away!

Passing backwards and forwards between the dining-room and the kitchen across the veranda that Angela had now realised was the most important part of the house because it was the only part that was shared by everyone, she watched the glory die out of the sky and the silence settle on the land. She watched the shadows in the trees down by the creek cease to be shadows when finally the sun went down.

All the time she was watching for Gilbert to come home because she had to watch for someone to come home and inhabit the empty chamber of her heart.

At last he came but Angela was by this time in her room changing for dinner. She did not hear his steps on the gravel but she heard them on the veranda. She heard doors opening and shutting and knew when he was in the bathroom, then later in his own room. She knew when he went up to the sitting-room to wait for the call to the dinner-table.

Just as Angela entered the sitting-room and Gilbert stood up and Nellie, prone on the floor, lifted her head from a music score she had found in the piano stool by the piano, the telephone rang.

"Excuse me," said Gilbert. He waited for Angela to enter the room and then went out down the passage to his office where the telephone bell gave another peremptory three rings. He hadn't even said "Good evening."

"Three rings is Naroo Downs," said Nellie without looking up again. "One is Enmore Station, two is Milga Station, three is Naroo Downs and four is Winderup. I know them all."

"You are a very fast learner, Nellie," said Angela, sitting down at the piano. She began softly and delicately to play, "To a Wild Rose." "How are the aches and pains?"

"Oh, so-so," said Nellie. "Do you know this is the score of *The Mikado*? It's got all the words, too. I think I could learn to play it."

"Of course you could. We must both do our practice. It seems years since either of us touched a piano."

"There's lots of music in the stool under you. And all those books along the wall too."

Gilbert's footsteps were coming up the passage. They were slower and when he came into the room his head was bent and he was reading something on a piece of paper.

Angela guessed at once what it was. A telephone message when it was relayed through several stations was always written down because it had to be read back to the person relaying it. That way each sender along the line knew that it had been received correctly. Gilbert had received this call from some station beyond Milga Station. He was reading it again.

There was a heavy frown between his brows. He stood just inside the door and finished reading the note, then he folded it and put it in his pocket.

Angela's hands dropped from the piano and she sat watching him, not daring to interrupt his thoughts, but wondering if he was going to speak.

"Any messages for me?" asked Nellie from the floor. She still did not raise her head from the music score in front of her.

"I imagine you and Enmore must have said all you have to say to one another over the air, surely?" said Gilbert.

Nellie shrugged.

"There's never enough time to say *everything*," she complained.

"How wonderful to have so much to say to one another that one went on for ever," Angela thought. For the first time she had a feeling of release where Nellie was concerned. Nellie was building a world and a life of her own. It sounded as if it might be a happy one.

Angela, pondering this thought, looked up to Gilbert's face. He was still standing just inside the door.

"That was from Red Gorge," he said to Angela. "The invasion is on. Hopkins and Smart will be out here on Friday. Stella Winton will motor over from Winderup. She is flying straight through to Winderup from the south by mail plane. They have an airstrip there."

Angela's eyes were on his face. She had not moved and had she but known she made a lovely picture sitting there on the piano stool, her body turned towards the door, her hands lying in her lap and her back beautifully straight. Her simple white dress hung over her knees in graceful folds reaching nearly to the floor. The shaded light on top of the piano cast a rosy flush over her face and her partly bared shoulders and her arms.

Nellie broke the silence.

"Why do they all have to come?" she said. "Why does Stella Winton have to come? Who asked her?"

"This is a business conference, Nellie," Gilbert said shortly. "Now if you will kindly get up from the floor I think we will go in to dinner."

As Nellie stood up she winced.

"And don't make faces," he added. "The price of first-class horsemanship is high and you don't groan when you pay the price."

"Will I be first-class?" asked Nellie, going to the door.

He held her back with his hand so that Angela could go through first.

"Oh, Angela's only my sister," said Nellie petulantly.

"She also happens to be my wife," said Gilbert quietly.

Over Nellie's head his eyes met Angela's.

CHAPTER THIRTEEN

At the dinner-table Gilbert Lawrence added one more piece of information that had come through with the telephone relay.

As he lifted the covers from the dish and disclosed a beautiful browned sirloin of beef, he said:

"The mine office in Red Gorge decided to provide Smart, he's the government geologist, with some staff." There was a studied silence as his knife bit into the side of the joint. "They are sending Kevin Richards."

It took Nellie less than a minute to digest this.

"Oh, goody!" she cried. "Whacko! Golly, Angela, you've got a *friend* coming to visit you."

"I thought Angela would be pleased," said Gilbert, continuing to slice beef on to the top plate in front of him.

"I am," said Angela because she thought it was the only possible thing to say.

Nellie looked at Gilbert mischievously.

"You and Stella, and Angela and Kevin! Golly, won't you have fun! Can't the Sullivans come over from Enmore for me?" She paused, aghast at a sudden discovery. "I've said it all wrong, haven't I? I ought to say 'You and *Angela* and Kevin and *Stella*, oughtn't I?"

"Do all young women of your age find it necessary to pair people off?" asked Gilbert of Nellie, coldly.

"Of course," said Nellie. "What's the fun without boys for girls and girls for boys?" She sighed. "I guess being married spoils everything for you." Then she brightened. "But there's Mr. Hopkins, isn't there? Maybe we could find someone for him."

Gilbert's voice was expressionless. "Will you serve the vegetables please, Angela?"

"Let's see," continued Nellie conversationally. "How many shes and how many hes will there be. Why, Angela, there's more men than women. You could have a lovely time."

Angela felt by the atmosphere at the top end of the table that Gilbert was not amused. Why couldn't Nellie feel that too?

"Nellie," she said, "pass me your plate. And it's not very good form to talk that way. Men and women, when they're grown-up, like to enjoy meeting one another and having conversation without . . ."

"Then how does anyone ever get married?" said Nellie, taking back her plate after Angela had served it with vegetables. "Kevin's got to marry someone now you're gone. Gilbert, would Stella Winton be too absolutely slashing a person for Kevin? At Enmore the Sullivans said she was the slashingest person ever."

Gilbert looked at Nellie.

"You may drop that topic as conversation, or leave the table. Whichever you like, Nellie. Please decide."

"Why . . .?"

She looked up and caught the expression in his eyes. Even Nellie knew he meant it, and that he was very angry.

"All right," she said weakly. "If you feel that way."

"I do."

The silence that followed during the rest of the meal was painful to Angela. Gilbert had been able to silence Nellie because already to-day he had cracked that stock-whip, both metaphorically and in fact, for Nellie's benefit. Nellie recognised his authority and now she bowed to it. She wasn't unhappy, however, for she ate a good meal. It was the first time Angela had ever seen Nellie face a meal without a display of fad and fancy.

When they rose from the table Gilbert turned to Angela.

"Mrs. Cummins will bring the coffee to the veranda, Angela." Then to Nellie he said, "Don't forget your duties in the kitchen. After that I don't want to hear from you again to-night. Be at the stables at half past seven to-morrow morning. Wear a hat."

He held the door open for Angela, and then followed her down the passage to the veranda. He had not looked at Nellie while he had spoken to her.

All this shook Angela very much for she had been brought up in a home that dictated tenderness and care for the feelings of the young.

Gilbert had been just, for while he reprimanded Nellie flatly and set her household work as a duty, he had also undertaken to give her her heart's desire—riding lessons. Perhaps Nellie in her haphazard childish mind recognised that justice.

Gilbert held Angela's chair for her as she sat down in her usual place on the veranda. He then went to his own chair. He stretched his feet out before him and dug in his pocket for his cigarettes.

"I would like to be able to say—*Now for an hour of peace*," he said. "However, there are a few things I will have to discuss with you. Nellie first."

He paused to select a cigarette and then light it.

"I'm afraid I haven't been quite successful in keeping her from under your feet . . ." Angela said.

"That remark of mine before we were married, about keeping out of the way, was theoretical sense, but not practically sound," Gilbert said. "I recognise that. You are both members of my household and must be treated as such. Nellie for instance must be given responsibility, plenty of activity and then some vocational work to do. If you get in touch with Meekatharra Air Station you will find out about lessons over the air. You'll understand more about that sort of thing than I do." He paused and then went on, "You will probably be able to supervise her work. If her work is not up to standard there'll be no playtime for Nellie. Either here or at Enmore. I'll deal with her in that regard in the morning."

He stopped again, this time to tip the ash from his cigarette into the ash-tray.

Angela wanted to ask him did he dispose of human beings as he might dispose of chattels. Yet there were people in the world who loved their chattels. Her own mother had loved her china and she, Angela, loved the ferns, and especially Redbella, as Aunt Kara must have loved them before her.

She could not argue with Gilbert because her own position

here at Naroo Downs was invidious. She was here on suffrance. She had to take his word as law just as a hired hand might have to do, in silence.

"With regard to these men coming out here on Friday," Gilbert went on. "Hopkins, who will stay in the house, represents a multi-millionaire industrial organisation. He is interested in getting an option on the manganese for this company. The other man is a geologist and is a different kettle of fish. He is sent here to watch the Government's interests in any mining that might be undertaken." Again he stopped and stubbed out the cigarette.

"Yes, I understand," said Angela.

"I don't think you do," said Gilbert. "Pastoralists and graziers in this State own only what's on the surface of the ground. Twelve inches below the surface of the ground, everything in it, belongs to the Government . . . until the Government allocates a right to mine. A Miner's Right, in other words. These men have been here some time and are coming back again this week-end. The conference is to decide whether or not I, with or without partners, take out a Miner's Right on this lease."

"And your visitors want to go into partnership with you?"

"Exactly. The Government on one hand, and Hopkins's organisation on the other. In short they are rivals of one another."

And where does Stella Winton come in? Angela wondered. The woman in the piece! It sounded very melodramatic yet Stella had to play a part in this quartet somewhere and somehow. Otherwise why would Gilbert allow her to come just at this time? Angela began to see how her own and Nellie's presence at Naroo Downs had interfered with Gilbert's plans. That was why Mrs. Cummins had said that finally, in death, Aunt Kara had got her own way. She had wanted to stop something, and Angela in the picture and Stella Winton out of it would have stopped that something.

Had Aunt Kara lived Gilbert would have been too strong minded to bow to Aunt Kara's decision as to whom he should marry. In death, duty to his own good name and duty to two rather luckless girls, had brought about the marriage Aunt Kara had wanted but which Gilbert had intended to resist.

Yes, Angela could see much more than Gilbert gave her credit for.

"I must ask you to keep as far away from these matters

under discussion as possible," Gilbert was saying. "You could, inadvertently, confuse things. The matter is serious to me. Do you understand, Angela?"

"Yes," she said. "I understand."

Keep away from Mr. Hopkins and the geologist; and, of course, Stella Winton. Let Gilbert play his own hand his own way!

"I have had business training," Angela said quietly. "I understand perfectly the importance of not interfering."

"Thank you."

Angela wondered how a real wife, a true wife, would have accepted this situation. She would have been on her husband's side, and have helped him, of course. But then she would have known what her husband wanted, and what was in his heart.

The only way Angela could help Gilbert was by keeping out of sight and mind.

A small sigh escaped her.

There was a different note in Gilbert's voice when he spoke next.

"I would be glad if you would help Mrs. Cummins out in the role of hostess. She is an excellent cook but does not like to meet or mix with guests inside the homestead. You could perhaps do that for me."

"Yes, of course," Angela said, and then allowed herself one remark to show she was not a complete cipher. "On the principle that I, like Nellie, must have some activity to keep me busy. Some vocational work, such as hostessing." She had meant to say it laughingly but her little rebellion fell flat in her own ears for on the last word there was a catch in her voice.

Gilbert moved his feet restlessly. At that moment Mrs. Cummins came out on to the veranda with the coffee.

Angela poured it into the small cups and they sat in silence and drank it.

When Angela put down her cup she stood up.

"I think I will go inside now, Gilbert."

He too had risen. It was very dark on the veranda. The starlight barely lightened the shadows and as there was no moon the garden all around them lay in darkness.

"Have you been out of the homestead to-day, Angela?" Gilbert asked. There was a new and unexpected note in his voice. It was almost one of concern—except that Angela could not believe that to be the case.

“Half-way to the stables to meet Nellie.”

“Then I think we'll take our evening walk.”

He moved round behind the chair and a minute later he was standing beside Angela. His hand was cupped under her elbow. She would have drawn away but with a quick movement he took her hand and put it under his arm. He held her firmly imprisoned.

“It's rather pleasant walking at this hour of the night . . . even when there is no moon,” he said, guiding her towards the edge of the veranda and the three steps that led to the path below.

They walked in silence to the bottom of the garden. Then Gilbert released her hand and he stood leaning over the fence, looking out over the dark ocean of the plain to the distant stars on the far western horizon. Angela too leaned her hands on the fence. Neither of them spoke but after a little while Angela felt herself grow still and quiet, as she too became relaxed.

Yes, he was right. It was peaceful to be here, alone, at night. There was peace in silence too. She understood why this evening walk was a universal habit in the out-back.

Angela felt glad she was not much of a talker, and that she had had so little to say to him. He didn't want speech, he needed silence, and perhaps someone who could be silent with him.

Perhaps Aunt Kara had talked too much? One day she would ask Mrs. Cummins.

“Shall we go up?” Gilbert asked at length as he straightened himself.

“Yes, I think so,” Angela said in a composed voice. “It is rather lovely down here by the fence at night. I'm glad we came.”

“One gets things in proportion,” Gilbert said. He seemed to know where, in the dark, her arm was. As they turned to walk towards the house he once again took her hand and placed it in the crook of his arm. This time he did not have to hold it imprisoned for Angela made no attempt to draw it away.

When they reached the darker shadows of the veranda he dropped her arm.

“Do you like to sit in the sitting-room at night, Angela, or are you going to your room?”

“I . . . Would you like me to sit in the sitting-room with you, Gilbert?”

“Heaven forbid. I would have both Nellie and the radio.

That I couldn't stand. It was *your* company I was thinking of."

Angela stood still. What did he mean? What could he possibly mean? How did she reply? What did she say? He wanted *her* company!

"I have never been in your office," she said at length, simply not knowing how to answer him.

"Time enough for that," he said brusquely. Apparently he did not intend to explain his cryptic comment about her company. He opened the wire door and stood aside for her to go in. He followed her and as the door of her own room was open to allow a passage of air through it he put up his hand and switched on the light for her. He pressed the lower of the two buttons and only the shaded lamp on her bedside table lit up. It cast a soft glow all over the room. Gilbert stood in the doorway looking at it.

"You have made this look pleasant," he said. "I hope you are comfortable."

There were lace mats on the tables and Angela's ornaments put about here and there. The red flower in its tiny painted pot on the dressing-table struck a note of vivid life.

"Oh, yes, thank you. And I like reading in bed. I found plenty of books on the bookshelves in the sitting-room."

Gilbert took a few paces into the room.

"There is a scent in here," he said. "What is it?"

"It's the pot plants on the veranda outside the french doors. There's daphne, and a sort of dwarf magnolia and some camellias. And all the ferns, of course. But I think it is the frangipani that is the most exotic."

Gilbert walked across the room and stood in the doorway of the veranda.

"Very nice," he said. As he turned to recross the room he noticed again the little red flower on the dressing-table.

"That's Redbella," Angela explained. "My best friend. She shares my bedroom with me. It's not so lonely . . ."

She stopped suddenly. *That was the wrong thing to say.*

If only he would go. Every moment he stood in this room was agony to her. He had every right, of course, but it filled the whole atmosphere with the silent cry of her own desolate heart. It made the room talk to him and tell him something she did not want him to know. It was like bringing dangerous unuttered words to the verge of sound.

"Please go, Gilbert," she said in desperation. "I'm dreadfully tired."

Anything to terminate the embarrassment of them both standing there in a sweet-scented room that spoke for itself!

"So early?" he said, looking at her.

Why wouldn't he go? He looked as if he might say something more, and whatever it was she couldn't bear to hear it. If it was to offer to stay with her she knew she could not give herself, the whole of herself, in a loveless marriage. If it was to cast her back into the role of the clever little adventuress who had managed to gossip herself into a marriage with him, she could not bear that either.

No, she would rather have his silence, his displeasure, and the loneliness.

"Please excuse me, Gilbert," she said. "I have much to do. I want to get my clothes ready for the . . . well, for the visitors on Friday. I need to sew some buttons and some straps . . . and . . . well, things like that," she finished lamely.

"Do you think that in a matter of clothes and dressing you have to compete with someone like Stella?" he asked. "Don't try because you never could. Stella has a flair for clothes. In addition . . ." He stopped short.

He had been going to say, "In addition she spends a fortune on her back," but he remembered in time that that might be to another woman an unkind cut. Stella had a great deal of money, and this young girl standing there, her two hands clasped together, her face in a poignant agony of doubt, had had no money to speak of at all.

"No, I would not try to compete with Stella," Angela said, filling the awkward silence. "I couldn't could I? That is what you have said, and what in your heart you feel. But there are others coming. I need to look my best. The man from the Government . . . and Kevin . . ."

Kevin! Why had she foresworn the love that Kevin might have offered her to stand here, like a prisoner before the bar, excusing herself to this man whose name she bore but whose heart was a strange mystery to her. She pulled herself together.

"I will do my best about the hostessing for you, Gilbert," she said. "I won't intrude on your business affairs. You need have no fear about that."

"Thank you," he said slowly. His shoulders had slackened a little as if he was tired. He straightened them now and looked round the room once again.

"I'm glad you are comfortable," he said and walked to the door. Once again he stopped as if he would turn and say something. He changed his mind for he went out, closing the door behind him. He did not say good night.

Angela stood where he had left her and listened to his footsteps receding down the passage. She walked to her bed and sat down on its edge. She looked down at two hands that had involuntarily entwined themselves in her lap. She felt tired, also released, as from a current of electricity that had been dangerous.

CHAPTER FOURTEEN

On Friday Mr. Hopkins, Mr. Smart and Kevin Richards arrived together but each in a different vehicle. Three dust clouds had rolled across the plain on the track from Enmore and Milga Stations. Angela, watching from the veranda, thought of them as three giant red balls bowled along by the wind. Presently the dust clouds materialised into a jeep, a big tourer and a utility truck. The last, the utility truck, she recognised as belonging to the mine office in Red Gorge. That would be Kevin Richards. She knew the jeep would belong to the geologist because it had a four-wheel drive and would go over anything . . . trackless plain, brush scrub and pindan. Those were the kinds of places that geologists investigated. The big tourer then must belong to Mr. Hopkins, the man representing the multi-millionaire firm.

Funny how the bush made fellow travellers of men who were deadly rivals! But then that was the nature of this strange almost waterless desert of a country.

Mr. Hopkins came straight up to the homestead and though Angela would have liked to go down to the garages to meet Kevin Richards she felt unexpectedly self-conscious about it. How would he greet her? With a laugh or a reproach? Also she had immediate duties to perform for Mr. Hopkins.

He was a tall pleasant man in his middle forties with a deceptively quiet voice. In the deep recesses of his friendly brown eyes Angela read that here was a man of purpose. He meant to get that manganese option and one way of going about it was to be charming to the lady of the house. He was carefully charming, not overdoing it by one word or gesture. Yet he set out to win Angela.

She showed him his room, forgetting he had been here before

and that he already knew it, and then as he was dusty from the long drive asked him if he would like a shower while she prepared some afternoon tea for him.

In her anxiety to do exactly the right thing for Gilbert's sake, and hide from Mr. Hopkins that already she had seen through his charm and its purpose, she went again to the trouble of showing him where the bathroom was, and how the three taps, the hot, cold, and warm-bore water, operated.

Mr. Hopkins took it all smilingly, not once spoiling this little lady's moment of wifely responsibility in the house by telling her he knew it all better than she could know it herself. He had been at Naroo Downs much longer, and more often for that matter, than she had herself.

Then Angela hastened away to help Mrs. Cummins with the tea. Gilbert had so effectively tyrannised Nellie into doing some work that even the sound of visitors arriving did not bring her from the floor of the writing-room where she was drawing a giant-size map of Asia, putting in all the rivers and place names in perfect print. One blot, one misspelled word, one unshapely printed letter and she would have to do the whole again. Nellie had more than met her match in Gilbert, and she knew it.

The thing that astounded Angela was that Nellie bowed in silent acquiescence to this discipline. She very clearly had a wholesome respect for Gilbert. Already, within a few days she had ceased to exaggerate in her talk. She was careful that what she said was accurate, or else she remained silent.

Gilbert had pulled her up on this score once and so scathingly that now Nellie thought twice before she said anything at all.

In the kitchen Angela and Mrs. Cummins peered through the window to see if Gilbert was bringing the other two men up for tea. Mr. Hopkins had driven his own car alone right up to the garden gate.

As Angela looked through the window she saw other dust clouds coming along the track. Some were big and some were small.

"Whatever's coming now?" she asked.

"That's the stockmen returning," said Mrs. Cummins. "They wouldn't have enough money left to stay the week-end in Red Gorge." She sighed. "Stockmen are always like that," she went on. "They pour it all away as fast as they can, and then come home."

" But aren't they disappointed at missing a few days?" asked Angela.

" No, because they do it again next time," said Mrs. Cummins. " And you know, Mrs. Lawrence, they never really like the town for long. They're true bushmen or they'd never stick station life. Their home is out there on horse-back, coming to terms with the sun and the plain. That's their real life."

Half an hour later the whole aspect of Naroo Downs had changed. There were men and horses everywhere, down at the saddling paddock and up and down the red roadway that ran between the outhouses down to the creek. A haze of dust enveloped everything beyond the garden fence.

Motor engines could be heard roaring and voices could be heard calling out to one another above them.

There were two strange men who came up to the homestead and who in their rolling gait went round the side veranda uninvited and then into Gilbert's office. Angela could hear their voices as they talked first to one another, then over the telephone. Presently one of them went down the passage to the sitting-room and turned on the transceiver set. He proceeded to talk over that.

Angela, politely drinking tea with Mr. Hopkins, had eyes as large as pansies in her face.

" What," she said, " goes on? Nobody knocked at the door . . ."

Mr. Hopkins smiled reassuringly.

" You are now seeing Naroo Downs in operation, Mrs. Lawrence. Last week must have been very quiet for you, with all the staff away."

No wonder Gilbert had talked about peace and quiet.

Those two men in the house for instance! They thought nothing of calling out to one another from one room to another.

" The storekeeper and the head stockman, I think," said Mr. Hopkins by way of explanation and watching with amusement the expression on Angela's face.

" Will you excuse me, please," said Angela. " I will just make sure Gilbert is not coming up for tea."

They had been sitting on the front veranda. Angela now went down the passage and through the dining-room where she had almost to jump sideways to avoid bumping into a short nuggety man in dusty clothes and dustier boots who was coming in the opposite direction—rolling in a true horseman's manner of walking.

"'Scuse me, missus," he said with a grin and went on into the house.

Angela turned round and watched him in astonishment. Her house . . . and with all that dust on him . . . and no by-your-leave!

She hurried to the kitchen.

"Mrs. Cummins," she said, "do they always live like this? I mean, in and out of the house, making all that noise?"

"Not in Mrs. Anstey's day," said Mrs. Cummins, shaking her head. "And they don't do it when Mr. Lawrence is around. Not inside the house like that unless he tells them. Of course the storekeeper and the head stockman go into the office."

"Then why do they do it now?"

"Well, you see, there was a week when Mr. Lawrence was away and he had to go down about Mrs. Anstey's death. And to look for you and Nellie. That's when Miss Winton came. She came to see Mr. Hopkins and the geologist. She likes a lot of people around. Mrs. Anstey had been very strict and Miss Winton thought they might as well get free of *that*."

"But it wasn't her homestead."

"Then Mr. Lawrence had to go backwards and forwards to Red Gorge, and to Carnlow too, I believe," Mrs. Cummins continued, "to see you."

"Didn't you say anything to the men, Mrs. Cummins? I mean, all that dust coming in the house!"

"They didn't take any notice of me," said Mrs. Cummins, shaking her head. "You see, I haven't got a very loud voice. And Miss Winton said, 'For heaven's sake let them come in. The place is empty—and useless. If I were here I'd build a new homestead.'"

Angela stood by the kitchen table thoughtfully.

"Mrs. Cummins," she said at length. "Would you have said the house was empty and useless since Monday? I mean, is it dull *now*?"

"Not with you and young Nellie around. Nellie's full of life. And your door open, with the scent of all those flowers coming through the house, is lovely. And . . . well, if you don't mind my saying . . ." Mrs. Cummins hesitated shyly. "You make me think of a flower yourself. You're so fresh and young, and that beautiful complexion of yours! It's lovely to see you round the house. I think Mr. Gilbert thinks so too. But then so he should. Oh, look there! I see him coming up from the garage. He's got a young man with him, and it's not the geologist."

Angela turned and looked through the window.

"No," she said quietly. "It's Kevin Richards from Red Gorge."

Beyond Gilbert and Kevin she could see the track that came into the homestead from the north. Along it was bowling another car clad in its dust cloud.

"And I think Miss Stella Winton is not far behind," she added.

The short nuggety man with the dusty boots rolled through the dining-room door on to the kitchen veranda and then seeming to remember something he had forgotten he turned and went back into the house.

Mrs. Cummins shook her head from side to side.

"I wonder if my voice is louder than yours, Mrs. Cummins," Angela said thoughtfully.

"I don't think so. Besides . . ."

"Besides what?"

"Well, Miss Winton told them you were only a young girl. That was when Mr. Lawrence flew off into Red Gorge to see you. *No experience of station life*, she said. I think they have more or less decided to do as they please now. Unless Mr. Lawrence . . ."

"Mr. Lawrence likes peace and quiet," said Angela firmly.

She turned and went out of the kitchen. In the dining-room she encountered the short dusty man again. She did not wait to ask him his name.

"If you want Mr. Lawrence will you please go to the office door? The veranda door," she said quietly. "He is not in the homestead at the moment."

"I only wanted . . ."

"The office door on the veranda, please," said Angela. She stood quite still and looked at the man steadily.

"Well, if you feel like that. I mean, how was I to know?"

"If you would knock any time you want my husband, or anything in the homestead, I could perhaps help you."

Surprised, the man left through the outside veranda door. He looked back once and Angela nearly laughed at the comical expression on his face.

She now went to the sitting-room. The transceiver was on full blare. A man sat before it, his knees spread, and he was rolling a cigarette. The ash of an earlier cigarette was lying on the carpet.

"Are you the head stockman or the storekeeper?" Angela asked politely.

"The head stockman, missus," he said, lazily getting up. "Just listening in to see what goes on in Hedland this afternoon."

"Is it something important?" Angela was still gently polite.

"Well, no. But Gilly—he wouldn't mind."

"Mrs. Anstey would have minded, wouldn't she?"

He laughed uneasily.

"We had to keep to hours with her."

"Will you please keep to hours with me? I'd be so glad to have your help in that way."

"Well, if that's how you feel about it . . ."

"Yes, that is how I do feel about it. Will you please tell the storekeeper and the other men under you? If anyone wishes to see Mr. Lawrence he could go to the office."

The man looked at her so surprised that his mouth opened and shut without saying a word.

"Mr. Lawrence has just come up now," Angela said with a smile. "You will find him at the office or with Mr. Hopkins on the front veranda."

"Okay. I'm sorry if I intruded."

"It's all right," said Angela happily. "You won't forget to tell the men, will you?"

"No. I'll tell 'em."

"Thank you."

She listened to him thumping across the passage through the dining-room and away. She felt like dusting her hands together. She could imagine Gilbert's anger if he had found his homestead invaded, dusty and full of noise like that!

Now she must put on another smile and go to the front veranda again. Not only would there be Mr. Hopkins's amused, friendly but perspicacious eyes to watch her, but there would also be Kevin Richards and Stella Winton.

Angela wondered how she would make out. She was grateful for the little brush she had just had with those two men. Her victory gave her confidence.

"Some more tea, please," she said to Mrs. Cummins, putting her head in the kitchen. "We have visitors galore. Invited ones. I got rid of the uninvited ones."

Mrs. Cummins smiled and nodded her head in approval.

"Mr. Lawrence wouldn't have liked it at all," she said.

Angela withdrew her head and went back into the house in the general direction of her own room and the front veranda. She would just run that comb through her hair again and put one more touch of lipstick on her mouth! By the time Stella Winton arrived on the doorstep she meant Stella to find her groomed, composed, behind the teapot, and mistress of her own home. She felt sure Mr. Hopkins wouldn't mind her prolonged absence when he knew how easily she had restored serenity in the inside of the homestead.

When Stella arrived, Angela was pouring tea from a large silver teapot over which she had to look to greet Stella. Kevin Richards was on one side of her and the ubiquitous Mr. Hopkins, taking his second and deferred cup of tea, on the other. Gilbert had gone to the gate to meet Stella and carry her suitcase to the veranda for her.

For one proud moment Angela felt she was queen of the situation. Then by a simple gesture, an easy pleasant laugh, and a completely natural, "Hallo, Angela. How lovely and fresh you look behind that nest of creepers!" Stella had conquered Angela again.

"She's *nice*," thought Angela. "She's just a nice person. She likes me, and she doesn't mean to do me any harm. How . . . how do I compete with someone who is beautiful and who is *nice*? And why should I think of competing? What for?"

What stupid inaccurate pictures she had built up in her mind! In her imagination she had turned Stella Winton into a siren, and here she was as Angela had first met her, lovely, friendly, natural, the centre of all attention, including Gilbert's attention, for he stood watching her. His face, if not smiling, was relaxed and he was interested in Stella's delightful way of making herself completely at home.

It was Nellie's appearance through the front door that broke up the tableau.

"I've finished it," Nellie said to Gilbert smugly.

"Hallo, brat!" said Stella laughing. She sat down and crossed her legs and showed a beautiful pair of nylon-covered ankles. "Don't tell me Gilbert's been cracking stock-whips round your young and curly head already?" she asked.

"Yes, and *some*," said Nellie.

"I bet you liked it . . . in the end," said Stella. She laughed as she spoke and her white pearly teeth shone between the delicately rouged lips. "We all do in the end. The strong man has a way with him."

She looked up at Gilbert and flicked one eyebrow in interrogation.

"Have you been kind to Angela?" she asked. "No stockwhips in that direction, I hope?"

"Look at her and see for yourself, Stella," Gilbert answered, sitting down by her. "Angela looks well, I think."

"She looks lovely," said Stella. "Pour me some tea, Angela, and I'll know from the tea leaves just what kind of a housewife you are."

"Of course," said Angela, finding her voice. "Do you take milk, Stella?"

"Yes, please."

Stella immediately engaged Mr. Hopkins in conversation across the table. Angela could see that Mr. Hopkins liked it and there was an easy, almost conspiratorial compatability between them.

Gilbert was asking Nellie about her work and Angela turned to Kevin.

"She's gorgeous, isn't she?" said Kevin, nodding his head in Stella's direction. "But don't be taken in, Angela. She's a designing woman." He said all this with a grin. He had greeted Angela as if nothing had ever taken place between them and for that Angela was grateful.

"You said that once before about Stella," said Angela reproachfully. "You are not right, and you are not very kind. Stella is a very nice person."

Kevin leaned forward so that his words were for Angela's ears alone.

"Don't be so easily taken in," he repeated teasingly.

"Why don't you like her?" countered Angela.

"I do. I just know what she is up to."

"What is she up to?" asked Angela.

"Ask Gilbert," Kevin said, flicking his glance at the other man. "At least he's not so stiff-necked he doesn't know."

Kevin leaned his head closer to Angela so that he was whispering in her ear. At the same time his eyes were on Stella.

"She's clever. She's hooking Gilly in now, just by being charming to another man. That takes talent, Angela."

Angela's eyes were not on Stella who she knew was talking easily across the table to Mr. Hopkins. Her eyes were on Gilbert. He had sent Nellie away and was watching Stella's face with an intentness that meant he did not for the moment notice anything else around that table. It was as if he was gathering to himself every word, every fleeting expression.

"That's rocked you," said Kevin, again with a tease in his voice.

Angela turned back to him.

"Kevin," she said, looking anxiously into his eyes, "do you have to be as unkind as all that?"

"No, Angela. Not when you look at me with those blue reproachful eyes. I'll tell you a secret . . ."

Neither of them now noticed that Gilbert Lawrence was no longer watching Stella's face but was looking at them instead.

"I don't want Stella to win," said Kevin in an undertone. "I'm on the other side of the fence. How's that for a faithful friend? I want to save Gilly from a fearful fate."

"Don't talk rubbish," said Angela in a low voice.

"I'm not. Gilly's got the fight of his life on his hands with that enticing dame from Winderup. Let's back him up, hey? You use your influence by the domestic hearth and I'll throw all mine in while out at the mines. Is it a deal?"

"It would be a deal if Gilbert were in danger," said Angela. Her eyes went back to Stella, then returned to Kevin.

"You talk rot, Kevin," she said firmly. "And don't ever bring the subject up with me again. She's lovely, and she's nice."

"You bet," said Kevin, leaning back in his chair and fishing in his pocket for cigarettes. "That's why she always wins. Being a nice person is an even more powerful weapon than beauty when dealing with an intelligent man."

"Then why don't you succumb yourself?" asked Angela.

"Dear girl!" Kevin had the grace to look surprised. "I'd lose my job. And as I'm going to get married I need to keep it."

"Married?"

"Don't ask me who. Wait until this mighty knot tied up round Naroo unravels itself. And if I win out . . ." He laughed. "She's a grand girl, and you know her very well," he finished.

Were there ever so many conundrums tied up in one afternoon's conversation? For the first time in their acquaintance it occurred to Angela that Kevin was a little mad. He couldn't possibly know the terms under which she and Gilbert had married. She had wanted to tell Kevin but loyalty to Gilbert had tied her tongue. And here he was talking about unravelling the knots as if it was as easy as all that.

Could that be why he kept drawing her attention to Stella's apparent intentions?

Dinner that night passed off easily. All the travellers were tired and the conversation was light and of a general character. Stella, who had a portable radiogram in her car had had it brought in and she and Nellie chose a long-playing record they both liked, and set the machine going. It provided a kind of background music and every now and then Stella would turn to Nellie and consult her as to how she was enjoying it. When that record concluded Stella invited Nellie to go and choose another and put it on.

Quite clearly a quick and happy friendship had sprung up between the glamorous and friendly woman from Winderup and the very impressionable Nellie. The young girl could hardly take her eyes from Stella's face.

Each time Angela's eyes strayed round the table it was to find Mr. Hopkins's quizzical eyes on herself.

He knows everything, she thought. She wished he would go away for she felt he was the one who was the real danger to Gilbert.

In between charming Nellie, Stella also bestowed her easy natural smiles on Kevin. He responded readily and naturally too but once he turned and winked at Angela. Mr. Hopkins intercepted the wink and once again Angela was aware of a deep amusement in his eyes.

After coffee on the veranda, over which everyone lingered a long time, it was decided all would retire early.

Angela had dreaded this hour. She didn't want Mr. Hopkins and Stella, who were guests inside the homestead, to know of the surface nature of her own marriage and somehow she had to contrive to retire last in order to draw the least attention to herself.

Seeing Nellie off to bed was, for once, the easiest of all the chores. It gave Angela time, and while she was with Nellie she hoped the others would have gone to bed themselves.

When eventually she left Nellie's room it was indeed to find Mr. Hopkins absent but Stella's bedroom door, which was opposite Angela's door, was open. The light flooded across the passage and Stella called Angela in.

"I've been waiting for you," she said gaily. "Come and sit on my bed and talk to me while I get undressed."

It would have been ungracious to refuse and, in fact, Stella's friendly manner and the quick way she went on talking did not give Angela a chance to refuse.

At least, Angela thought, she would be seeing Stella safely into bed and safely out of sight.

She sat on the bed and while Stella chatted she watched the beautiful nylon and lace nightie come out of the suitcase and equally breath-taking nylon and lace undies reveal themselves as Stella pulled her dress over her head. Presently she slipped unobtrusively into her nightie.

Next the long golden hair was unpinned and fell in waves around Stella's shoulders.

Stella stood in front of Angela, a hair brush in her hand. As she talked she added shine to shine on that lovely hair.

How could anyone so beautiful, so absolutely beguiling in that delicate enticing nightie make another's heart feel so low!

Don't compete with Stella, Gilbert had warned. It was perhaps a certain feeling of hopelessness in comparison rather than an unkind envy that made Angela make a final decision as she sat on the bed.

She would not try to replace Stella in anybody's heart. Not even in Nellie's heart for it was clear that Nellie now had eyes and ears and talk for only one person. Stella Winton. Stella had swept the susceptible Nellie into a state of silent round-eyed adoration.

Even Angela could only sit on that bed and say:

"Stella, you are very beautiful."

Admiration might have been wrung from her heart but it was genuine, unalloyed, and honest. She had to say it.

Stella ceased sweeping her golden hair with her brush and sat down on the bed beside Angela.

"Darling girl," she said. "What's beauty compared with that?" With the handle of her brush she pointed to the gold wedding ring on Angela's finger.

Angela, knowing what that wedding ring really meant, flushed.

"If I had that on," said Stella, "Naroo Downs wouldn't this minute be cluttered up with all these people. Sweet Angela, do you know the opportunity you have to rule, with just that little circle of gold?"

"What do you mean? Gilbert is not a man to be ruled!"

Stella laughed.

"Don't I know! Mrs. Anstey certainly tried. But she couldn't win. I nearly married him myself just in order to get my own way with him."

"Then why didn't you?" asked Angela, also gravely.

Stella sighed.

"An absurd, out-dated sense of chivalry intervened." She made a wry face at Angela, then went on with mock sorrow. "A girl . . . I can't call her woman for she is too naïve . . . accidentally got herself talked about too much. Old Gilly, who has always had a touch of the Sir Galahad about him, couldn't permit that." Stella's tone changed again, this time to one of mock severity. "And he didn't like himself being talked about, either, I might add."

Her radiant smile came back unexpectedly.

"I haven't got a broken heart, child. Don't look so sad. It was his manganese I was after. I'll take Gilly too, like the proverbial pound of tea, if you'll . . ." Her smile faded and she looked straight into Angela's eyes. "If you'll throw in your weight on that option. What can be achieved on the nuptial couch is easier won than round the conference table, my sweet."

Angela was at least relieved to know that Stella thought there was a nuptial couch.

She was, nevertheless, astonished at this planned scheme put forward in Gilbert's own house.

"How do you take both the manganese and the pound of tea?" she asked out of sheer curiosity as to how Stella's mind worked.

Stella, sitting there beside her on the bed, began to brush her hair again.

"Sweet Angela," she said, "I have both ears and eyes too. You won Gilbert in a rather neat way but you regretted it before he even came good with a proposal. You fell for our friend Kevin Richards. And I know how that happened too. The first man to put his arms round a lonely girl's waist generally wins." She looked at Angela archly. "And he was the first, wasn't he? You have a very 'untouched' look about you, Angela, and I think the Kevin Richards incident was a case of heart winning in spite of the head ruling, wasn't it?"

Angela was silent from sheer surprise.

"On the whole you were very naïve, Angela, weren't you?"

"Yes," said Angela, thinking of how she had herself been a victim of Stella's charm. She had thought Stella really was a nice person while all the time it had been Kevin who had been right. Stella was designing, but oh, so very clever with it.

"Yes," agreed Angela thoughtfully. "I was rather naïve."

"And of course I was as much aware of that heart-to-heart

conversation you and Kevin were having on the veranda this afternoon as was Gilly," Stella went on, swishing the brush through her hair. "The solution is very simple. Win Gilly to that option idea and I'll take both it and him off your hands. You and Kevin will be rich for life for I'll see that you come in on a small partnership too. As a matter of fact you can make that a condition on Gilly yourself. I suppose you know that option is for ten thousand pounds? And if they take up the manganese itself there's three million in it?"

Angela ignored this last remark.

"Tell me, Stella," she said curiously. "How *could* you take Gilly off my hands?"

That magic word "Gilly" again. How catching it was when everyone else said it so glibly!

Stella stood up. She walked over to the mirror on the far wall. She threw the hair brush on to a chair and then flung back her head so that the wonderful long golden waves rippled down her back. She turned round and faced Angela and at the same time raised her arm lazily as if about to yawn.

"Dear child," she said. "*Look*, and work it out for yourself."

Yes, thought Angela, who had not moved from the bed. Gilly is a man like all other men, and who could resist *that*?

"I think I'll say good night," Angela said, standing up.

"You'll think it over, Angela?" Stella said, coming to the door with her.

"Yes, you may be sure of that," said Angela in a flat voice. "I'll think it over."

She crossed the passage into her own room. The door was ajar and the sweet scents of ferns hung gently on the air. Gilbert was sitting in a chair under the front window; a cigarette was in one hand and Redbella was in the other.

He leaned forward and put the flower back on the table. He stood up and turned to Angela.

"And what was Stella so interested in?" he asked. He was looking at her with grave unsmiling intent eyes.

"Manganese," said Angela.

"I asked you not to discuss that."

"I had no option. Stella discussed it."

"And you continued?" He took two steps forward as if to come close to her but he stopped short. Then abruptly he turned away and went to the veranda door. He stood in the opening, his back to Angela and the room.

"How much do you really want money, Angela?" he said in a harsh angry voice. "As I get to know you I cannot understand that you . . . *this Angela about the house* . . . is the same person who so adroitly saw that she married for security. And who now has even greater ambitions."

He broke off and turned round. He walked back across the room and took Angela's shoulders in his hands. He thrust her backwards a little so he could stare into her face.

"You did marry me for security, didn't you?"

Angela's face was very white.

"Yes," she said. "I told you at the time. Nellie was sick. You were angry. I might have lost my job."

He almost threw her away from him.

"Sick be damned," he said. "I've tried her out. She can stand up to anything."

"Is that what you were doing when you took her out? Trying her out? It wasn't from kindness?"

"No. I was trying to find out the right and the wrong of what you two girls were up to."

"I see," Angela said. She felt suddenly dreadfully weary. Poor Nellie! Gilbert and Stella had both won Nellie's heart but they had only been fooling her. It was all a sham.

"We shouldn't have married," Angela said, turning away to the small table by her bed. She began to take off her wrist-watch and then reluctantly, sadly, her wedding ring.

"I agree," said Gilbert. He walked to the door. He turned and stood with his back to it. "Since you've been here . . ." he began, then stopped. "That's the damn' stupid part of it," he went on. "I must have been mad. For four days I thought . . . Well, it doesn't matter what I thought. When I saw the look on your face when Kevin Richards was talking to you this afternoon, I knew I'd been wrong."

"You were wrong," said Angela. "Bitterly wrong. This afternoon, I mean."

Gilbert was too angry to follow her meaning.

"Of course a person such as myself doesn't fall in love in four days. I know that. I'm not a fool," he went on. "But I would like a settled home. Peace. I thought we might do it. I like . . ." He paused. Then from across the room he said quite softly, "I liked this room, Angela, and the thought of you in it. Do you think it's too late, even now, for us to accept one another's motives for what they are and leave it at that. To make some arrangement . . ."

"Without love?"

"Without love, if you like. I don't know what to call whatever it is between us."

"I'm not that kind of person, Gilbert."

There was a long silence.

"I see," he said at length. "Good night."

"Good night, Gilly."

It was only after he had gone through the door she realised she had used that name.

She stood by her bed, her eyes closed.

"Good night, Gilly," she said again to herself. It sounded strange. Strange, and something else she couldn't name. It made her feel as if she was a different person, someone years older than the girl who had driven into Red Gorge in a high-powered truck.

CHAPTER FIFTEEN

In the morning Mr. Hopkins and Kevin disappeared in the jeep with the geologist. Angela did not ask whether or why. She was very scrupulously not going to mind the manganese business, in spite of what Gilly thought and Stella desired.

Nellie, full of exuberant spirits, was dressed in her jeans and blouse and riding-boots. Angela did not have the heart to tell her those riding jaunts were probably over. Gilbert had found out all he wanted to find out about the Burns sisters. Angela's only interest, he thought, was in money and Nellie's only occupation was in being interesting and attracting attention by any means at hand. It was sickness if nothing else offered. As horse riding was offering at the moment; when falling dramatically from a horse . . . while her mentor cracked stock-whips . . . was occupying Nellie's attention. Alternatively there were the Sullivan brothers at Enmore Station, and Stella Winton a guest at this one.

In addition to the riding-outfit Nellie had put a lavish slash of lipstick on her mouth and had asked Mrs. Cummins if there was any peroxide in the house. She wanted to turn her hair into the same colour as Stella's hair.

Gilbert, dressed in his customary khaki drill riding-clothes and wearing the wide-brimmed hat that shaded the eyes from the brilliant sunlight, had gone down to the horse paddock by the time the rest of the household sat down to breakfast.

During that meal Stella kept Nellie entertained with accounts of her own riding experiences. Angela could see that Nellie now not only wanted to jump fences and mount a running horse as Gilbert did but she wanted to win the ladies' jumping events at the Royal Show. She saw herself sailing over the six-foot hurdles and the water jump as in imagination she saw Stella doing it in the past.

After breakfast Nellie helped Mrs. Cummins in the kitchen at such break-neck speed she dropped and broke a cup.

"Don't tell Gilbert when he comes up, will you?" she begged Angela later when she confessed. "No one's ever allowed to make even one little mistake with Gilbert."

"He's not so free from mistakes himself," said Angela with a touch of anger as she helped Nellie put the silver away in the dining-room.

Even Nellie, who was never accustomed to thinking of Angela first, stopped what she was doing and looked at her sister in concern. She had not expected to hear criticism of Gilbert from *Angela's* mouth.

"But you never make mistakes with him," Nellie said, almost accusingly. "You're *perfect*, Angela. I won't ever be like you, I know." This last she said with regret.

"No one is perfect and everyone makes mistakes," said Angela.

She shut the silver canteen and put it away in the cupboard of the sideboard. When she stood up her face was a little flushed.

"Try not to exaggerate, Nellie. That is your biggest mistake. You don't have to exaggerate, you know. You're interesting enough as a person without that. And sometimes people believe you. Then it is not you alone who suffers . . ."

"When did I say anything that hurt anyone else?" demanded Nellie indignantly.

Angela was rearranging the silver dishes on the sideboard and she did not turn round because she did not want to see that "wounded" expression on Nellie's face.

"When you told people on that ship coming up the coast that I was going to marry Gilbert," Angela said. "That hurt me, and it hurt Gilbert. That is one of the mistakes that Gilbert has made. He thinks I did say that, and at that time he had not met me."

"But he did marry you. And you wanted to marry him, didn't you, Angela? And how did you know I said that anyway?"

"Everyone on the ship knew that one of us said it, Nellie. Never mind about it now. It is all over. But it hurt." She shook her head at her sister. "Do try, please, Nellie, for all our sakes."

"But you like being married to him, Angela, don't you?"

"Yes, dear, very much." *Now who was exaggerating?*

"And you love him, don't you?"

"Of course I do, dear. Don't be silly. I love him very much." *The things we say to put the minds of children at rest!* "Now you can run along, Nellie. Oh, I forgot . . ."

"Forgot what?" Nellie asked dubiously. Somehow Angela's manner had been curiously unconvincing and Nellie felt an uneasy twinge in her conscience.

"I'm not sure Gilbert will take you riding to-day."

"Why not? Oh, I can hear him coming up now." She ran to the door and on to the veranda. "Gilly, Gilly! I'm going riding, aren't I?" she called.

Angela could not hear Gilbert's reply but she heard Nellie's voice. "Angela's gone bats this morning. She said she didn't think you would take me."

Angela fled through the other door into the passage and down to her own room. Once inside she shut the door and childishly put the chair against it. As soon as she realised what she had done she took the chair away again.

All the same she wouldn't answer if anyone knocked.

She made her bed and tidied up her room, putting things away so neatly she was alarmed at her own thoroughness. Nellie's words . . . "But you're perfect, Angela" . . . ran through her mind. A perfect person was not really the best person to bring up a young girl. Perhaps that was why she had failed with Nellie. She had unconsciously rebelled by falling down on the job on the strength, or weakness rather, of sickness.

Angela wished she had read a book on psychology. Perhaps that would have helped.

And, of course, she herself wasn't perfect. How much of her inner self had she hidden? It would have been better, and more human, to have shown her sister her own true faults, the inner longings and girlhood dreams which were no different from Nellie's surely. Nellie lived them, melodramatically, but Angela had dreamed them, also melodramatically. How would she have the courage to live them more honestly when she was with Nellie?

Well, she could begin by opening that door and facing the life that was going on in the homestead. Hiding wouldn't prove anything to anybody, not even herself.

Angela brushed her hair, giving a rueful smile as she remembered Stella's operations with a hair brush last night.

What, she wondered, was she going to do with Stella all day.

She kissed the tip of her finger and touched Redbella.

"Wish me luck," she said. "I've a long, long day to endure, but I'll do it with a smile just to take a leaf out of poor Nellie's copy-book."

She went down through the dining-room towards the kitchen. From the veranda she saw Gilbert and Nellie riding over the crest of the plain beyond the creek.

"Mistake number one that I've made. He did take her after all."

After she had spoken with Mrs. Cummins in the kitchen she fetched a hat and set off down the red roadway between the outhouses that formed the homestead environs. She was going to find out all she could about Naroo Downs. And live it. Go forward to meet life. *Another line out of Nellie's copy-book.*

Everywhere there were sounds of activity. The clang of steel in the smithy's shop, the clattering of iron in the windmill workhouse. The engine house delivered up a rhythmic hum and in the horse yards there were men running colts around on the end of leashes. Two men were loading wool bales on to a truck outside the woolshed and along the brow of a hill Angela could see some cattle moving in front of a man on horse-back. Down by the creek the lubras were hanging out their gaily coloured cottons on the bushes. She could hear their chatter and laughter from where she stood in the middle of the red dusty road.

Yes, it was a big place, and a busy place. No wonder Gilbert had enough on his hands without worrying about manganese too. And there were the asbestos mines operated from Red Gorge in addition.

Strange, but before she came here, Angela had never thought of a station as being a large and costly industrial unit. She had just thought of sheep and cattle and stockmen.

When she walked back towards the homestead garden she paused to stand in wonder again before the solar hot water plant. What a wonder was that! Almost as wonderful as satellites surely. Here a bright frame caught the rays of the sun and heated the water as it ran over it in black pipes. And regulated the heat too!

When she turned into the garden she saw Stella coming down the three steps of the veranda to meet her.

"Looking over your domain?" Stella asked with a friendly smile. Angela, gazing at that lovely face with the clear friendly blue eyes, forgave herself for being taken in by Stella. The deception was complete. There was no flaw in it.

"I've been looking over it," said Angela. "But I don't know if one would call it a 'domain.' It's very interesting, isn't it?"

"You must come over to Winderup sometime. It's like this, only we have more. A better homestead, for instance."

"I like this one," said Angela, hoping she did not sound defensive. If Stella had such a wonderful homestead why did she want more?

"Let's sit over here under the hibiscus," said Stella. "As soon as it gets too hot we'll have to go inside."

"You didn't go out with the geologist?" Angela said, politely complying with Stella's suggestion.

They sat on two weathered garden seats by a flat-topped stump of a tree that served as a table.

"They've only gone out to the camp to get the seismograph reports," said Stella. "It's a nasty trip, but at least they'll know before I do how deep the manganese is out there."

"And that is important?"

"Of course. They've been mapping it during the last week. Did you sound Gilly about that option last night, Angela? I meant to warn you to go about it subtly. Gilly is a canny brute . . ."

"But a naïve person is never subtle, surely?" asked Angela.

Stella laughed.

"I didn't hurt your feelings, did I? I'm sorry, Angela. You're really rather a sweet person, you know. And only a woman would see through you. A woman, if she goes about it the right way, can always pull the wool over a man's eyes. That's why Mrs. Anstey did everything but bring in machine-guns to keep me off the place. She, being a woman, *knew*. Gilly was going to be protected. Now tell me how Gilly reacted?"

"Gilbert will not discuss the manganese project with me, Stella. He wants to work that out for himself."

"But, my dear child, there are ways of getting at a man. Don't you understand . . .?"

"I'm afraid I don't understand the manganese thing at all. You tell me."

"It's as simple as A B C. You've worked in an office, you ought to know how these things go. There's stuff out there. Hopkins's company will pay a ten thousand pound sum down for the option over what covers Winderup and Naroo Downs. If the manganese is in there deep they'll *buy* the Mining Rights for three million pounds. Think of it, Angela. Three million. Think of what you could buy, dear girl."

"Who actually gets the three million?"

"Hopkins's company pays the three million and they've got to pay it to us. I want Gilly to take out a Mining Right in partnership with me. Hopkins wants that too. He doesn't want the Government to set up a competitive mining show, which they can legally do if Gilly doesn't take out the Right. The Government just keeps it."

"Why don't you take out a Mining Right by yourself, Stella?"

Stella took out a cigarette and lit it.

"The stuff on Winderup is surface stuff and costly to treat. Hopkins doesn't want it unless he can take the option on Naroo too. And the deep stuff is on Naroo boundary . . . where they've gone this morning."

"Why does Gilbert hesitate?"

"He's got enough money. He likes cattle. He can't stand the idea of big-time operations on his lease. On the other hand, he doesn't want to do me out of a big sum of money and he doesn't want to lose this State the opportunity of big capital from overseas being invested here. Got it all? The tug and pull are about equal. He's waiting for the reports to see just how much he would be depriving the State, and incidentally me, if he turns the proposition down."

"Fair enough," said Angela thoughtfully.

"What is fair enough?" asked Stella curiously. "That he should take it or turn it down?"

"That he should deliberate. It isn't a matter of being his own gain or loss. He has to make the decision to deprive others."

"Or make the decision to share with others."

"Or share with others," conceded Angela. She looked up at Stella again. "And Aunt Kara didn't want it?"

"Aunt Kara, as you call her, didn't want Gilly to marry me," Stella said with a laugh.

"You are very frank, Stella," said Angela. "Am I allowed to know why she didn't want that?"

Stella really laughed this time.

"Do I look the kind of person who would have been run by the Aunt Karas of the world?" she said. "No, my dear Angela, there would have been only one woman on Naroo Downs if I had married Gilly, and Aunt Kara knew very well who that would be."

Angela was very thoughtful for a minute.

"I don't think I can do anything to help you, Stella," she said at length. Then she added, "I think that the reason why Gilbert doesn't want to talk with me about it is because he may be just a little tired of women attempting to direct his life. This time, with this woman, he means it to be the other way round."

"Very shrewd, my little Angela. Not so naïve after all. Nevertheless you don't love Gilbert and I've put a fairly good proposition before your innocent business-like eyes. Help me pull off this deal and I'll take Gilly, and his affairs, off your hands."

"Supposing I don't want the proposition either? And that I don't want Gilbert taken off my hands?"

Stella drew in a breath. The blue eyes once again had that cold Arctic look that Angela had noticed on the first night she had met Stella.

"Careful, Angela," Stella said softly. "I may take him willy-nilly. Just to teach little girls not to play with millions . . . carelessly."

"You are very confident," Angela said after a long silence.

Stella's laugh was clear and natural once again. Her eyes were friendly. She was just a nice person.

"Look at me," she said. "And when you go inside, look in the looking-glass. Also don't forget I have the know-how. I've played that sort of game before."

"How?" asked Angela curiously.

"Winderup," said Stella. "I got it from a second cousin. He broke his heart and went away. Do you want the details?"

"No thank you," said Angela politely.

"Don't think you'll spike my guns by warning Gilly. You'd be surprised how much attraction that sort of thing adds to a woman in a man's eyes. And in any case, I hold the ace of trumps, Angela. I know a thing or two about you that Gilly wouldn't like to hear."

"For instance?"

"Your announcement on the ship that you intended to marry Gilly . . . before he had any such intention himself. Add to that a romantic meeting each night with Kevin Richards, while you were in Red Gorge, and *after* you had announced the fact you were going to marry Gilbert Lawrence of Naroo Downs. In brief, you were playing two men, Angela. Something not liked, when it's found out, by either man. You stand to lose them both."

"I see," said Angela. She stood up. "Shall we go up to the house now? It is about time for morning tea and my walk gave me quite a thirst."

Stella stood up gracefully. She straightened herself, throwing back her head as she did so, and drew in a deep breath.

"Gorgeous smell of wild hibiscus," she said gaily. "Don't you love it?"

Angela was wise enough to know that Stella's remark had been an excuse to make a gesture with open arms and head thrown back that would once again draw attention to her lovely figure, the curves of her throat and the sheer danger of her beauty.

Stella picked one of the pale mauve flowers and playfully tucked it behind Angela's ear.

"There you are, my sweet," she said. "Now, go in and win. Don't forget you get a man and a big sum of money out of this. If you lose . . ." Stella shook her head ruefully. "No man and no money. Heavens, what a catastrophe for little Nellie!"

Angela wondered why she felt so calm and unmoved. It was probably because she still couldn't quite believe that anyone as natural and charming as Stella Winton could be so unscrupulous.

Mrs. Cummins brought them tea on the veranda and they chatted idly as if nothing had happened. Angela hadn't any idea what she herself would do next but of one thing she was quite certain. She was never voluntarily going to mention the subject of manganese to Gilbert.

She did not think it was the least bit necessary to mention this to Stella Winton.

Nellie, for whom Stella Winton shook her head so dolefully, was not enjoying her riding lesson. Nothing dramatic like falling off, or even pretending to be about to fall off, happened.

The trouble was that Gilbert was setting too slow a pace. As he always took the lead, Nellie could not stage a gallop away from him.

Also he was thoughtful and silent, giving no instruction this morning. Nellie found it altogether boring.

She let her hat fall off.

"Gilly," she wailed, "I've lost my hat."

Gilbert reined in. He turned in his saddle.

"Then ride back and get it," he said. "You'll get sunstroke again without your hat in this sun."

Nellie had at least caught his attention. One thing Gilbert was adamant about. A hat had to be worn on all occasions in the sun.

Nellie wished she had ridden farther before she announced her loss, then she could have ridden back out of sight and pretended to get lost. As it was, her hat was showing a white blob on the side of the track.

If Gilbert were a gentleman, she thought, he would get her hat for her. As it was, he sat as if he was glued to his horse and let her get it for herself. It would serve him right if she did have a bad accident while out riding with him. How would he look if he had to carry her back wounded and unconscious, and confront Angela with a lifeless body?

So engrossed was Nellie in these thoughts that she failed to free one foot from the stirrup as her weight came over the saddle in the act of dismounting.

Her horse, disliking the awkwardness, reared slightly. Nellie fell to the ground on her back and her foot was still caught in the stirrup. The horse plunged forward.

"*Steady!*" came Gilbert's voice in command.

The horse, obedient, stood motionless while Gilbert galloped up. He was off his own horse before it had ceased to move and in less time than it took Nellie to blink her eyes he had one hand on her horse's mane and one hand on her foot where it hung twisted in the stirrup.

"All right, Boy, steady," said Gilbert again in a voice quiet with authority.

The horse froze into a stone statue. Gilbert bent and carefully released Nellie's foot from the stirrup.

"Move, Boy."

The horse moved forward a few paces. Gilbert lowered Nellie's foot to the ground. She lay on her back, watching him. When he had touched her foot her face had gone white. When he lowered it to the ground she shut her eyes and gritted her teeth but she did not utter a sound.

Gilbert knelt down beside her and examined the foot.

"That's not so good, Nellie," he said. He shook his head.

"I'll have to cut away that nice, very elegant, boot." He looked down at her. "I'm going to lift you up and carry you over to that clump of trees. It will be cooler there. How about it?"

Nellie nodded. He stooped, gathered her up carefully and carried her in his arms to the tree shade. Then with unexpected tenderness he set her down, her back to a tree.

"How's that?" he asked. "Comfortable?"

Again Nellie nodded. The pain in her ankle was excruciating but somehow she didn't want to make a fuss about it. Intuitively she knew that Gilbert would never make a fuss if he were injured. What he could bear, she could bear.

And she loved him being so nice to her this way. He hadn't roared at her for losing her hat, and worse, for dismounting carelessly. He was just being kind. And he had a gorgeous smile. She'd never noticed Gilbert's smile before. She couldn't remember seeing him smile at all. Or hadn't she been looking at the right time?

As he took a jack-knife from his pocket and knelt beside her and with delicate gentle strokes began to cut away the leather of her riding-boot, she found herself watching for that smile. Every now and again he looked up at her. First there was a query in his eyes and then when she nodded he smiled.

"Golly," she thought. "Angela must be mad about him!" Little thrills of excitement went up her spine as she thought of Angela being able to look at him as often as she liked when he smiled. And he'd smile an awful lot for Angela. He'd love her, wouldn't he?

Angela had said he made mistakes. He was hurt because of that silly rumour on the boat . . . the one she, Nellie, had set going just to make that silly stewardess pay her some attention. She *had* paid attention, too. She'd stopped treating Nellie as if she were no more than a silly ignorant schoolgirl. She had started straight away treating her as "Miss Burns of Naroo Downs." She'd even called her that several times.

"Gilly," said Nelly contritely. "I dropped my hat on purpose."

He nodded his head.

"I know," he said as he began carefully to loosen the remnants of the boot.

"You didn't growl at me."

"I used to do something like that myself when I was a boy. Just to get Aunt Kara's attention."

"Did you really?"

"Yes. She whacked it out of me." He turned round. "That hurt much, Nellie? You've got a whopper of a swelling there. Want to look at it?"

Nellie liked looking at his smile best but she thought her ankle might be interesting too.

The swelling was coming up even as she looked at it.

"It's a beaut, isn't it?" said Gilbert.

"Why don't you growl at me?" asked Nellie.

"You've had all the whacking you need, young Nellie. Now you're entitled to be interesting."

"Is that what you were doing when you growled at me? Whacking me? Like Aunt Kara used to do to you?"

"She did hers with a stick," said Gilbert. He was sitting back on his heels looking at Nellie as he spoke.

"I bet you never did things as bad as I've done," said Nellie.

"You start first and tell me. Then I'll tell you."

Nellie looked at him with grave eyes.

"I told everyone on the ship Angela was going to marry you. Angela didn't say it at all."

The near-smile on Gilbert's face gradually froze away.

"Go on, Nellie," he said quietly. "Tell me some more."

"Angela said that was fairy stuff dreamed up by Aunt Kara and I was never to mention it. She said she wasn't even likely to meet you."

"I see. And why did you say it, Nellie?"

"I wanted people to take notice of me. And Angela, too. Angela was so shy and nervous. She wasn't having any fun. We were lost really and didn't know where to go. Red Gorge was the only place in Western Australia we'd heard of so Angela just sort of went on there. She didn't want me to know we hadn't anywhere to go so she pretended. So I pretended too."

"And who was the best at pretending, Nellie?"

"I was. You can always tell with Angela because she gets a sort of anxious look in her eyes. She had it this morning."

"Why did she have it this morning?"

"Because she loves people and she's shy. I don't think she knows how to say it. She just shows it by doing things for them. You don't let her *do* things for you much, Gilly."

Gilbert picked up a leaf twig and flicked away a sergeant ant that was creeping dangerously near Nellie. His face suddenly looked drawn.

"Are you going to whack me, Gilbert?" Nellie asked.

"Not this time," he said, shaking his head. He looked back at her and the shadow of that smile came back into his eyes. "You're really, truly interesting this time, Nellie. So I don't have to whack."

"I asked all the people to the wedding, too," said Nellie. "I wanted Angela to have a lovely wedding. Me too."

There was a long silence.

"Now you tell one," said Nellie.

"I used to say there was a big snake down by the creek to frighten everybody. After a while they didn't take any notice of me but one day I did see one. And they wouldn't take any notice . . ."

"What happened?"

"A little black boy got bitten."

"Did he die?"

"No, but he very nearly did."

"Did Aunt Kara whack you?"

"With a stick as big as the snake, and for a long time. But I never did that sort of thing again, Nellie. It was a lesson to me."

"Me, too," said Nellie soberly.

"You mean that?" asked Gilbert, looking into her eyes.

Nellie nodded.

"Cross my heart," she said.

Gilbert stood up and straightened himself. Then he bent down and scooped Nellie up in his arms. She put her own arms round his neck, hiding from him her wince of pain.

"Smile again, Gilly," she said. "I like you best when you smile."

He really smiled this time and Nellie giggled, then nuzzled her head against his shoulder.

"I love you," she said.

"I'm keen on you too, Nellie. Shall we call off all whackings?"

"For keeps?"

"For keeps."

CHAPTER SIXTEEN

When later in the morning Gilbert carried Nellie into the homestead it was to confront a white-faced Angela.

"You let her fall off," she said tight-lipped.

"No, he didn't," said Nellie, so quick to Gilbert's defence that Angela looked startled. "I did it all myself."

Over Nellie's head Gilbert looked at Angela with more expression in his eyes than she had ever seen. He, too, seemed lost for words. Now there was in the look on his face a touch of remorse and something else, very impersonal, which Angela could not interpret. She turned aside and led the way into the homestead and to Nellie's room. Gilbert followed with Nellie and placed her gently on her bed. With great care he bent over her and straightened her legs.

"Alternate cold and hot water for that swelling, I'm afraid, Nellie. It will be painful but healing. I think you can stand it. Yes?"

Angela saw this exchange of comradely glances between them and her own heart twisted painfully at the new Gilbert she saw being so kind and encouraging to her thirteen-year-old sister. She didn't know how to express her gratitude for that without betraying the emotion in her voice so she spoke only to Nellie.

"Darling, I'll get the bowls of water. Mrs. Cummins will get you some tea too."

She hurried from the room without looking again at Gilbert.

"You see? She just *does* things," said Nellie. "Actually, she's having a million fits because I'm injured."

"Yes, I see," said Gilbert. "I think I'd better go and help with those bowls of water."

"No, please, Gilly. Just let Angela do it. She'll be happier that way. And I'll tell her how it was my fault and that I'm not going to be naughty any more. I'm not even going to peroxide my hair to look like Stella either. I'll just stay the way I am."

Gilbert rumpled Nellie's hair.

"I'll tell you a secret," he said. "I like light brown hair as worn by a lady in a famous song, and the two Burns sisters."

"Truly? But Stella's hair . . ."

"Suits Stella but not Angela or Nellie."

He went to the door, turned and lifted his hand, the forefinger and thumb making the sign of a circle. Nellie had been in Australia long enough to know that as a victory sign. She made a circle with her own fingers and smiled back at him from the bed.

On the front veranda Stella was reclining back in a cane chair, one knee crossed over the other, one foot pointing casually into the air.

"Sit down, Gilly," she said. "I've news for you."

There was an arresting note in Stella's voice and Gilbert, after a moment's hesitation, sat down. He took out his cigarettes and offered one to Stella and then took one himself. He lit them, leaning forward as he did so and not looking at Stella as he put the match to her cigarette.

"I saw you carrying in the accident case," said Stella. "I didn't come to your rescue. That sort of thing is more Angela's line than mine. And I can't stand sick people."

Gilbert said nothing and Stella paused. She looked at him curiously.

"You certainly took on something when you took on that pair," she added.

Gilbert stretched his legs out in front of him and half closed his eyes as he looked out into the blinding light of the midday sun. His eyes were no more than slits.

"Was that the news you had for me, Stella?"

"No. The seismograph chart had been completed by the men at the boundary camp in our absence . . . your absence getting married and mine taking a fashion jaunt down south. One of the boys came in with it. He passed Hopkins and company on their way out there. They're coming back."

"And can you read a seismograph chart, Stella?"

"I didn't have to do that. The boy told me the gist of it."

He sat still, legs stretched before him, his narrowed eyes watching a cloud of dust that was heralding the approach of a vehicle along the track from the north.

"The manganese is in scattered lodes. There's no widespread area of it at any depth. Surface stuff only. Costly to treat and so of no great commercial value. That make you happy?"

Gilbert expelled a long breath of cigarette smoke. He removed his eyes from the dust cloud that was materialising into the jeep bringing back the geologist and his party.

"For your sake I'm sorry, Stella. But for mine, very relieved."

Stella twisted one nylon-clad ankle in the air. She examined the slim tapered toe, one of a lovely pair of white shoes.

"We had the pleasure of Hopkins's company out of the venture anyway," she said with a laugh.

"He is an unusual man," Gilbert conceded.

"Tell me, Gilly," said Stella casually, herself now looking

out to the approaching jeep. "What would you have done if the big stuff had been there?"

"I haven't the faintest idea. I always cross my bridges when I come to them. Not before."

"I wish to God I had your patience," concluded Stella.

They sat in a thoughtful silence for a long time and Stella who had finished her cigarette and ground it out in the ash-tray asked for another. Gilbert gave it to her. This time as he lit her cigarette he looked straight into her eyes.

"I hope this little fiasco won't affect our friendship—as between neighbours," he said with a conciliatory smile.

Stella shrugged.

She watched the jeep at the bottom of the red road that ran between the outbuildings of the homestead area disgorge its three passengers. Hopkins went with Smart the geologist into the storekeeper's house where a temporary office had been set up. Kevin Richards came on up the dusty road in the direction of the homestead garden.

"Your real problem is just coming up the stretch," Stella said, watching Kevin. "Does it appear to you, Gilly—having appeased the tyrant convention—that you might be doing two people a kindness by releasing Angela from this rather silly marriage?"

Gilbert's face froze and his mouth tightened into a grim line.

"What I have is mine," he said. Then he looked at Stella. "You ought to know that better than anyone, Stella. You have tried often enough with those Rights on the boundary."

Stella laughed.

"Your Aunt Kara was a tyrant," she said. "But I think she met more than her match in you. What a good job, in the interests of the cold war between you, you both had the same feelings about that manganese. Oh, well . . ."

She yawned and stretched lazily.

"It was Angela I was thinking about," she said as she rose slowly and patted down the creases in her linen skirt. She looked at Gilbert out of friendly eyes. "She is a young woman, with human feelings, just like the rest of us. She's rather sweet and I like her. I'd like to see her happy. Well, here comes Lothario and he hasn't got enough money to interest me. I'll leave him to your tender mercies."

She went to the doorway into the homestead and then made her parting shot.

"Hopkins is the man of the moment for me," she said.

" There's more than manganese on Winderup. Ilmenite, topaz, zircon. Who knows? I might bring down the lion yet."

Kevin Richards came up the three steps on to the veranda.

" You've heard the news?" he asked.

" Yes," said Gilly. " I think it calls for drinks. Are Hopkins and Smart coming up?"

" Shortly. Meantime I'd like to borrow Angela. Is she about? No, I won't sit down, thanks, I've a bucket of paper work to do to get those reports back to the mine office."

" Angela is attending to Nellie. Nellie has sprained her ankle."

" You been cracking stock-whips again?" asked Kevin with a grin. He was not abashed by Gilbert's cold silence.

" If you'll excuse me I'll go in search of Angela. I think I can wean her away from Nellie's side," Kevin said.

He went into the homestead.

Gilbert stood up and walked down the steps into the garden. He turned on an area of reticulation that watered the shrubs. Slowly he went back to the veranda. As he reached the top steps Angela, carrying her hat in her hand, came out of the front door with Kevin.

" Nellie's all right. I've bound her ankle," she said to Gilbert. " She's feeling sleepy so I think it is quite all right to leave her for an hour or two. Kevin needs my help."

" Then if Kevin needs you . . ." said Gilbert, looking searchingly into her face.

" Oh, he does," said Angela, avoiding meeting his eyes. All the time she had been attending to Nellie she had listened to Nellie's rapturous account of Gilbert's kindness. And she couldn't forget the look in Gilbert's eyes when he had carried Nellie in; and his kindness and compassion when he had lain the young girl on her bed.

Angela was afraid to look at Gilbert now for fear he read that knowledge in her own eyes, and the deep way in which it had affected her.

" If you don't mind I won't be here for lunch," she finished lamely. " Kevin said the storekeeper will give us a snack. We've quite a lot to do and I'd like to be back here when Nellie wakes up."

Kevin picked Angela's hat out of her hand with his forefinger and thumb and dropped it on top of her head.

" Words, idle words," he said. " Come on, Sweetie Pie, we're wasting precious hours. Nay, even minutes matter between me and thee."

"Thee and me," corrected Angela, pulling her hat on properly. She offered Gilbert a half-veiled, half-rueful smile and went down the steps and through the garden with Kevin.

Gilbert sat down in the chair, took out another cigarette and lit it. He remained looking through slitted eyes out across the plain.

"You see," Kevin was saying as he and Angela walked down the road to the storekeeper's office. "The storekeeper has got this old typewriter. A hell of a job really but I think you can make it go. Get that report off for me, sweet Angela, and I can get it all checked and signed etc., etc., by the geologist. The wool truck is heading for Red Gorge to-night. Then we don't have to travel in the hot sun of noon to-morrow. Understand? You will have my eternal gratitude."

Angela nodded.

"Of course I'll do it for you," Angela said. "And please don't be grateful, Kevin. I'd do that and more for you."

"Would you, indeed?"

"I'll never forget how kind you were to me in my first two days in Red Gorge. And when I came down to the mine office to get a job. You could never understand what it felt like. I was a stranger. I knew no one . . ."

"I had a low-down ulterior motive," said Kevin, rubbing his chin. He glanced sideways at Angela. "Want the bitter truth?"

"Yes, you might as well tell me."

"That first night in the hotel. You were the niftiest-looking piece of peach bloom that had ever arrived to compete with our sun-tanned girlies up here in the north. And Janette . . . you know . . . Janette Wells? She would keep playing off all her other boy friends against me. So I thought two could play at that game."

"Oh!" said Angela, looking at him, shocked.

They were in the middle of the road outside the storekeeper's office.

Kevin stopped and shook a finger at Angela.

"Don't get me wrong, Angela. I fell for you quite hard. I had a pretty bad time of it. Two loves! The old and the new! Which? You've no idea what sort of a fix that puts a man in. Janette seemed to settle it for me by giving me the extra hard brush-off and going out with those other two Lancelots. Then in walked Gilly Lawrence and I'd got neither. See what I mean?"

Angela nodded her head gravely. Then suddenly she burst out laughing.

"Oh, Kevin! What a pair we were! Isn't love a terrible thing really?"

"Well, it's all turned out okay now. You've got Gilly right round your little finger and Janette now says she'll have me. See why the hurry back to Red Gorge? I've got to nip that little bird right into a matrimonial cage before she sees someone else better looking than I am."

Angela had blinked her eyes when Kevin had said that about Gilly being right round her little finger. It would make Kevin happier to believe that. She let it pass and instead smiled at him.

"I do love you in a way, Kevin," she said. "You're so delightfully and slangily frank."

"Good. You'll be the first godmother on the list. Shall we shake on it?"

They stood there in the blazing hot sunshine clasping one another's hands and smiling. Kevin leaned forward and kissed Angela on the forehead.

"That's for ever!" he said.

Angela put up her free hand and drew his head down and kissed him on the brow too.

"Same for me," she said. It was with a half-sad thought she recollected Kevin was the only man she had ever kissed.

Up on the homestead veranda Gilbert Lawrence watched them take hands and, in spite of the heat, run into the storekeeper's office like a couple of children.

"Do you mind if I shake the dust of Naroo Downs off my feet later this afternoon, Gilly?" said Stella, leaning through her bedroom window. It opened on to the front veranda near the table where Gilbert sat. "I might even take Hopkins with me, if I can interest him in ilmenite, topaz, or zircon."

"Taking Hopkins off my hands will be a blessing," said Gilbert without turning round in his chair. "I'm sorry Naroo Downs is so inhospitable, Stella."

"I have a temporary mood about it," she replied. "Doubtless I'll get over it. It will give you breathing space to resolve the matter of that little duet down by the store office."

Gilbert had known that Stella had seen from her bedroom window what he had seen from the cane chair on the veranda. He made no comment.

"Don't tell me what you have is yours," laughed Stella. "If I read Angela's soft heart right you'll need more than money and good looks, Gilly. She's got that awful thing called 'integrity.'"

"I know that," said Gilbert.

"My share as well as her own," said Stella. "Supposing I ask Mrs. Cummins to bring us a tray of drinks? I see Hopkins and Smart on their diplomatic way to call on you. They might as well drown their sorrows and I might as well get up some pep to beguile Hopkins."

"I'll get the drinks," said Gilbert, getting up from his chair. "I see you're bent on gilding the lily. You've met your match in Hopkins. I think he is a downy bird, Stella."

"More zest to the hunt," said Stella and withdrew her golden head between the muslin curtains of her window. Gilbert went inside to get the drinks.

At sundown the homestead stood silent in the brooding stillness of the evening. The last of the shadows had gone from the trees along the creek bed and the western sky waved its last crimson banner for the day. The bougainvillaeas were etched in graceful festoons against it.

The cockatoos were crowning the ghost gums at the bottom of the homestead road like white flowers. A goanna raced across the red road heading for its hole in the creek bed. Down in the waterhole a fish jumped and circles eddied in the water until they washed with a gentle lap against the banks. A lubra was singing an aboriginal song as she brought in the washing.

On the north track leading out of Naroo Downs was a dust haze left by Stella Winton's departing car. True to her word, she had taken Hopkins with her.

Kevin Richards had made his farewells and was keeping company with the truck drivers who might leave with the wool clip at any hour after dark. Smart, the geologist, was secluded with his maps and his figures in the store office. He too wanted to finish up and be away as soon as possible.

Mrs. Cummins basted the roast beef in the kitchen while Gilbert sat on the front veranda and sipped his "sundowner."

Angela had come up from the store office only a few minutes earlier. She had gone straight in to see Nellie and when she found that her sister was both happy and comfortable she went to have a shower and change her dress for dinner.

She felt unaccountably nervous now that she was alone again in the homestead with Gilbert. Only now she realised that the company had been a support. She had been reluctant to say good-bye to Kevin for she felt she was losing a friend. She had enjoyed her afternoon's work at the typewriter with Kevin. It took her mind off Gilbert, and that look of tenderness and compassion he had had on his face when he had lain Nellie down on her bed. It had revealed a different man, one that caused her own heart to flip dangerously.

It had opened up whole avenues of conjecture as to Gilbert's real nature. What was he really like behind that hard walled exterior?

His potential for kindness and tenderness suddenly became more frightening than his frigid formality.

She put on the white dress, splashed with gold roses, which she had worn the night she had first had dinner with Gilbert in the Red Gorge Hotel. It was the dress that Nellie called "Angela's dress with the golden roses." It gave Angela confidence. Her little black suède shoes gave her confidence too, and so did the tiny touch of perfume on her lace handkerchief. Redbella seemed to approve of this dressing up and that gave Angela even more confidence.

"I don't feel such a 'stray,'" she confided to the red flower, and she was quite sure Redbella nodded her head in agreement.

Before she went to dinner Angela went in to see Nellie again.

"Oh, Angela! You've got on your golden dress. You do look scrumptious."

"Do I? Not too dressed up?" asked Angela, suddenly anxious.

"'Course not," said Nellie. "Do you know what that man Mr. Hopkins said to me? He said . . . 'If I had a million dollars I'd put them all on my wife's back. But mind you, I'd expect her to look like it.' Wasn't that funny?"

"He says some very sagacious things," said Angela, brushing back Nellie's hair from her face. "I don't think Gilbert will mind if you lie out on the lounge on the veranda after dinner, dear. You seem to get on so well together now and it's very hot in here."

"I'm not coming," said Nellie firmly. "I'll have Gilbert in the mornings. You can have him at nights. Besides, I find lovers stuffy."

"Thank you. And what about Messrs. Sam and Bob Sullivan of Enmore?"

"Gilly talked to them on the transceiver for me this afternoon," said Nellie with a sly smile. "Did he tell you? I'm going over there next week to recuperate. That's a big word, isn't it? But Gilbert told me what it meant."

"He didn't tell me," said Angela startled. "I mean about Enmore."

"He will," said Nellie, nodding her head. "He does things his own way. But then it's a nice way."

"You must have won his heart," said Angela gratefully. "He is going out of his way to do things to make you happy."

"It's for you as much as me. He wants to be alone in the homestead with you."

"With me?" said Angela startled. Her old nervousness came back. But then she'd been alone with Gilbert last week-end, after their marriage! It hadn't been frightening then. It had been peaceful. Yes, peaceful. Gilbert had liked it!

"And Mrs. Cummins is coming too," Nellie finished with a flourish. "For three days. Gilbert said so."

Angela's heart raced into a panic of speed.

"Oh, Nellie," she said, then pulled herself together. "I must go and have dinner now. Mrs. Cummins will bring a tray to you." She fled from what further alarming pieces of intelligence Nellie might have to impart.

What could it mean? Nothing, of course. It was just Gilbert and his quest for peace and quiet. This week-end of rest had been stolen from him in the matter of the manganese. Now he would fix the calendar to suit himself. He was going to make a week-end of Monday and Tuesday to make up for lost time.

"Tell Gilly I want him after dinner. *By himself,*" called Nellie after her. "I've got something special to tell him."

Gilbert coming down the passage heard her and he put his head in the door.

"Five minutes between dessert and coffee, Nellie," he said. "Will that cover it?"

"Less," whispered Nellie conspiratorially. She held up a circled finger and thumb as a sign.

Gilbert replied with the same signal.

Dinner was not such a stilted affair as Angela feared. Gilbert talked to her a little of the failure of the manganese project and of his own relief.

"I've all the money I want," he said quietly. "I was concerned for Stella and of course it is in the State's interest to attract outside capital. I had a duty to Stella as my neighbour, and the state as my country. It would have been a hard decision to make if the stuff had been there at consistent depths."

"I see," said Angela quietly. "I'm glad you told me. I'm afraid Stella will be disappointed."

"Not really," said Gilbert. He looked up as he went on. "Stella is very fond of money but fonder still of playing around with big business. She is a woman of quite considerable financial ability and she likes to match her wits. Now she's got the wits of Mr. Hopkins to preoccupy her."

"I think he might know, or guess . . ."

"Quite, but he's a man for all that. He likes beautiful women as well as high finance. And someone like Stella, who has both brains and beauty, would be a pleasant partner."

"Do you *mind*, Gilbert?"

He looked at her in surprise.

"Why should I mind?" he asked. "Stella without occupation is an annoying neighbour. With plenty on her hands she keeps out of mischief. My mischief, anyway."

"Your mischief?" asked Angela puzzled.

"My manganese mischief if you like to put it that way."

"Oh!"

Gilbert had opened a bottle of white wine for their dinner. He now added a little to Angela's glass.

"Shall we drink to peace and quiet, Angela?" he asked and raised his glass, looking at her over the top of it.

It brought an unexpected flush to Angela's cheek. She thought of that moment last night in her room with Redbella looking on and the scent from the potted flowers and ferns pervading the room. Was this going to happen again? Love without love?

She lowered her eyelids to hide her anxiety as she raised her glass and sipped the wine.

There was no court of appeal. She had married him. She would have to take the consequences.

If only he felt for her that terrible burgeoning in the heart that she was beginning to feel for him!

After dinner Angela went down the passage to the darkened veranda alone, leaving Nellie and Gilbert to their conference. If there was one thing that lightened her heart it was this unexpected friendship and understanding that had sprung up between them. She felt almost tearful with gratitude to Nellie for somehow having accomplished it.

When Gilbert came into her room Nellie jumped in her bed and then gave a small screech of woe as her painful ankle responded with a sharp reminder that injured girls stay still in their beds.

"She's got on her dress with the golden roses," whispered Nellie. "It means she's nervous and she wants to look nice. She's doing it for you, Gilly. When Angela does things . . ."

"Don't talk about your sister in her absence," said Gilbert sternly. "And Angela's always doing things. She sponged and bound your foot for you. And she worked at typewriting for Kevin Richards all the afternoon."

"Pooh, *him!*" said Nellie pouting. "He's going to marry Janette Wells, and he wanted to get back to Red Gorge in a hurry."

Gilbert was standing by Nellie's bed. He looked down at her, his face suddenly remote, the old veiled look back in his eyes.

"Who told you that, Nellie? You're not exaggerating again?"

"I said I never would exaggerate again," said Nellie crossly. "You're not fair to say so. Angela told me. You ask her. Kevin told her and she told me before she went to have her bath. She said Kevin had grown an extra size in hats and Angela is to be the first godmother. She's thrilled to bits . . ."

"About what? Kevin being married?"

"Yes, and about being a godmother too. Kevin was Angela's first friend and best friend in Red Gorge, except Mrs. Smith at the hotel, of course."

"Friend?" said Gilbert quietly. "Is that what he was?"

"Of course. He got Angela the job down in the mine office. That's why she's grateful. That's why she did his typing for him. I told you. Angela *does* things . . . she can't *say* them."

"Nellie, would you like a horse of your own to ride? And a slice of the moon?"

"Now I know you're joking."

"Not about the horse anyway." He leaned forward and pushed his fingers through her hair. "I don't know what I'd do without you, Nellie," he said.

He went to the door. Once again they exchanged that signal —a thumb and forefinger making a circle in the air. They were conspirators.

He went down the passage with a tread that made Nellie cock her head and ask herself . . . "I wonder what's got into him?" Then she smiled wisely. "I know. It's the dress with the golden roses!"

Gilbert walked out on to the veranda. It was not quite so

dark now, behind those clustered creepers, for a new moon was rising in the east.

Gilbert stood by Angela's chair and held out his hand. It was a strangely compelling gesture and Angela found herself putting up her own hand. Gilbert took it, and holding it so she could never release it drew her up to her feet.

"The coffee can wait," he said. "There's a new moon rising. Angela, I love you."

"*Gilbert!*"

She tried to pull her hand away but he held it too firmly. He drew her against his body, his hand releasing hers only to put his arms around her. He held her imprisoned, her body rigid against his.

"Say '*I love you*,' Angela. Say it and learn to believe it," he said roughly into her ear. His face was pressed against her cheek as he bent his head and somehow forced back her own head. It hurt her.

"Say '*I love you*,' Angela." He could feel her tenseness. She shivered. "Don't just do things for people, sweetheart. Say them too. Say '*I love you*,'" he commanded again.

She felt as if he would break her in two.

Suddenly, all her resistance slackened and seeped away. Her body of its own accord surrendered to him, softly, like a quiet and glorious defeat.

"I . . ." But the words, long cabined in her heart, would not come. Instead she turned her head a little and her lips met his lips.

Whatever she had dreamed in the years of her lonely girlhood, she had not known that love was like this. This tall stern silent man was kissing her with a love and passion that overwhelmed her.

"Put Redbella out where she belongs," he said. "Put her out with the other flowers." He held her away from him but neither could see very much except the pale shadow of their faces in the moon and starlight that was filtering through the vines. "Because," he said, "I'm coming in."

Again she tried to say something and failed. Instead she went back into his arms and buried her face in his shoulder.

Aunt Kara had brought them, Angela and Nellie, safely to harbour at last.

Neither of them noticed that Mrs. Cummins had decided this was not the right moment to bring the coffee. Instead she went back down the passage and shared it with Nellie.

Nellie was planning a dress with golden roses for herself. That would bring the Sullivan brothers to their knees, she told Mrs. Cummins, for sure!

Out on the veranda as the new moon came up in the eastern sky Gilbert still held Angela in his arms. Neither had yet found their voices, and there was time enough later for explanations. Love and desire were explanation enough for the moment.

THE END

ALSO AVAILABLE IN FONTANA BOOKS

SMOULDERING FIRE

D. E. Stevenson

In the romantic setting of loch, mountain and ruined castle this popular woman's author weaves a delightful story around the startling happenings at Ardfalloch Glen.

WINTER AND ROUGH WEATHER

D. E. Stevenson

James and Rhoda Johnstone return from their honeymoon to their hill-farm on the Scottish Borders—and to the dramas of their many neighbours . . . "Miss Stevenson knows just how to draw a full measure of amusement from every situation." *Scotsman*

BRIEF SUMMER

Mavis Heath-Miller

The charming story of what befalls Jo and her fiancé one brief summer when a famous actress and her brother come to stay in the village . . .

RETREAT FROM LOVE

Maysie Grieg

Ann had to become a model in order to get to the bottom of her family's unhappiness—and becomes deeply involved in the world of fashion and its strange personalities . .

ALSO AVAILABLE IN FONTANA BOOKS

KATE HARDY

D. E. Stevenson

An attractive young woman novelist finds a world of rivalries beneath the surface calm of Old Quinings . . . "Charming, true and sincere." *Observer*

THE BLUE SAPPHIRE

D. E. Stevenson

"A romantic and delightful novel about likeable people . . . I was sorry to part with Julia when the book came to an end." *Evening News* "Miss Stevenson writes of London life with authority and charm." *Books of the Month*

TAKE THREE DOCTORS

Elizabeth Seifert

A raging fire . . . a serious epidemic . . . three men have to face catastrophe in order to find themselves.

LEGACY FOR A DOCTOR

Elizabeth Seifert

Behind Charlotte were years in an orphanage, and an unhappy girlhood with a jealous spinster . . . ahead lay the drama of a doctors' world.